# THE
# BROKEN
# ONES

'Ma... ...ith comp...ing characters and an ending that left me awestruck. Put this one on your 2020 list!'

Samantha Downing, Richard & Judy bestselling author of *My Lovely Wife*

'I really enjoyed the style of writing. It really drew me in and I had to keep reading. I also loved the mystery of it and was never quite sure who to trust. I found this cleverly written, intriguing and twisty. It definitely kept me turning the pages.'

Karen Hamilton, *Sunday Times* bestselling author of *The Perfect Girlfriend*

'Ren Richards has crafted a story fraught with suspense that weaves back and forth through time and keeps you guessing. An engrossing tale of secrets, regret and redemption. *The Broken Ones* is an emotional rollercoaster right up until the final page. I devoured this book.'

Sherri Smith, author of *The Retreat*

'Darkly atmospheric and haunting, *The Broken Ones* had me hooked from page one. I adored the characters and raced through it, desperate to uncover all their secrets. A brilliant ending that I'm still thinking about…'

Vanessa Savage, author of *The Woman in the Dark*

# THE
# BROKEN
# ONES

## REN RICHARDS

VIPER

First published in Great Britain in 2020 by
VIPER, part of Serpent's Tail
an imprint of Profile Books Ltd
29 Cloth Fair
London EC1A 7JQ
*www.serpentstail.com*

1 3 5 7 9 10 8 6 4 2

Typeset in Palatino by MacGuru Ltd
Printed and bound in Great Britain by CPI Group (UK) Ltd, Croydon CR0 4YY

A CIP catalogue record for this book is available from the British Library.

ISBN 978 1 78816 406 1
Export ISBN 978 1 78816 606 5
eISBN 978 1 78283 642 1

MIX
Paper from
responsible sources
FSC® C020471

# THE
# BROKEN
# ONES

# 1
## NOW

Murderers are human too. That's the part people forget. Look at this photo of the Widow Thompson. She is a middle-aged woman with grey hair and a disoriented sort of smile. Her eyes are distant. She looks ashen and strange, but objectively human. She has teeth, cheekbones, clavicles that peek out from the collar of her olive-coloured dress.

Now you find out this woman is a murderer. Suddenly the eyes are not human. The smile is evil, depraved. The skin is not covering a skull and bones and muscle. Something has changed, and you tell yourself that you had already suspected this. You'll turn to the person next to you and say, 'I knew it. I knew something was off.'

There is no bone, no piece of connective tissue or strand of DNA that separates a church mom from a woman who drowns all eight of her children in a bathtub. And that's what the woman in this photo has done. She started with the oldest, who was eleven. Eleven is bigger than one or three or even nine. An eleven-year-old can weigh about ninety pounds and put up a good fight, rake their nails across their mother's face, rip the towel rack from the wall trying to climb out of the shallow porcelain grave. Pieces of drywall and fractured tiles turned the water grey.

But the Widow Thompson was stronger. Not by much, but enough to get the job done. The other children were smaller, easier. The thirteen-month-old was last. She took no effort at all. As her mother carried her past the bodies of her siblings – all laid out in a silent row on the bedroom floor – she stared curiously, wondering why none of them looked up to pay her any attention.

Babies are easy to kill. That's what the Widow Thompson said in her interview with police. She smiled and said that it was peaceful. Her older children hadn't known that this was the right thing to do, but the baby had. She just slipped underwater and closed her eyes.

You only have a photo of the woman, though. You don't have the forensics photo of the baby in the tub; you just have to take the woman's word for it, and you'd be stupid to believe it happened like she said. But don't kid yourself. The hands she used to do it were shaped just like yours.

CTRL + S, and the story was saved to Nell's hard drive. *The Widow Thompson* would be her second true crime novel, the most controversial, and as of yet, the most lucrative.

It was five minutes to midnight. She sat in the dark with the blue glow of the screen lighting up her face. The tea in her mug had gone cold. The cream was curdled and pungent, like metal in the air.

She opened an email to her agent, attached the file and hit send, meeting her deadline with four minutes to spare.

Sebastian slept in the bed beside her, turned away, the muscles of his back creating lines in his shirt.

'Hey,' Nell whispered, and leaned over to kiss his ear. The laptop slid and she grasped it before it slid off the bed.

Bas groaned and shifted.

'I finished it,' she said.

Bas turned to face her, and his eyes opened, heavy-lidded. 'Just now?'

She closed the laptop with a resolute slam. 'Just now.'

He coiled his arms around her and pulled her to his chest. 'What's it like in your head?' He tucked her hair behind her shoulder. 'All those fucked-up stories floating around all the time.'

'They're not my stories,' she said. 'I'm just reporting the facts.'

He buried his face in the curl of her neck. He smelled so good, like laundry fresh from the dryer. It was the consistency of his presence – his smell, his touch, even the soured breath from hours of sleep – that Nell loved the most. Consistency was a foreign

3

country whose maps eluded her. Two years of sleeping beside this man and she was still waiting for the morning she would wake up and find him gone.

It was a thought that left her fearful of the dark, as though he would disappear in the blackness between the city lights that dotted the windows. But every morning he was exactly where she'd left him, and the longer he stayed, the more their lives braided together. She could almost believe that he was permanent. This frightened her more than anything the Widow Thompson had done.

Sebastian's eyes were closed now. He tightened his hold on her, and her body rose and fell with the waves of his breathing. 'How does it end?' he asked.

'The Widow Thompson's mug shot,' Nell said. 'That's what made me want to take this story. It was just so – sad.'

'Yeah. Eight kids drowning in a tub because their mother is one Froot Loop away from a full bowl is pretty sad,' Bas snorted.

'I didn't write a book about the kids,' Nell said. 'We already know their story. They were all over the news. Little Stacie in her ballet photos and Caleb getting baptised in his tuxedo with the sleeves that are too big for him.' Indeed, there had been a dozen two-hour specials in the three years since the crime had occurred. The story had been interred in the endless tomb of the world's tragedies, only to be ripped open anew by the Widow Thompson's appeal case.

Society had seen fit to let her rot in the New York state pen on death row, but a women's rights group successfully won an appeal to have her transferred to a mental healthcare facility two months ago. It sparked outrage, and the news was plastered with the photos of her dead children, forever frozen in time. Blowing out birthday candles and holding up Fourth of July sparklers and – in a tragic bit of irony – splashing each other in the public pool.

But nobody talked about the Widow Thompson. Nobody talked about the husband who died when his tractor-trailer veered off the road after a forty-eight-hour shift to provide for the children he'd insisted they conceive in bulk. Nobody talked about the postpartum depression the Widow Thompson had been displaying for a good five years before the crime, ever since the birth of her twins, Spencer and Lillian.

*Someone had to,* Nell thought.

For the first half of this writing endeavour, she wondered if she would be demonised for daring to see such a wicked woman as human. And for the second half, she'd ceased to give a fuck. The truth came out hard and fast and ugly.

'You're going to get a lot of letters,' Sebastian said. 'They won't be like the ones you got for your last book.'

'Mm,' Nell agreed.

It had been five years since the true crime novel

that jettisoned her to literary acclaim. That hadn't been the goal. She just wanted to tell the story, and it had taken her several years.

Nathan Stuart. Nine-year-old victim of the Syracuse Strangler, a man with a clean record. He had been luring children to his '64 Cadillac Eldorado for a decade. The car was an antique, bright blue and in mint condition; it drew the eye. Children especially had only seen such a thing in pictures and often wanted to climb inside, as though it were a sort of time machine. Nathan Stuart was the first of his victims to ever be found – half of him, at least. His legs were never recovered, though the Strangler confessed to throwing them in a landfill outside of Rochester in exchange for a plea deal.

While every journalist in the city covered the story, Nell had been the only one to drive to Rochester to meet with the Stuarts. They were in no mood to speak to reporters, but Nell was a baby-faced college junior with a splash of blonde freckles across her nose and a small, unassuming sort of presence. The heaviness of her leather jacket nearly swallowed her up, and her pinstripe leggings made wrinkles where her ankles were too bony to fill them.

Later, Mrs Stuart would say it was the freckles that won her over. She showed Nell the photos of Nathan's freckled smile, plucking the four school portraits from the mantel and laying them one at a time in Nell's hands. Nathan at six. Nathan at seven.

Nathan at eight, holding a baseball bat and missing a front tooth. Nathan at nine, in the photo that made the news all summer long. Nell handled each with care, as though she were holding what had been found of the child's bones.

The interview with Nathan Stuart's mother and sister was a thousand words long and posted on her university's bimonthly page in the town gazette. There it sat stagnant for a month, until a literary agent called the university to find out how to contact this Nell Way, who had somehow managed to capture an entire lifetime in a thousand words. He had never read such a compassionate account of something so brutal. 'You have a gift, Ms Way,' he'd told her. 'You're not like those vultures who show up looking for a fast story and a faster dollar. You bring victims back to life. You make them human again.'

For three years, and under her agent's guidance, Nell turned the Stuarts into a humanising true crime novel with a finesse every reporter on the case would come to envy. And at twenty-nine years old, Nell had at last completed her second opus, this time favouring the perspective of the villain. Her agent had been so enamoured with the Widow Thompson project that it had already found a home with a publisher who'd agreed a contract for seven figures.

The number still didn't register to Nell, though

Sebastian had hoisted her up and spun her around the living room when she told him. Her agent said she'd realise just how much money she'd made the moment she hit send.

But as Nell lay awake, Sebastian dozing beside her, she was thinking of Marina Thompson, tucked away in a dreary room, fated to a life of pills and construction paper hand turkeys. How silent it all must have been, to have grown used to a house filled with children, and to now be in a place where no child would ever visit her again, except in her nightmares.

# 2
# NOW

Morning light hit the tea in the crystal mug on the nightstand.

For a moment Nell thought that she could collect the morning itself in that little mug, the way she'd caught grasshoppers in her hands when she was young. She could keep this warm feeling in her stomach, keep the reflection of Sebastian sleeping in the tangled white sheets, skin flushed.

She would like to take little sips of this morning throughout the rest of her life and remember this feeling, because she knew too well that it wouldn't last, that everything good in the world must eventually be traded for something sour. That was the bargain.

The alarm buzzed. Seven fifteen. Bas's arm fell heavy over her hip and he moaned into her neck. 'Aren't we too rich to work yet?'

Her fingers moved across his hair. 'Is that why you've been sleeping with me?'

His teeth grazed her earlobe. 'There are other reasons.'

She pretended this didn't cause her blood to rush

from her feet to her chest. It was a sort of game she played, hiding how much she loved him, what he did to her.

'Get up.' She slapped his thigh. 'Linds is going to be here soon to drive with me to King's.'

Royal King's State Penitentiary was a two-hour straight shot up Industrial Highway 95, and a trip Nell and her sister had taken every Christmas since Nell was born on the floor in the women's housing unit. The labour had been too quick and the prison guards too impassive to get Bonnie to a hospital. Who could blame them? She had faked labour nearly a dozen times for an ambulance joyride. The boy who cried wolf, and all that.

Bonnie had been eight months pregnant when she shot her husband with a hunting rifle as he napped in his recliner. During trial, sympathy generated by Bonnie's pregnant belly was what saved her from death row, her state attorney maintained. It also helped that her husband survived the attempt on his life. He'd come to court hissing mad and demanding that she fry for it. You can't be charged with murder if your victim is present to testify against you.

Nell was born two weeks after the sentencing, hitting her head on the concrete floor of the cell. The blood and fluids broke her fall. Bonnie had been crouched there for hours, screaming as her cellmate quoted scriptures and sang 'O Come All Ye Faithful' because it was the only religious song whose words

10

she knew by heart. 'Fucking simpleton,' Bonnie said in her later retelling of this story. 'Good pipes though.'

Shortly after her birth, Nell was dumped into the arms of her four-year-old sister, and Lindsay had never entirely let go of her since. It wasn't enough that their mother was serving 25-to-life and their father hadn't been sober since his teens; the sisters also had the misfortune of having nothing but headstones for grandparents. Two died young of cirrhosis, Grandpa Jake died in a house fire in '83, and Grandma Isabelle killed herself in '82. From the start, Nell and Lindsay had only each other. This fact nettled at them with every argument, every screaming match where one came away with a fistful of the other's hair. Every slammed door, every peal of rubber tires when one sped off in a fury. *Fuck you. I hate you. You're the worst. Go die in a well.* And then always, always, a contrite creaking open of the door, and: *I love you, you asshole.*

Foster homes changed like painted settings in a school play, each one as flimsy as the one before, but Lindsay was all four points in the weathervane of Nell's childhood.

'You with me?' Bas slid his hand down the slope of her waist, across her stomach, between her legs. Nell rewarded him with a shuddered breath, and she could feel his triumphant grin against her jaw.

It was a morning that she wanted to keep forever, but she knew that she couldn't, and with her next

11

breath she was pushing him away. 'Up,' she ordered again. 'Are you showering first?'

'Sure,' Bas said, not turning to look at her as he made his way across the room. He paused to stretch, his rippled arms silhouetted against the windows. Nell forced herself to look away. She pressed her palms against her stomach and stared at the ceiling instead. She liked to linger in bed after Bas had left her side. She liked the feeling of being deprived of him, the way her blood moved about under her skin in search of his fingers.

She heard the rush of water in the shower, and at last she forced herself to get up and contend with the dirty dishes. It was an open-concept penthouse apartment, perfect for parties if one liked having people in one's home, which Nell didn't. The view alone was worth the rent. She had been here for two years, and she could afford better, but she wasn't sure that she wanted to move, though Bas often left the newspaper open to real estate in the suburbs.

The bathroom was the only room without a view, but like the rest of the apartment, it had fourteen-feet ceilings, exposed pipes making up a map of brass and steel. Everything was sweating with condensation, and the room smelled like Sebastian, his firm presence and flowery sweet cologne. This was why Nell always showered second, wrapped up in the warmth he didn't know he left behind.

As she was wringing out her hair over the sink,

she heard the doorbell. 'Lindsay must have forgotten her key,' she called, her own voice breaking the spell she'd fallen under.

'On my way out anyway.' Bas poked his head into the bathroom, his grey-brown eyes sincere. 'I hope the interview goes well.'

She put her wet hands on his shoulders and kissed him. She straightened the collar of his shirt as he said it again: 'I really hope it goes well.'

'Do I look nervous?'

'You look cool as ever,' he said. The doorbell rang again, and he turned to leave. 'Love you,' he said. Nell gave a gentle, firm kick to his backside as he went. It left a dark wet imprint on the ass of his grey twill pants.

It was more than an 'I love you.' It was better.

Lindsay entered the apartment like a shark in its own current. Focused, ready. She was holding three glasses by the rim in one hand and a pile of discarded laundry in the other arm when Nell came out of the bathroom.

'Such a slob,' Lindsay said.

For sisters, they didn't look alike. Where Nell was short, plain and easy to lose in a crowd, Lindsay was petite with a commanding presence. She had sharp eyes and gold hair; today it was drawn into a bun, gleaming under a gallon of hairspray. Her lips were painted bright pink, her eyelids shimmering with hints of silver. It was a deliberate sort of beauty, meant to prove a point. Nell didn't comment on it;

13

when it came to Lindsay and Bonnie's tense reunions, she preferred not to get between them.

Silver, the colour of knives. Lindsay was the sort of woman who made you wonder what she might have been like if she weren't so clearly broken by the events of her life. Her heels made a hard slapping sound as she paced to the kitchen sink. 'What are you going to do with your hair?'

Nell picked up a chunk of her damp brown hair and then let it fall to her shoulder again. Lindsay had been pestering her for months to get highlights. 'I thought I'd leave it like this. It's eccentric. They always expect me to be eccentric.'

'Honestly,' Lindsay said, tossing the dirty laundry into the hamper, 'your life would fall apart without me. It would fall to utter shit.'

'I will forever and hereafter do everything you say,' Nell said, being mostly sincere. It had been Lindsay's idea, after all, to interview the Widow Thompson and write her story, and the endeavour had paid handsomely.

But Lindsay was wary of today's interview with Easter Hamblin. It was evident by her flawless makeup and new outfit – denim leggings and a white cowl neck whose buttons were the size of fists – that she was only coming along for the unseasonable visit with Bonnie. Lindsay's love for their mother was all hostility and aggression, with only a perfume spritz of desperation.

It was no accident that Nell had dressed down for the occasion. She wore jeans and a grey sweatshirt. She did this so that her sister could feel secure in her role as the beautiful one. Today especially, Lindsay would need the power this implied.

Lindsay was out of breath as she stood upright, gave the blankets a final smoothing over. 'Ready?'

✳

They took Nell's car, a decade-old Buick with scratched blue paint, parked sombrely behind Lindsay's Red Obsession coupe. It had already been established that Lindsay's tires would never touch the asphalt of the prison parking lot. Nell didn't mind making the drive; fixating on the road took her mind off of the anxiety that was starting to mount now that she'd turned in the manuscript that had haunted her for two years. There was something terrifying about the months between the send button and the box of hardbacks that would arrive in the mail the week before publication.

'Hey,' Lindsay said, buckling her seatbelt. 'Did you send it off?'

Nell put the car in drive. 'Yep.'

'So that's it,' Lindsay said. 'You're a millionaire?'

'Two thirds of a millionaire, after Jasper's fee and taxes.'

'You smug little shit,' Lindsay said. 'Just let me be proud of you.'

Nell smirked at the road ahead. Lindsay's pride meant even more to her than Sebastian's love, but she wouldn't let her have the satisfaction.

They turned onto the highway and Lindsay cranked the radio to a volume that was wholly inappropriate for such an early hour. If Nell had her way, she would be sleeping for at least another three hours, as per usual. But Lindsay was a relentless morning person, and she had no qualms being obnoxious about it.

Besides, if Nell was going to interview Easter Hamblin, now was the time. Royal King's had a problem with overcrowding and new convicts were often transferred further upstate. Better a two-hour drive than a seven-hour trip one way.

This was Easter Hamblin's story: She murdered her twin sister and assumed her identity for a year. The twins were born in Russia, conjoined at the hip and forearm. Unable to pay for their separation surgery, their parents eventually forfeited them to some charity organisation that flew them out to America. They were promptly adopted and a doctor was able to separate them, leaving each sister with mirrored scars and a body of her own. To go with their new identities, the twins chose American names for themselves.

The twins never spoke about their lives in Russia.

Not a single mention of their biological parents, despite having lived with them for the first ten years of their lives. In the months leading up to the trial, several child psychologists had come out to give interviews to the press, speculating that the twins had been abused. Attachment disorders. Post-traumatic stress. Things that would slip through the cracks in the adoption system that brought the twins stateside.

But a physical separation could not undo the effect of their years spent sharing an identity. Autumn flourished while Easter shrank into herself and became increasingly reclusive. At twelve, she was accused of setting a litter of pit bull puppies on fire. She denied this and the murder of many other small things found in the twins' wake.

By their twenties, the sisters lived in a shared apartment, having never been apart. Because Easter had been famously agoraphobic, their neighbours thought nothing of only seeing one twin at a time.

It was a year before Easter was found out. She'd taken great lengths to hide her identity, always wearing long sleeves to conceal her scar, which was on the opposite arm to Autumn's.

Even after Autumn's skeleton had been found, picked clean by woodland creatures, Easter tried to maintain her sister's identity.

Two years ago, it was the most talked about case in the country.

Nell had followed the case with the sort of

romantic obsession of a girl in love. She held her breath when television shows were interrupted with newsbreaks; when she retrieved the morning paper, her heart was in her mouth.

But she hadn't written about it. She hadn't planned to. She was waist-high in mothers who had drowned their children and spurned lovers who poured arsenic into their partner's tea.

'Bonnie's block doesn't have visitation until three,' Lindsay said. 'So I'm coming with you.'

Lindsay pitched this as a coincidence, but Nell knew better. Lindsay considered herself to be Nell's unofficial manager, not just of her career, but of her life. When things started getting serious with Sebastian, Lindsay happened to be in the city rather often. She had to stop by Nell's apartment to pee, or to borrow a coat.

So Nell had been expecting her sister to be present for the potential dawning of her next big thing.

'I haven't decided if I'm going to take her on yet,' Nell said. 'She reached out to me with an outlandish story that her murdered sister is secretly still alive. It was oddly lucid – not the rambling delusion you'd expect from a story like that.'

'She sounds nuts,' Lindsay said. 'Imagine if I murdered you and just walked around living your life for a year until someone figured it out.'

'It would mean you have to write the book,' Nell said. 'Sounds like I'd get the better deal.'

The parking lot of Royal King's State Penitentiary was predictably crowded. The prison itself was sanctioned as a city by the state of New York, with its own zip code and grid of streets that all led to the same destination: the sprawling granite building surrounded by guard towers that resembled grim castle spires, and barbed wire fencing.

The streets beyond the parking lot were jammed with parked cars – spouses and heartsick mothers coming from out of state to visit their loved ones. Nell and Lindsay used to be among those sleeping in their cars overnight before they'd moved to New York. It was murder on the spine, but worse was being turned away when they found out Bonnie had violated a rule and been denied visitation. That meant another night in the car, hoping they could get in the following day.

For Nell, growing up with a parent in prison was like having a piece of herself always in a cage. The smell of the place soured her for days after, and she thought about all those women who were trapped, making little animal sculptures out of toilet paper and water, fashioning eyeliner from the grease under the windows so they could look like they had when they were free.

Nell and Lindsay were shuttled from one foster home to the next throughout their childhood, and every time Nell stuffed her clothes into her backpack and climbed into the social worker's car, she wondered if she'd be sent to prison too. It seemed inevitable, like there were only a finite number of homes in the world and eventually she'd burn through them.

That sick feeling of dread was with her even now as she pulled into a parking space.

If Lindsay felt any discomfort, she didn't let on. She pulled down the visor and pursed her lips at her reflection, making sure her lipstick was even.

They were an hour early, but it would take that long to get to the front of the line anyway. In addition to being the most crowded prison in the state of New York, Royal King's also housed some of the most famous prisoners in the tri-state area. They seldom stayed permanently; they were usually shuttled elsewhere. But there were always visitors for famous felons: journalists, writers, beautiful women whose fathers hadn't loved them. And in the women's section of the prison, thousands upon thousands of love-struck men who were lured in by the siren song of these dangerous women. Women who looked like their mothers, or a girl they used to lust after in middle school. Women who looked lonely and small, or powerful and dominating.

Nell had seen every type. She had interviewed dozens of convicts searching for her next story. Sebastian was the one who had set up a PO box for her after the letters started coming in. Attorneys looking for writers to humanise their clients before an appeals case, parents swearing their child was wrongfully accused, inmates themselves looking for commissary money. Most lost interest in being interviewed when Nell told them they wouldn't be paid.

Easter, being a convicted felon, would be entitled to no percentage of the advance if the manuscript sold. That was some cold irony, Nell thought. Her punishment for her crime was that she could never profit from her story, but without her crime she would have no story to tell. Nobody was going to buy a book about a well-mannered twin who lived a quiet little life arranging flowers.

Lindsay draped her arm around Nell's shoulder, hanging on her like a sleepy toddler, her hyper morning verve suddenly gone. She hadn't made Nell stop anywhere for coffee, and it was starting to show. She stayed like that until they were called.

Visiting a convict is a dehumanising experience. Pat-downs, metal detectors, the deadpan CO drawling out the same rules about not bringing gifts or engaging in physical contact. The physical contact rule wasn't relevant anyway. Easter was a high-profile case being housed in solitary for her own protection. This meant all her visits were partitioned off by a sheet of bulletproof glass and a phone.

Nell waited on the ruptured vinyl bench whose stuffing was billowing out like a polluted cloud. Lindsay made room for herself on the edge of it. The sisters never needed much space for themselves;

that came from a lifetime of sharing bunk beds and dining chairs, being crammed together in minivans packed with foster siblings like clowns in a VW.

Easter Hamblin was brought to her side of the glass, shuffling with the hobbled gait of an inmate in chains. She was forty years old, and her features couldn't seem to agree on how her face was supposed to look. Her skin was leathery, aged, and her lips were pale and thin. But her eyes were large, bright green, with long lashes that would have made sense on a younger and prettier face. Her hair was limp and brown, dulled by the neon lights, but it still held the hint of curls.

*She's a set of twins in one body*, Nell thought.

Easter sat and considered Nell and Lindsay. They looked nothing like twins, surely, but Nell realised now that she and her sister were sitting the way that Easter and Autumn had when they were conjoined. She shifted, but there was little room for her to change this.

Easter picked up the phone, and Nell held her receiver between herself and Lindsay so they could both hear.

'That your manager?' Easter asked. She had a thick Russian accent, not at all smoothed over by her decades in America.

'Sister,' Nell said. 'She's just here to observe.'

Easter laughed. It was the humourless, exaggerated bark Nell had heard from Bonnie. Maybe there was something about this place that changed the sound of laughter.

'Observe,' Easter echoed, taunting. 'Like a watchdog looking for a thief to bite, she observes.' Easter bared her teeth, animating her imagery.

Lindsay said nothing. If Easter meant to unnerve her, it would take more than that. Besides, it was true. Nell's presence made Lindsay fierce. A social worker had tried once – only once – to separate the sisters when the group home got too crowded. Lindsay, who was eight, went rabid. She lunged into the driver's seat and bit his neck. His cries were drowned out by her screaming. A merciless, shrill sound that Nell wouldn't hear again for another decade.

'Me and Autumn came to America when we were ten,' Easter said, not missing a beat. Like most of Nell's interviewees, she had a mind for details. 'My brother Oleg visited sometimes. Kept in touch.' She waved her hand as though swatting at a mosquito. 'Our American mother had the email then Facebook.'

Nell wove the pen between her fingers but didn't take notes. She rarely did. She had a strong memory for details, but the ideas needed to be written down immediately. Those disappeared forever if they weren't captured.

'What did Autumn think of Oleg?' Nell said. 'Did she get along with him?'

23

She had only met the brother once, a brief chat over coffee in preparation for visiting Easter. He had given her a stack of childhood photographs, carefully presented in a crisp white envelope. They had looked through them together, laying them out on the sticky table. Infants turned in slightly different directions. Toddlers, one looking sullenly to the left while the other stared transfixed by something to her right. Sepia memories of little girls in dresses whose arms were pinned together.

'Sometimes I think they are the real twins,' Easter said. 'Joined at the hip.' She flashed her teeth in a taunting smile. 'She hates most people. That's something you don't see in papers. Beautiful smile. She would always talk to the neighbours. "How are you? How is work? How's that cute little poodle? Is your mother good after her surgery? Maybe I bake her some muffins."' Easter's face changed as she adopted her sister's persona. Her eyes made sense as the rest of her features brightened. She pouted her lips so they looked fuller. Then the illusion deflated and she looked weathered and old again. 'But she didn't mean it. That's what you call an act, like in a play.'

'Why?' Nell asked.

'What do you do when you have a secret?' Easter countered. 'You bury it in the dirt, hope no one will dig it up, or you dye it a pretty colour and wrap it around your shoulders like a shawl, so nobody will see how ugly it is.'

'Psychotic,' Lindsay said. 'The word for what you're describing is psychotic.'

Nell cut her sister a vicious glare. Lindsay pretended not to see it.

Easter laughed, not at what Lindsay had said but Nell's reaction to it. She pointed a finger from one sister to the other. 'The blonde one is older. I can tell, even though she's smaller. She thinks she's the boss, but it's you.' She was looking at Nell, but then her eyes moved to Lindsay. 'Ask my neighbours and they say I was psychotic. Didn't dress nice or say hello. But what is the first thing anyone says about a psychotic person when they learn what they've done? "I never would have expected." Autumn is like this.'

'I notice you keep referring to Autumn in the present,' Nell said, diverting the attention away from herself, as she always did when her interviewees started to pry. She shared as little of herself as possible. This was why she never invited Lindsay to tag along; Lindsay had her own ideas about what rules should apply to her, and she had never been especially good at keeping her thoughts to herself.

'Past tense is for the dead,' Easter replied. 'Autumn is alive.'

Autumn was very much not alive. Nell had seen the crime scene photos and the dental records that confirmed the pile of bones lying by a woodland river was Autumn Hamblin. The twins' brother saw

25

fit to share this alongside their childhood photos. He was willing to help Easter convince Nell to take her on. But he had no illusions about her.

Nell didn't challenge Easter, however. She sat in patient silence, waiting for her to go on. When she didn't, Lindsay said, 'You're saying Autumn was the evil twin.'

Easter laughed. 'If you like to word it this way, yes.'

Below the range of the window, where Autumn couldn't see, Nell was clutching Lindsay's knee, her nails boring into the denim. *Mouth shut*, she was saying.

Easter took on Autumn's expression again. It was eerie how she could do that, become someone else entirely. She curled her fingertip around the rigid cord of the phone. 'Do you talk about your little girl like she's alive, or dead?'

The room went silent.

Easter leaned back, as though lounging in a recliner rather than the empty space behind her stool. 'You don't talk about her, do you?' she said. 'You're the type to bury secrets in dirt. But bodies always come back up.' She said those last three words slowly, and they popped from her mouth like she had been sucking on a lollipop. Like the words had a taste she could savour.

Lindsay snatched the phone from Nell's hand and slammed it back on the receiver. 'We're done.' She grabbed Nell's wrist, but Nell didn't move. She was staring at Easter, who was still holding the phone, her eyebrows raised expectantly.

The receiver clattered against the hook when Nell reached for it; her hand was shaking.

Lindsay was standing over her now. 'Nell!'

'Shut up,' Nell said. She pressed the receiver back to her ear.

'You're not the only one who does research,' Easter said. 'There are thousands of newspapers in prison library. And there is all the time in the world to read every word, to find the right person to tell my story. You changed your name, grew out your hair. Maybe I wouldn't have found you if I wasn't looking, but you resemble that girl in the newspaper too much to be coincidence.' She smiled, and her eyes were dead. 'You've been careful. No author photo on your book. No interview. The only recent photograph I could find was in a local article last year.'

Nell remembered that interview perfectly. The young journalist had fawned over her like an excited puppy, and she'd insisted on taking Nell's picture at her editor's behest. It was a small interview in a local paper with no online archive, and even then, Nell had been reluctant.

She could deny it, but something about Easter's gaze had her frozen. Nell still hadn't answered the question. Did she talk about her daughter like she was alive, or dead?

Daughter.

In truth, she hated the word.

Easter shrugged. 'I want you to tell my story. You want me to tell you my story so that you can get more money in your piggy bank. The least you can do is be honest—'

'I don't talk about her,' Nell said. 'Not in the past tense, and not in the present.' It was the truth. In the ten years since it happened, she thought about her child constantly, counting the days and bundling those days into years, keeping them in neat little piles in her brain. And behind all of that organised mourning was the child's name: Reina. Reina, rusted like an abandoned hubcap on the side of the road, half covered over with dirt as the world rushed by.

But she didn't talk about her.

Nell could feel Lindsay's worry. It was palpable, like the air after someone had just thrown up. Humid and sick. 'Nell.'

'Sometimes the papers say you're innocent and sometimes not,' Easter said. 'Maybe you have your own secrets.'

Nell was aware of what the papers said. One morning she was the dim-witted teenage mother being controlled by her wealthy boyfriend and his influential family. The next, she was the girl who had snapped. The next, she had been plotting the child's demise since her birth, had punched herself in the stomach when she was pregnant. Sometimes she was covering up an accidental drowning, or a backyard accident. Sometimes she had beaten her child with a shovel and hidden the body. The story shifted like hues in a mood ring, never fully coming to form.

When all goes as planned, people pour their cereal and drive to work and daydream about the beach on their desktop wallpaper. Everything is safe. But when a child goes missing, suddenly they remember that any horrible thing is possible. Everyone is a killer or a rapist. There's a sort of desperation when it's a child, and the theories get uglier and more brutal as time passes, until there's nothing left to do but be angry.

Nell had lost her child. That was true. That was all anyone knew. Staring at the photos of that chubby-cheeked little girl would yield no answers; they had all been taken before it happened.

'Did you kill her?' Easter asked.

'No.' Nell's voice came out hoarse and hushed. She cleared her throat. 'No, I didn't kill her.'

Easter considered this. When she spoke again, it was with a flawless American accent. 'Maybe you're telling the truth. Maybe all of those papers are telling lies. Just like they're telling lies about me. My sister is still alive, and I know I didn't kill her, just like you know you didn't kill your little girl.'

It had been nearly a decade since any newspapers found Nell worth writing about. In an industry that thrived on tragedy, there was no shortage of merchandise. Still, Nell swiped through the papers on her iPad every day, looking for Reina amid reports of unidentified bodies.

In the first weeks after Reina disappeared, Nell wondered at what exact moment her child had died. As Nell spoke to reporters, as she and Ethan forced themselves to eat from the covered dishes brought by neighbours and church members, as everyone said nice words, Nell could feel her child decomposing somewhere. She could see it sometimes. She could see the skin going cold, then pale, then shrinking down as though the soil were absorbing it. But what she couldn't see was where her daughter was. She couldn't draw a map to that spot. And no search was complete until the lost thing was found.

Easter was still searching her face. 'All right,' she said. 'Take your notes. I'll tell you my story.'

# 3
# NOW

Lindsay was all dressed to impress Bonnie. She'd even gone to the salon for acrylic tips, the French manicure accented by painted red fleurs-de-lis. But by the time Bonnie was brought to the visiting room, Lindsay was too subdued to bother with her.

Bonnie noticed it right away. She sat on her side of the round table, looked Lindsay up and down, then turned to Nell and said, 'What crawled up her ass?'

Lindsay's face was downturned, but she raised her eyes to give her mother a sour glare.

'Hi, Momma,' Nell said. Her attempt at recovering civility.

'Hi, baby girl.' Bonnie spoke with a surge of affection; she patted Nell's hand. She could switch it on and off, her warmth in one moment as believable as her coldness in the next.

Across the room, a CO said, 'You know the rules, Baker.'

'All right, all right.' Bonnie waved without turning to look at him. Baker was the maiden name she'd reclaimed after her conviction. No sense keeping the name of a husband she hated so much she'd tried to murder him. 'Motherfucker,' she mumbled.

Lindsay moved her finger to her lip, about to chew on her nail before she remembered the acrylic tips. Nell worried. Lindsay prided herself on her appearance; not just the cosmetic aspects, but the overall presence of a woman who had her shit together. A woman who awoke each morning smelling like a lilac sprig. Very rarely did the nervous foster child surface in these little gestures. Nail biting. Fidgeting. Repeating words like a dementia patient.

'I finished my book,' Nell said. 'Just emailed it off this morning.' Nell was sparse in the details she shared with her mother. The money never came up. She craved Bonnie's approval, and simultaneously she knew that no good would come from telling her about any of her achievements. She'd made that mistake with the first book, and Bonnie had managed to talk Nell into adding money to her commissary. Bonnie had even faked a heart attack for the guilt factor; the trip to a brightly lit hospital with a private TV in her room was just an added bonus.

'Email,' Bonnie echoed. She had been in prison for twenty-nine years. She had never even owned a computer.

Ten years ago, when Reina went missing, Nell considered it a blessing that Bonnie couldn't access the internet. While the newspaper articles and television segments were brutal, at least they ended. The internet never forgot a thing. You could search for the story of a missing four-year-old and her eighteen-year-old mother and find all sorts of theories. Crudely drawn amateur depictions of theories, videos whose comments discussed all the ways that mother deserved to die, get raped, be sent to Gitmo Bay. *Give me five minutes with that bitch, I'll do what the state's afraid to do.*

'I'll mail you an early copy when I get them,' Nell said.

'You know I love your writing, baby,' Bonnie said. 'You write ugly things but they sound pretty when you tell it.' Her gaze shifted to Lindsay. 'Who's the new man in your life?'

'There is no new man,' Lindsay said. She'd straightened her posture now, but her eyes were still mean.

'No?' Bonnie said. 'I just assumed there was. It's been a couple years since you burned through the last husband. You're about due for a third.'

'Okay.' Lindsay's chair scraped against the linoleum as she pushed away from the table. 'I don't have to take this. I'll be outside.'

That word was its own revenge. Outside. Lindsay could step through a pair of glass double doors and Bonnie would never be able to follow.

'Linds—' Nell began, but she was already gone. Nell blew out a hard breath, pushing the hair away from her face. 'Why'd you have to put her in a mood? I'm the one who has to ride home with her for two hours.'

In truth, Nell wasn't dreading the ride home. But she liked to make out that she and Lindsay weren't as close as they were. Bonnie was jealous enough that her girls had freedom; knowing they had each other would make her spiteful.

'She was in a mood when she walked in.' Bonnie held her hands up, as though that somehow implied they were clean.

# 4
# NOW

In Missouri, there's a little town called Greendale Park. Population 200,000. It has an elementary school with a library wing donated by the First Lady in 2004. There's a video rental store that continues to survive despite streaming media. There's a lake where it's illegal to fish, and a bike path, and several blocks of little split levels that went up in the sixties. And on the corner of East and Sutland, there's a telephone pole in front of a church.

When Nell last saw that telephone pole, her child's face was stapled to it in a glossy high-resolution photograph that Mrs Eddleton had printed. Below the photo in big bold letters: JUSTICE FOR REINA.

Teddy bears and mason jars of tea light candles surrounded this pole. The sky was filled with little trinkets for the world's missing children, and when nobody was looking, those pieces rained down on that spot one at a time. A blue stuffed lion. A grey elephant. A bear holding a white heart that said 'I love you' in purple taffeta.

*Sorry*, these gifts said. *Sorry that you hadn't been someone – anyone – else's child.*

Maybe those offerings were all still there. Maybe the pile had grown and swallowed up the entire town in an avalanche of cotton batting and prayers.

✻

Lindsay was already in the car when Nell returned to the parking lot. She was shivering in the November chill, her breath misting before her.

'Jesus,' Nell said as she climbed into the driver's seat. 'You could have waited in the lobby.'

Lindsay shook her head. She was staring at the prison yard beyond the barbed fence. 'I didn't want to be in that hellhole a minute longer.' She turned to face Nell, who was glancing at her mirror as she backed out of their spot. 'You can't work with Easter Hamblin. She's fucking insane.'

'People want to read about the insane,' Nell said.

'No, I mean like actually insane,' Lindsay emphasised. 'Straitjacket grade.'

'She murdered her twin and then pretended to be her, Linds. Were you expecting a Victorian debutante?'

'How did she find those articles about you? How did she even know it *was* you? You changed your name. You changed everything.'

'I didn't change my face,' Nell said. 'And my picture was plastered all over the newspapers when it happened.'

'I'm disturbed by your level of calm,' Lindsay said. 'You should be freaking out.'

'I plan to,' Nell said, craning her neck to see past a Camaro parked across two spaces. 'But is it okay with you if I get us out of here first?'

Once they were on the interstate again, Nell stretched her fingers and then renewed her grip on the steering wheel. 'Okay,' she said. 'I'm terrified that Sebastian will find out.'

Early on in their relationship, Bas had revealed himself to be of the open-book persuasion. On their second date, he told Nell about his mother's two rounds of chemotherapy and his sister's douchebag boyfriend. A month later, Nell knew about all his ex-girlfriends and how he liked his coffee, and that his preferred genre of movie was 'so bad it's actually good.'

In exchange, she began offering small bits of herself like anniversary presents tied up with dollar-store ribbon. She told him that her father had lost custody when Nell was two, after he was pulled over driving drunk with his daughters in the back seat. Nell hadn't been in a car seat because they didn't own one, but they had been wearing seat-belts. This was Lindsay's vigilance. It would have been all the same to their father if they jumped around or strangled each other. And her first kiss was with a boy at her group home when she was eleven. It was on a dare, and she had to use her tongue because that was part of the deal. He tasted like pickles.

Slowly, they both unfolded for each other. Awkward confessions over dinner turned to hushed revelations in the bedroom. At first she kept him at a distance. But while she wasn't paying attention, somehow he came to fill her hair, the tight crags between her teeth, the darkness at the back of her throat. He could not be separated from her so easily. If he left her now, pieces of herself would tear away with him. Her fingers. Her cheek. The bone in her hip where he rested his hand as he slept.

She lied to him sometimes. Little things, like that her new laptop had cost less than she'd really spent, or that she had eaten something other than coffee and Cheetos for breakfast. But the only big lie she'd ever told had been about the dull scar that ran from her pelvis to her breastbone. She'd told him that she had gotten pregnant at fourteen, and that they'd had to cut her open because the baby had tangled herself on the way out and nearly killed them both. All true. But the next part of her story was only what she wished had come next: a nice couple came with one of those car seats that converts into a stroller. They whisked their new adoptee away, to a life of private school and piano lessons, and there she remained to this day. Nell didn't worry about her, she said, and the adoption had been closed. She didn't want them to find each other.

Surely Sebastian had seen Reina on the news when she first went missing and in the months that followed, but he had no reason to remember the teenage mother who hurried past the news crews, trying to cover her face with her coat. She had changed over the years, taken pains to adjust her hair, her clothes, even her posture. And like most people, he was inoculated to the tragedy of missing children. He had likely muttered his disgust, poured himself a cup of coffee, and gone back to whatever had mattered to him all those years ago. Turned on the radio and gotten snared by the lyrics of a song and forgotten all about it, most likely.

'Fuck,' Lindsay murmured. She looked like she was going to throw up. 'Okay. Okay, you know what? Don't panic.'

'You're being inconsistent, Linds.'

'Easter tells stories. She murdered her sister and then told us that her sister is alive. She's a loon. Nobody is going to believe her even if she does blab about you.'

Easter wouldn't have to convince anyone that she was telling the truth about Nell. The evidence was right there in the papers. Dozens of photos of Nell falling apart, or faking calm, or walking to her car with a bag of groceries. She had changed her name and she had moved to a new state, but there was no such thing as anonymity in 2020. Easter was right. Buried things always unearthed themselves.

Now Nell was the one to whisper, 'Fuck.' The word came out squeaky and cracked. She had the sense that she might cry, but she refused.

She took a deep breath. The calming effects of deep breaths were overrated. Deep breaths when Ethan Eddleton first tilted her chin and kissed her. Deep breaths as she ambled into the hospital with an arm wrapped around her stomach and water trailing down her legs. Deep breaths when Reina's constant tantrums rattled around in her skull until she felt sick with them. Deep breaths when she sat in the courtroom, her hair pulled back to show the judge her baby features in the hope of a merciful verdict. Deep breaths when she sped over the Missouri/Illinois state line.

Deep breaths now, as she drove this road that felt like an executioner's walk.

'I wonder what medications Easter is taking,' Nell said. 'The state provides such shitty alternatives to anti-psychotics to cut costs.'

'What?' Lindsay said. 'Who gives a fuck, Nell? Why are we talking about Easter?'

'I don't know, Lindsay. I'm trying to pretend I still have a life left to salvage, is that okay with you?'

The mania of Nell's tone made Lindsay realise that they were both hysterical. That wouldn't do. One hysterical sister was manageable, but that meant the other had to be that much more reasoned. Lindsay slipped into her old familiar role like a well-worn dress. On a normal day, Lindsay and Nell were sisters. But when the rare need arose, Lindsay became the mother she had learned to be when she was four.

'Let's imagine the worst-case scenario one piece at a time, and we'll figure out how to deal with it,' Lindsay said, her voice calm. 'Let's say Easter contacts Jasper and tells him who you are.'

'Jasper won't care.' Nell realised this was true as soon as she'd said it. Her agent had been in the publishing industry for nearly as long as Nell had been alive. He was slim with a salt-and-pepper halo around his balding crown, and he had the vocabulary of a burly sailor. He took nothing personally, saw setbacks as personal challenges and hung up on clients if they started crying. 'If I took a machine gun to an orphanage tomorrow, he'd be contacting a lawyer to make sure I could write the story from my cell.'

Lindsay nodded. This sounded like an accurate depiction. 'The press,' she said.

'The press would be a nightmare.' Nell raked a hand through her hair. 'I'd have to move.'

'Fine,' Lindsay said. 'Fuck that apartment.'

Nell loved her apartment, but it wasn't worth the hell of being locked inside with the curtains drawn while reporters waited for her to take out the garbage so they could paw through it. Nothing was worth that. There were plenty of other places to live.

Nell had learned that the world could be endless. If it had been possible for her child to slip through a tear in the atmosphere and be gone forever, it was also possible for Nell to elude the press. It would take time, but she could do it.

'Bas,' Lindsay said.

Nell's vision blurred. *Sebastian.* If he found out what happened all those years ago, she would lose him forever.

'How much have you told him?' Lindsay tried again.

'I told him I had a baby fifteen years ago and gave her up for adoption. He hasn't pressed for more than that.' Of course he hadn't. Nell's account of Reina's birth came out during a fight. For the first year of their relationship, they'd fought all the time. Heated, screaming marathons of impassioned anger that lasted for days, until they came up gasping and desperate and, somehow, even more in love.

The fight had come about because Sebastian was frustrated by Nell's secrecy. It wasn't that she didn't tell him where she'd been all afternoon or who was on the phone – he didn't care about things like that. Rather, he always sensed that there was more to the woman he loved than what she presented. He wanted the parts of Nell that she'd just as soon leave for dead. And not only did he want to know her entire life story, he also needed to know how she felt about it. What had it been like, visiting her mother

42

in a state pen? What was she thinking about when she couldn't sleep? Nell had not been prepared for someone to care about these sorts of things. No one had ever asked.

It didn't frighten her that he asked. It frightened her that she wanted to give him the truth. She wanted him to know everything about her, just like she knew everything about him and his family. His mercifully ordinary family, from which he couldn't possibly have been given the tools to understand her own.

She wanted to tell him all about Reina, and the day she disappeared, and that it was her fault. She wanted to show him the articles and scream, 'There. There it is. Are you happy?'

But by then she had grown too attached to the idea of loving him. And what was the point in changing her name and starting anew if she didn't embrace the role of Nell Way, born and raised in Rochester, NY? This Nell Way had never been to Missouri. Had never heard of Greendale Park. And that awful teenage mother who lost her little girl? She was just a headline from long ago. A story heard on the news and then forgotten about as the earth churned up new tragedies and more candles were lit.

'I had a baby,' she'd blurted out, pulling up her shirt to show him the scar that he had seen a hundred times before. And when she broke into tears and he put his arms around her, she told herself that this

43

had to be enough. This little lie, this bit of comfort, had to be where the truth came to an end just like a clamp on an umbilical cord. Without that clamp they would bleed to death.

'Sebastian will leave me if he finds out,' Nell said. She hit the steering wheel.

'Don't do anything rash,' Lindsay said. 'Easter doesn't have contact with the outside world. The most she can do is write letters, yeah?'

Nell nodded. 'Jasper would open a letter from Royal King's. It could be a query. But if Sebastian saw a letter from a prison, even if it were addressed to him, maybe he would assume it was for me.'

'You're the one to check the mail anyway,' Lindsay said. 'Your address isn't public. Letters go to your PO box.'

'Right.' Nell's breathing had slowed. The overwhelming heat in her blood had settled, and things felt manageable again. There was no need to panic. Not now, anyway.

'This day sucks,' Lindsay said. 'Let's get some fucking pancakes.'

## 5

# THEN

Two things commonly expressed about childbirth:

It hurts.

It's worth it.

Already at age fourteen, Nell had committed these sentiments to heart and trusted that they were true. She had been to five school districts, in shitty towns and in nice towns, but they all had the same two types of girls: the ones who secretly pined over their crushes, writing their initials in their notebook and dreaming of their first kiss. And the ones who talked about finger banging at the school dance, either because they had done it or they were pretending they had.

There were some grey areas between the two, but most girls could place themselves neatly into Column A or Column B.

Nell, however, was spending her study period googling things like 'is it true you poop when you give birth' and 'do stretch marks go away.'

By the ninth month, she was covered in stretch marks. Dark, angry gashes in shades of purple and deep red. She had stopped looking at herself in the mirror or in the shower. It was too dangerous to face what she had allowed to happen.

It hurts.

It's worth it.

There were millions of women who had given birth, and you'd never know just by looking at them. Did all the traces of pregnancy go away, or was it just possible to hide them? Nell couldn't imagine that she would ever look like a normal person again. She imagined her enormous stomach deflating once it was empty, sagging down to her knees. All those gash marks. The greasy skin. Swollen toes.

When she finally went into labour, it was actually a relief. She succumbed to the stabs of pain that shot up her spine and down her stomach. When she screamed, it was the release of all those months of worrying, of questioning her decision, of thinking she had made a mistake.

Here's what Nell hadn't been told: teen mothers do not give birth surrounded by chariots of angels. No one places a flower crown on your head when you're fourteen and you stagger into the ER in the middle of the night. No one congratulates you or asks if you have a name picked out. It was a busy night for emergencies and the nurses were harried. For more than an hour, Nell twisted in a plastic chair in triage, her legs and arms going numb with shock.

When the pain rendered Nell unable to scream, it was Lindsay's turn to make a commotion. She

From her penthouse apartment, Nell could see the western half of it. The aerial view of Rockhollow was a famous one, having been featured in a two-page spread of *Time* magazine in 1984; a peaceful photo, which has been forever interred on the walls of physician waiting rooms.

She knew every crag of this city. Not just the bright and glimmering bits, but the ugly parts too. Eight million people were crammed in this small tear on the map. So many people you could drown in them. Babies and bodies appearing like offerings.

Nell had worried for a long time about being recognised here, but it never seemed to happen. Unlike Lindsay, Nell had an ordinary face. Plain, generic. Neither ugly nor pretty. She had narrow shoulders, a small nose and mouth, eyes that were blue without being bright, and dark brown hair without any hint of red or blonde even in the sunlight.

When she'd first moved to the city, she noted the work shifts at all her favourite delis and rotated her visits so she didn't encounter the same cashiers often. She ordered different things until she'd exhausted the menu, and then she started again.

The news circuit exists in a pit of quicksand, and soon enough nobody cared about Reina. The Eddletons still tried mercilessly to keep the case afloat. November 2019 had marked nine years since the date of Reina's disappearance, and approaching a decade had been enough of a landmark to warrant a feature on some evening news programs. Nell was pointedly absent from the family photos, thanks to the efficacy of her state attorney all those years ago.

Still, she'd kept the TV off for months, and recycled the newspapers before Sebastian could get to them.

She'd fallen in love with a man who had little interest in the world's tragedies. On a news and cultural level, he only cared about the stock values, whether it was a buyer's market, and occasionally what was going on in the local art scene.

Nell had learned that most people were like Sebastian. Most people turned on the news in the mornings and at night, letting the anchorperson tell grim stories while they made their coffee and unclasped their jewellery and fed their children. It was just background noise, easily forgotten and occasionally earning a 'that's so sad' or 'people are so sick'.

And now, Nell sat curled in her recliner, cradling a mug of tea and staring out at the city while the television prattled on.

Sebastian was watching a documentary about online gaming culture, something that was especially dear to his heart. This had its own world of gore and guts. No matter how realistic the graphics were, though, players could always resurrect from the dead and the monsters weren't necessarily human. You had mythical creatures to fill that role.

'Hey,' Bas said. Nell blinked owlishly at him. 'You okay?' he asked.

She gave him a half-smile in answer. Her way of dodging the truth.

'You never said how the interview went,' Bas said. He lowered the volume on the TV.

She had been in the shower when he came home from work, which hadn't been coincidence. Then she'd breezed out of the bathroom still wrapped in a towel and said, 'Should we order in for dinner? I'm craving Thai.' And then she had asked him about his day and made sure that there was always something to fill the silence. The TV, or the whir of the Keurig dispensing hot water for her tea.

But that could only last for so long. Of course he wanted to know how the interview went; she'd made such a big deal out of getting it.

'I'm going to write it,' Nell said. 'I haven't told Jasper yet.' She didn't like to pitch ideas to her agent until she'd at least done her preliminary interviews. For the Widow Thompson this had taken a month. The widow's siblings didn't return phone calls at first, and Nell had to start with a cousin, slowly working her way into the family's circle of trust.

'I'm going to reach out to Easter's adoptive parents and see if they're willing to speak to me,' Nell said.

'Her brother is working with you, right?' Bas said.

'Yes,' Nell answered. 'But he's very close to the

project and he'll be biased. Better to get a dynamic array of participants.'

'"A dynamic array of participants",' Bas said, grinning. 'God, you sound so professional.'

She raised her chin. 'Don't I?'

Everything she'd said so far was the truth, but it didn't stop the hot flutter of nerves in her stomach. A feeling like this wasn't going to end well.

A car alarm was blaring in the street below. Maybe it had been doing that for a while. Nell grabbed the remote and raised the volume, even though it was a commercial.

Her tea had gone cold, but she blew on it like it was still hot. Suddenly the thought of Sebastian getting up to refresh her tea was unbearable. Any small act of kindness would have felt like spiders on her skin.

Tomorrow, she would contact Easter's adoptive parents and get to work. She would pretend that everything was fine, and eventually this would be true.

The car alarm wailed on. Then came the distant sirens, the honk of a fire truck.

Sebastian got up and went over to the window. The penthouse was thirty stories up and the altitude dulled the city commotion somewhat, but he had never gotten used to the noise.

'Hey.' Sebastian had one hand on the velvet curtain that covered the massive floor-to-ceiling windows. 'Where's your sister tonight?'

'Her monthly booze-and-painting thing at the country club,' Nell said. The churning in her stomach kicked up a level, and her chest started to hurt. 'How come?'

'That looks like her car that's on fire.' His tone was unbelieving: *nah, it couldn't be.*

Nell got up and followed his gaze.

If the coupe being devoured by flames didn't belong to Lindsay, it was the exact same model. It was the same shade of Red Obsession, which Lindsay had so haughtily corrected when Nell made the error of just calling it 'red'.

*It's not Lindsay's car*, she told herself. But for some undetermined reason she started running for the door, Sebastian on her heels.

Thirty stories isn't very high when you've got an elevator, especially late at night when nobody else is pressing floors and adding themselves to your descent. But in certain moments it can feel like an eternity.

Nell watched the buttons for each floor light up as the car dropped lower, lower.

Thirty.

Twenty-two.

Fifteen.

When the doors finally opened, she had already imagined what she would find. But that still didn't prepare her.

She ran through the polished, brightly lit lobby and endured another small eternity going through the revolving door to the outside, where the November cold bit at her skin. Even the heat from the burning car didn't reach her. The smoke found her, though, fogging up her vision with black plumes, making her eyes water. Through this, she could see Lindsay's licence plate still bolted to the bumper. That was when 'of course it isn't her' collided with 'I knew it was her'.

A crowd had formed, a mix of neighbours and passers-by, all standing across the street and at a distance, murmuring to each other and huddling.

The fire was already out. Above the ringing in her head, Nell could hear the rush of water through the hose. And then from somewhere very far away, a fireman saying, 'We've got a body.'

Nell was screaming. On some level she knew this. The eyes that had been gaping at the car were now gaping at her instead. Someone held her back, and it didn't matter that she fought or cursed or kicked. Someone was telling her to calm down, to just wait.

Smoke still wafted up like the fleeting thoughts that linger after a nightmare upon waking. And through it, Nell could see the body being pulled from the driver's side door.

Bodies, Nell had seen. Slight and unassuming as she was, she often wove her way between reporters when bodies were found. She was one of the people who showed up to stare, wondering if there was a story in someone else's tragedy.

But this body didn't make sense. The skin was melting. The hair was too bright and unreal.

Nell stopped screaming. She went still, and her feet landed on the sidewalk again.

The fireman dropped the body unceremoniously to the concrete and announced, 'It's a mannequin.'

Relief turned to confusion. It *was* a mannequin, its head turned to Nell at an inhuman angle, its eyes indifferent. Pert nose melting, cheeks charred, left ear still burning before the smoke chewed up the flames.

Sebastian was beside her now, wrapping his robe around her shoulders. He must have seen it too: the crude imposter of a corpse lying on the pavement.

All of her terror and shock turned fast into anger. She wanted to kick the thing, to crack its plastic head with the heel of her bare foot. She stomped over to her sister's car and looked in through the shattered windows. The seats were empty.

A firefighter took her by the arm. 'Ma'am, you need to step away.'

She drew her elbow back and hit him in the gut. It was a reflex. It had been more than a decade since anyone had tried to manhandle her but the venomous foster kid in her would always surface.

Sebastian was at her side now. 'Go upstairs,' he said. 'Try and get Lindsay on her cell. I'll talk to them.'

It was the exact right thing to say. It gave her just

55

enough perspective to move. She ran back for the revolving door, Bas and the firefighter's murmurings behind her.

The phone was ringing inside the apartment. Even before she'd opened the door, Nell could hear the melodic trilling, the vibration rattling the granite counter.

The name 'Lindsay' appeared at the bottom of the screen, below a photo of her sister wearing a Santa hat and staring through a giant fishbowl glass of wine.

'Linds.' Nell's voice was breathless when she pressed the phone to her ear. She was breathing hard, as though she'd run up all thirty flights rather than taken the elevator.

'Can you come down here?' Lindsay said. 'The cab just dropped me home and you're not going to believe this; some fuckwad stole my car right out of the driveway.'

'Okay.' Nell fell into a barstool, all of her bones turning to jello. 'I'll be there in ten minutes.'

For Nell, an estimate of ten minutes was code for 'an hour, maybe more'. But just this once, she tugged on her boots and was in her car in record time.

Just as Nell's life was contained to the bustle of Rockhollow, Lindsay's life was equally contained to the posh suburb just ten minutes north. It was a perfect metaphor for how their entire lives had been: close, but entirely different.

Past the bodega wedged between a neon sign

advertising palm readings and a package store, beyond the gridlocked apartments and brownstones, the chaos abruptly died. There were long, winding roads surrounded by trees and farms. Ritzy grocery stores and fresh fruit stands – all of which closed by 9 PM.

Lindsay was in her own dimension here. A dimension of leggings, fur-lined suede boots and perpetual latte-wielding. She never looked at price tags and she was always sporting some kind of diamond in her ears, on her wrist or around her neck. She had not amassed these financial gains on her own, but rather by way of her two failed marriages. Matthew Cranlin had been first. After that had been Robert Della, from whom Lindsay had acquired a modest suburban mansion with three empty bedrooms, none of which contained the children she ultimately couldn't give him. The country club with its boozy painting nights was a lingering piece of that catastrophic union. Nell liked Robert, but she hadn't let herself hope it would last. Lindsay never left her heart in one place for too long, not even if she was in love. Especially if she was in love.

Nell arrived at Lindsay's driveway to find her standing there waiting in the glow of her porch light, tapping at her phone. When she saw Nell's car, she waved and ran towards her.

'Christ, this night,' Lindsay said as she fell into the passenger seat.

Nell broke into tears. She didn't know why. She hadn't expected them. It was unfair the way they just sprang up without warning.

'What?' Lindsay's tone was grave. 'Is it Easter? Did that psycho do something?'

Nell shook her head. She swiped at her eyes. Took a breath. Put the car back in drive. But before she could move, Lindsay clamped a hand over the wheel. 'Tell me what happened.'

'I know where your car is,' Nell said.

❋

By the time they arrived at Nell's building, the crowd was gone. The fire truck too. There was only a lone police car parked behind the tow truck that had come for Lindsay's car. Lights flickered in black puddles on the street.

Lindsay saw the skeletal remains of her alimony checks and looked like she was going to throw up.

Lindsay cared greatly about *things*. She wasn't sentimental, but she was hungry for luxuries, hoarding them as though they might disappear if she didn't.

'No, no, no,' she said, and yanked open the door even before Nell had finished parking. She sprinted to the tow truck's driver side door and hoisted herself up to peer through the window. Doubtless she expected the driver to offer her some sort of explanation.

The mannequin was gone, though a wet tuft of synthetic yellow hair was lying in the street like drenched tumbleweed. No crime scene. Just litter.

Nell's eyes were drawn to it. In the periphery was Lindsay's silhouette against the flashing lights and the blur of cars passing by. She jumped when Sebastian rapped his knuckle on her window.

She opened the door, and when the air hit her she realised how cold the night was. She hadn't noticed earlier, when the world had stopped spinning.

'Did you find anything out?' Nell asked.

'They're going to check with some gas stations and banks to see if the joyride was captured on any surveillance cameras,' Bas said. 'But it looks like someone stole the car and set it on fire to destroy the evidence.'

*That doesn't make sense*, Nell thought. People stole cars all the time, but then they just abandoned them. Fires drew attention. Parking a stolen coupe under a bridge where it would be stripped of its parts did not.

And why the mannequin? Nell searched her memory. The mannequin hadn't been wearing clothes. The hair had been blonde. This was generic enough for a shop window mannequin, but it had been a wig. Why a wig? Why blonde? Was it meant to mimic Lindsay, or was that just a coincidence?

Nell didn't believe in coincidences, even when she wanted to.

# 6
# THEN

The year that Nell gave birth to Reina, Lindsay aged out of the system and moved into her own apartment. It wasn't much. The walls were thin, and now that Nell and the baby occupied the living room, the neighbours hated them.

Reina cried. And not only when she was hungry or she had made a mess. She cried indiscriminately, at every hour. And if someone picked her up, her cry changed to a keening pitch that no human had any business being able to make. She hated being touched, and Nell, in turn, hated having to touch her. She hated holding this small, quivering little body that was always hot, as though flushed with rage. She hated the feeling that she was going to break her, or that she already had.

Nell hadn't known what to expect from motherhood. She had hoped it would make her feel important, but it was proving to just be another in her long pattern of failures. She didn't know how to soothe her baby, and after a month and a half of the constant screaming, she was not sure she could even bring herself to love it.

Loving her baby was the one thing Nell had been prepared to do well. Love was free. She expected it to be the way family worked. She loved her father, even if she hated him at the same time. And she loved Bonnie, though she'd rather have nothing to do with her most days. And she loved Lindsay, though that love had been well earned.

But she did not love this baby. How could anyone love a thing that brought nothing but misery?

When she slept at all, she dreamt that Reina had disappeared, or even that she had never been born. She dreamt that she had taken the money her sister offered and just aborted Reina in the first place. Dreamed of Reina's little malformed hands and skull being scraped across her uterine walls like caviar.

Nell awoke from these dreams hating herself, not for the dreams but for still wishing them to be true. She had never known herself to be capable of such ugly thoughts, and she never told Lindsay about them. She never told anyone. Hatred turned to fear and back again, over and over in her head, always trapped.

Neighbours pounded on the wall. Police came. Once, that old bat downstairs called social services to make sure they weren't stabbing the kid with hot pins. The social worker had been kind and sympathetic. 'It's tough when it's the first one,' she said. 'I have four.'

Lindsay had looked at Nell and said, 'I'll sew your vagina shut myself if you think you're having four.'

✦

# NOW

Nell didn't sleep. She sat at the desk she rarely used; she had never been good at keeping organised or committing to one spot. But right now, she was stationed there, thirty stories up from the rest of the city. A faraway siren wailed, and Nell took comfort that the sound was not for anyone in her own life. Sebastian was asleep in bed, and she could hear his rasped breathing through the open door.

Lindsay was a small bump in the chenille throw on the couch, also asleep. She could sleep through anything. As children, the sisters had sought out their own superpowers, and they discovered that was Lindsay's. She could escape to dreamland no matter how frightened she was.

Nell's superpower was that she could pretend nothing was wrong. Her foster parents thought she was dumb, or else easy, and she had escaped a lot of wrath that way.

Nell hadn't let Lindsay go home, and besides, in the morning Nell would have to shuttle her around to the police station, DMV and insurance office while they untangled this mess.

For tonight, Nell could only focus on the case that had already been solved. A photograph of Easter Hamblin's arrest was open on the front tab of her browser, the woman's hands cuffed behind her back. A police officer is pushing her into the back of a cruiser. Her head is raised in one final defiant look at the free world. She will never see it like this again. For the rest of her life, it will be in fleeting glimpses through prison bus windows as she's transported to and from the courthouse.

Nell switched to the next tab. It was an email from Easter's brother Oleg; they were scheduled to meet in a downtown café tomorrow, and she typed out a reply to let him know that she couldn't make it. The next day would be better. Or any other day this week. 'Schedule's free whenever you are,' she wrote.

She hit send.

She opened a new tab.

Here she hesitated, staring at the blinking cursor. She checked over her shoulder just to confirm that she was the only one awake, and then she typed her old name in the search bar.

Penelope Wendall.

It was a name she hadn't used since 2011, after it had been legally changed. She wanted to believe that she could abandon her past in a pen stroke. Register for college as a new person entirely.

Most of the articles that came up were old. Photos of her teenage self, when she had been rail thin with long hair. She looked like a child in all of them, eighteen years old with a dead stare in her eyes. She had felt so old back then.

If Sebastian saw this girl, would he recognise her? Back then, all the girls her age were on Facebook and MySpace. Their lives were chronicled in photos of parties, drives with friends, posing over plates of fajitas in restaurants. But Nell hadn't indulged in any of these things. She hadn't even taken pictures of Reina, much less herself. Who would she have shared them with anyway? She didn't have any friends. Even Lindsay had eluded her back then, lost in the fiery passion of her courtship with Matthew Cranlin. Nell pretended she hated her sister during those years, rather than accept that she had been abandoned by a third parent. And so the only photos of teenage Nell came from blurry surveillance footage and paparazzi candids.

Her blood went cold at the photo of Ethan with his arm around her. Her face was covered by the jacket of his suit as he ushered her down the church steps. It had been a long time since Nell had seen her child's father, and this photo was so clear. He was in focus: pale skin, dark blue eyes, black hair that he let grow almost to his shoulders. She could see in his face that he loved her then. This was the first vigil after Reina went missing.

She scrolled down, pushing the image out of her mind. She had learned to do that with Ethan. She tucked him away somewhere in her brain amid heaps of awkward social encounters and bitter regrets. He never went away completely, but neither did any other bits of the past. The present was just a slide show projected onto all the things people wanted to hide.

Her name appeared in no articles in the year after the trial. This was a credit to her defence attorney, who had managed to put a gag order on Ethan's parents, the Eddletons. They could discuss their missing grandchild all they wanted. They could hang flyers and muscle their way onto talk shows and stand on the roof shouting with a megaphone, but Nell was always to be blurred out of photos and her name was never to be spoken.

There were a few message boards dated as late as 2017. People trying to find Nell, wondering where she was, hoping she was dead and sharing rumours that she was. But it's no fun waiting for a witch to burn if the witch never shows, and the interest died away. There were new mothers to hate. Maggie Kitling, who shot her five- and seven-year-old daughters and made it look like a botched carjacking because her boyfriend hadn't wanted children. Elaine Yeates, who drowned her son in the family swimming pool because his ADHD was too demanding and her church forbade medications to calm him.

Even these women, with their confessions captured on police interrogation room cameras and uploaded to YouTube, were eventually forgotten.

Nell closed the tab and went back to reading about Easter and Autumn. The sisters had kept a low profile. There was no social media and no shared photos. The other tenants in their apartment complex had not even known they had ever been conjoined.

There was more information in the stack of photographs Oleg had given her. Maybe that was how Easter had learned who she was; they were both so good at hiding in plain sight.

She opened a new private tab and typed in SilverBars.org, a forum that came up somewhere in the search results of every case she researched. A collection of message boards for crime and punishment addicts, it boasted millions of threads, ranging from news and general updates on cases, all the way to prison groupies who discussed their favourite cases, which inmate was the most fuckable and tips for writing a letter that was guaranteed to get a response.

Nell typed 'Penelope Wendall' in the search field. There were no hits, but this was always the case whenever she checked. The website was founded in 2015 by a bunch of prison groupies who were kicked off of other social media platforms for violating their terms of service. And by 2015, Nell's own story had long since been buried under an avalanche of newer, more sensationalised stories of deceit and murder and unsolved disappearances.

She intended to keep it that way.

# 7
# NOW

The ride to the police station was silent, neither Nell nor Lindsay in any particular mood for chatter, both of them lost, for once, in their own separate worries. They were never without worries, but they were usually better at hiding them.

Lindsay still hadn't been home to change, and now her hair smelled like Nell's shampoo and she was wearing Nell's clothes: straight-leg jeans and a white sweater with wooden buttons. The plainness of Nell's wardrobe irritated Lindsay, but on her, somehow these pieces looked glamorous. The look was topped off with Lindsay's heart-shaped sunglasses and coral lipstick. Sometimes her beauty was polished and manicured, and other times, like today, it was haphazard and bohemian. But it always emanated strength and assuredness.

It was a marvel to Nell that they were related sometimes. Every good thing in Lindsay's life had been hard-won and meticulously planned. Even when it blew up, like her marriages, the pieces fell in a way that could still be utilised. Conversely, Nell came about all her good fortunes by accident,

69

without trying, and lived with the constant fear that she would inevitably fuck them up.

She parked in front of the station just as a car sped from the lot, siren blaring. Neither sister was unfamiliar with facilities of law enforcement, but this trip felt especially ominous.

Minutes later, they found themselves sitting in an interview room, waiting for an officer to speak to them. The air was dry and punishingly hot. Lindsay groused about sweating off her concealer. After several moments of fussing, she said, 'You look like you need a drink. I propose an early lunch after we're done here. We have another two hours before the appointment with the insurance agent.'

'Sure.' Nell pulled the phone from her purse and checked for messages. Nothing new since this morning. She turned off the screen and tucked it back amid wads of receipts and a pack of spearmint gum.

'Mrs Della,' an officer entered the room, pausing to close the door behind him. 'Thank you so much for coming down to speak with me. I'm Officer Greg Rayburn.'

'It's Ms Della, actually,' Lindsay said as she shook his hand. She had kept Robert's name in the divorce but dropped the implication that it had ever belonged to him. 'I don't understand why I needed to come down in person, though. Isn't this something that can be worked out through the insurance?'

'I'm afraid it's more complicated than that. Your insurance company will want to do their own inspection of the vehicle, but we're treating this as a threat of bodily harm.'

'A threat?' Lindsay blinked. 'Someone took my car out for a joyride and trashed it. I live in the suburbs, Greg. Lots of rich brats looking to rebel.'

The officer appeared flustered by her easy use of his name, but he went on. 'Where was your car parked, Ms Della?'

'In my driveway,' Lindsay said. 'There's a gate, but I don't lock it.'

'And where were you?' Rayburn asked.

'Out with friends.' Lindsay was deliberately vague. 'I wasn't driving. The car was missing when I got home. I keep a spare set of keys hidden under the back porch and they were gone.'

Rayburn laid his clipboard on the table, face down so his notes weren't showing. He leaned closer. 'Ms Della, can you think of anyone who might want to harm you? Threaten you?'

Lindsay shot a fleeting stare at Nell. In that instant, Nell saw the epiphany in Lindsay's eyes. *Shut up*, that look said. *Don't you dare.*

Nell didn't say anything. She wouldn't have, even without the warning.

'There's nobody,' Lindsay said. 'Like I said, I'm sure it was some bored rich kids looking for something to do.'

71

The officer unclipped a manila folder from his clipboard and slid it across the table to Lindsay. She opened it, and her expression almost resembled fear, before she laughed instead. 'What's this?'

'That's the mannequin that was pulled from your car last night. It was stolen from a women's clothing boutique on 45th and Main. We're still waiting on security cam footage from the store and the gas station across the street.'

45th was uptown, in the part of the city that flirted with the outlying suburbs. The absence of any nightlife scene meant it was reasonably quiet. For some kids looking to get into white-collar trouble, it was an unsurprising choice.

Nell scooted her chair closer and looked at the photo too. The mannequin was made of a durable plastic, with painted eyebrows and blue eyeshadow that gave it an eerily lifelike appearance. The wig was bright and garish; an unlikely choice for such an upscale shop. It looked like a costume store wig. A realistic wig was useless if it wasn't the right colour. Someone had made sure this mannequin had a cheap imitation of Lindsay's features.

'I don't know what this is supposed to tell me.' Lindsay slid the folder back to Rayburn. 'If I've answered your questions, I'll be going now.'

'Ms Della—'

'My insurance will be in touch.' Lindsay stood, Nell automatically following. 'Thank you for your work, Greg, and your concern. But I'm sure you'll get your camera footage and realise this was just a group of kids. Don't go too hard on them. Insurance will get me a new car; I'm not looking to press charges.'

Lindsay had never moved so fast. Nell trailed after her through the building and across the parking lot like a clumsy gosling following its mother.

'Don't,' Lindsay said pre-emptively as Nell climbed into the driver's seat.

'Linds, you should have told him about Matthew.'

'It doesn't matter.' Lindsay waved her arm at the steering wheel. 'Drive.'

Nell tugged the car aggressively in drive, but she went on. 'He was a monster, Linds.'

'Do you think I don't know that?' Lindsay turned in her seat to face her. 'That's why you aren't speaking to the current Mrs Cranlin right now. But it was a long time ago, and he has no reason to come back and make threats. I'm sure he's busy tormenting his new wife.'

Matthew Cranlin. That smug piece of shit. He was the only person Nell hated more than she hated the press, more than the vultures that had peddled her photos and pried into her life and accused her of murdering her missing daughter because it sold papers.

'You should have told him,' Nell murmured.

'Can we drop this now?' Lindsay said.

They came to a red light and Nell hit the brakes so hard they both jolted forward. 'No, Lindsay. No we cannot drop this. I saw your car last night and my heart just about stopped. I thought that was you being pulled out of the flames. I thought you were dead.'

They began moving again. Lindsay turned to look out her window. 'I'm sorry,' she mumbled. 'I didn't know you thought it was me.' An apology from Lindsay was a rare thing, but Nell was in no position to revel in it now.

'If someone is trying to hurt you, if there's anyone who has any reason to be pissed off, you need to tell me.'

'Matthew was a monster, like I said, but I can't think of a reason he'd come for me now. There's nothing to gain; I don't even collect alimony from him.'

It didn't matter if there was anything to gain. It had not been enough for Matthew simply to have Lindsay as his wife. To dress her up to impress his friends, fuck her any time he wanted. He had always wanted something more. To devour her whole, to own her fire and her spirit. It infuriated him how much he loved her. He wanted to keep her and kill her at the same time.

A divorce couldn't end something that powerful. Maybe nothing could.

But that hadn't been the worst part. The worst

74

part had been trying to make Lindsay understand this. It was like screaming in a dream, wondering why no sound came out.

Nell turned into the lot of the Gold Acropolis. As diners went it wasn't the ritziest, but they served alcohol at all hours and Lindsay liked their breakfasts.

Lindsay's distracted silence over breakfast gave Nell a greater feeling of unease than anything else to happen in the last twenty-four hours. Lindsay downed a tall stack of pancakes but didn't even feign interest in her mimosa. Nell hated to see her sister so worried, and moreover, hated not knowing what she was thinking.

'Linds, I don't want you to go back to the house.'

'Don't be dramatic. It's the safest place. There's an alarm on every window.' She was staring out at the busy divided highway. Over the past decade, the city had become so overpopulated that people had begun flooding the outskirts, desperate for more affordable housing. If they couldn't live in the city itself, they could at least have a view. The highway had doubled in size, and the air always smelled faintly of gasoline.

'I hate this time of year.' Lindsay's voice was soft. She was speaking more to her faded reflection in the glass than to Nell. 'At first, the air gets a little chilly, but then on days like these, the sun is out but there's a bitter cold that cuts through you. It doesn't matter what you wear. It doesn't matter if you hold your hands up to the vents with the heat going full blast. The cold gets inside of you.'

Nell felt a shiver move through her. She gave a lot of thought to weather like this. Days like this. The thing that truly made her restless and made eyes seem beady and intentions sinister was the anniversary that had passed without acknowledgement. Every year she moved over it like an odd bump on a dark road. This week was ten years since Reina had disappeared. Instantly, silently, the frozen white sky had devoured her whole. It was the cleanest explanation. They never found so much as a shoe. It seemed impossible that such a vast world filled with so many people had been unable to unearth even a missing child's fingernail. Somewhere in the cardboard archives of the police station, Reina was preserved in a folder like a dead flower in an old book. The box could be opened, the photographs and reports viewed a hundred times, a million, but there was no life there, and nothing left to bloom. Nell's child was a stunning rarity: one of the few things that didn't come back.

And it had been on a day just like this.

Nell reached across the table and grabbed Lindsay's wrist. She could feel how real and solid and warm she was. Lindsay was her constant. Reina had appeared one day and disappeared just as suddenly, but Lindsay had always been in Nell's world, and if she ever left, she would take that entire world with her.

Lindsay seemed grateful for the touch. She wasn't the sort to initiate affection, or to ask for it, but the lack of it would make her do desperate things – like marry Matthew Cranlin.

Nell's phone trilled in her purse, making her flinch. She fumbled for it and checked the number on the screen. 'Shit, sorry, I have to take this,' she said. She ran outside, a gust of icy wind blowing across the speaker and distorting her voice when she said, 'Hello?'

'Hello,' an uncertain voice replied. It was a woman. 'Is this Nell Way? I hope I have the right number.'

'Yes,' Nell said. 'Is this Mrs Hamblin?'

'I read your email,' the woman said, by way of answer. 'My husband doesn't want me to speak with you, but—' She cut herself off. The line went so silent that Nell checked the screen to make sure the call hadn't dropped.

'I can meet with you today,' the woman went on, still hesitant. 'Can you come to my house now? I'll email you the address.'

Nell looked at Lindsay through the diner window. She was using the camera on her phone to reapply her lipstick.

Mrs Hamblin sounded uncertain. If Nell tried to reschedule, she would lose her opportunity to talk to the twins' adoptive mother. But if she spoke to her now, maybe she could earn her trust, which would lead to further interviews, which would ultimately lead to a book that did justice to both Easter and Autumn.

'Yes,' she said. 'Are you in the city? You know what, it doesn't matter. Send me the address, and wherever you are, I'll be there as fast as I can.'

After hanging up, Nell breezed into the diner and began fishing for cash in her wallet. 'That was work,' she said. 'I'm going to drop you off at the insurance agency and from there you're going to have to take a cab back to my apartment.'

'Work?' Lindsay said. And then she went pale, and she whispered, 'Not the crazy twin story. I thought you were going to drop that one.'

'Why would I drop it?' Nell asked.

'Do you just want the immediate reasons, or should I sit down and compose a list?' Lindsay said. But Nell had already left the money on the table and was making for the door.

Lindsay sprinted to keep up with Nell. 'You aren't speaking to that crazy woman's family alone,' Lindsay said. 'I'm going with you.'

'No,' Nell said. 'You aren't. Yesterday you didn't keep your mouth shut, and I can't have you doing that, Linds, I just can't. Mrs Hamblin is very skittish about speaking to me. I don't want her getting scared off.'

Skittish, Nell understood. The Hamblins had made headlines throughout their daughter's trial. HEART-BROKEN PARENTS BLAME THEMSELVES. HAMBLIN MOM CONFIDES IN PRIEST FOR GUIDANCE. THE HAMBLINS A YEAR LATER: WILL THERE BE CLOSURE?

The media was ruthlessly parasitic. But Nell was not media. However chaotic she was in her own life, she approached the interviews with her subject's friends and family with finesse and compassion, things that had never been afforded to her when she was the subject of the same scrutiny. She would always ask them how they were doing, pause for the reply, thank them for their time.

Interviewing the subjects of her books themselves proved less formulaic. She hadn't interviewed Nathan Stuart, given that he was dead. But the Widow Thompson had evoked unexpected compassion from Nell. She had been very polite, even sweet. She often asked about the weather because her room, the hallways and the activity centre at her institution were without windows. She wanted to know if it was snowing or raining, or if the heat was of the humid or dry sort.

'You need to drop this project, Nell,' Lindsay said. 'There are a hundred other stories.'

Nell shook her head. 'A woman who murders her conjoined twin? There aren't a hundred of those.'

'The entire family must be crazy,' Lindsay said.

'Of course they're crazy,' Nell said. 'That's what makes the story so interesting.'

Lindsay was not used to losing arguments, and when Nell pulled up in front of the insurance agency, Lindsay's sourness was palpable. But they were at an impasse.

'Just be safe,' Lindsay said. 'And call me when you're done so I know this woman didn't murder you.'

'I promise not to get murdered,' Nell said.

Lindsay cut her a mean glare, but then she pushed forward and kissed Nell's cheek, and she was gone.

✻

The Hamblins lived in a brownstone in what Sebastian would call the sinister part of Rockhollow. But then, to him all cities were bubbling stew pots of crime and disease.

Nell thought it was pretty, with cast iron railings and rectangular gardens between staircases. The windows were tall and looked like half-closed eyes. The number 48 was bolted beside the front door in gleaming copper.

The door opened before Nell could knock.

'Ms Way?' Mrs Hamblin stood in the doorway. She was a tall woman, slim, with thinning blonde hair that had been teased back to fullness. She took pride in her appearance, that much was clear. Her face wore a coat of concealer and bronzer and blush, and her eyelashes were thick with mascara.

'Please call me Nell,' Nell said.

Mrs Hamblin nodded and moved aside to let her in. She did a quick sweep of the street before she pulled the door shut. 'Thanks for meeting with me on such short notice,' Mrs Hamblin said. She was leading Nell down a narrow hallway, past a staircase and into a study. Books lined the walls floor to ceiling. There was a piano, a fireplace and two leather armchairs. It was an impressive amount of furniture for such a small place, Nell thought. 'My husband is away visiting his mother. He flies back tomorrow morning, and he would be angry if he knew I'd agreed to speak with you. I'm still not sure why I agreed.'

'Well, thank you,' Nell said, sitting in one armchair while Mrs Hamblin took the other. 'I appreciate it. I know that it's difficult to establish trust after dealing with the media circus, but you have my word that nothing is on the record unless you agree to it.'

Mrs Hamblin gave a sad smile. 'Oleg has become a good friend to us, especially since the trial.'

Oleg was older than his sisters by five years. After his sisters were given up for adoption, he remained in Russia with their biological parents, but he never lost touch with his sisters. Visits, gifts, letters.

Nell offered a warm smile. 'It's good that you have him to talk to.'

'This has been hard on him,' Mrs Hamblin said. 'He was so close to Autumn. Even though he was only here once or twice a year, the two of them always picked up right where they left off.' She stared into the fire burning in the hearth. It made the house smell of cedar and camping. 'I don't know why I thought boys would be less open about their feelings than girls. I suppose that's unfair, isn't it? But I wanted a daughter because I thought daughters were supposed to be sweet.' She crossed one leg over the other and hooked her hands around her knee. She was so elegant, like a portrait in a gallery no one visited.

Nell wanted to ask what Mrs Hamblin meant by 'sweet' and if either of her daughters met the criteria. But she would have to choose her questions carefully so as not to startle her.

'We expected to adopt a baby. The waiting list is very long. Years. We were willing to wait, but when the agency called us about twins – I was overjoyed. They were older than what we expected. Ten. But one look at their faces and it was love.' Her voice fogged up with that word and she said it again. 'It was love.'

Nell wrote it down. 'What were they like?' she asked.

'Very shy,' Mrs Hamblin said. 'They came to live with us about a month before their surgery. We homeschooled for that first year so the girls could become more comfortable with English. They were both exceptionally bright. Autumn had a head for numbers; she was my little helper when I was balancing my chequebook or budgeting for groceries. And Easter had the most brilliant imagination. She could write entire plays in her head and perform them with her dolls. She even voiced the characters. But they were ... quiet, I suppose. Skittish for a long time.' Her voice lowered to a hush, though there was no one but Nell in the house to hear her. 'The social worker suggested that their birth parents used to hit them. So many times I thought of asking Oleg, but it never seemed right. He wasn't my child, after all.'

Nell thought of Easter switching between her Russian and American accents. If the conversation lulled, Nell was prepared to ask questions about the twins' relationship with each other and the outside world. But now that Mrs Hamblin had begun talking, she had a lot to say. She didn't sound like the mother of a murdered child; in her recounting of motherhood, she hadn't gotten to that part of the story yet. She was still the parent of two little girls with shiny blonde hair and sullen green eyes.

'I never knew when the girls were fighting with each other,' she said. 'Even as teenagers, they were very well-mannered. There were no shouting matches, but I would hear them whispering angrily sometimes at night. Some things they preferred to work out among themselves.'

'Do you have any examples?' Nell asked.

'Well, let's see.' Mrs Hamblin narrowed her eyes at the fireplace. Her gaze shifted to the mantel. It was decorated with a series of Precious Moments figurines and two candles, half melted in copper candelabras. There was an empty space at the centre; it would have been a perfect place for two framed photographs of identical children with matching scars. But there were no photos there, or anywhere else in the house that Nell had seen.

'There was that time with the mouse,' Mrs Hamblin said. 'The girls were nearly thirteen then. We found droppings in the cupboards and little holes in the cereal boxes. Bits of Cheerios all over.' A smile. 'Easter had the idea that she could catch the mouse and keep it like a pet. I said that would be fine, just so long as she got the damn thing out of my kitchen. She set about making little traps to catch it. But Autumn went into the basement and took a snap trap and baited it with peanut butter. She was only trying to help. She hated rodents and bugs – not because they scared her, but I think … well I think they reminded her of being destitute. She was a very tidy child and she liked things a certain way.

'We all heard the snap in the middle of the night. There was the mouse, dead in the trap, poor thing.'

Nell considered this. Easter had wanted a pet. That was typical for a child, and not at all typical for a budding murderer. Animals were the first victims of future killers. Small, easily broken things to whet the psychotic appetite for human blood.

But Autumn had been the one to kill the mouse. And she had used a trap. That didn't tell Nell anything at all; Autumn may well have been doing the practical thing: getting rid of a pest.

'What happened after that?' Nell asked.

'I'm not entirely sure,' Mrs Hamblin said. 'You could tell something had changed though.' She looked at her hands. 'Easter took her allowance and bought a guinea pig. I said it'd be all right. She took good care of it. It lasted almost ten years, I think. Pasha. She took it with her when she and Autumn moved into their apartment.'

There was a hitch to her voice when she said that last word. Here was where the story turned dark, with that one word: apartment. Once Autumn and Easter left this house, they ceased to be the children Mr and Mrs Hamblin had dreamed of. They became women. Their secrets flourished and festered and turned into something ugly.

If only they had stayed here. That's what Mrs Hamblin's expression said. Maybe they would have stayed little girls forever.

'I'm sorry,' Mrs Hamblin said. 'I have to ask you to leave now. I have guests due.'

'Mrs Hamblin—' Nell fought to keep her desperation in check. She knew this was the only interview she would likely be granted. This was the only time she would be welcomed into the home of the media's most infamous conjoined twins. 'This isn't just Easter's story. I would like to tell the world about your daughters as they really were. Before this happened.'

Mrs Hamblin fell silent and the air was tight. Nell felt her own pulse thudding in her temples. Had she just blown the interview?

'I didn't know what to expect, and that's my fault,' Mrs Hamblin finally said. 'I thought having children would be like the sitcoms I watched as a girl, and the poems on birthday cards.'

Nell was holding her breath. She didn't dare to make a sound, lest she ruin the momentum that had been built.

'They weren't easy children.' Mrs Hamblin tugged at her thin gold necklace as though it were tightening around her throat. 'I can only guess what sort of life they had in Russia. As I said, there may have been abuse. My husband and I tried to understand. In the twins' first year of high school, Easter would turn up with bruises all the time. I couldn't imagine how she was getting them because she wasn't the rambunctious type. Autumn came to me one evening in tears and said that Easter was beating herself with her hairbrush, burning her wrists with the curling iron.

'We put Easter in counselling immediately, but

I think – I think that was the wrong thing to do, because she shut down completely after that. And later that same year was when we found the wild rabbit head in the garden…'

She trailed off into silence, and the image hung suspended in the air.

'Mrs Hamblin.' Nell spoke gently. 'Who killed the rabbit?'

Mrs Hamblin's gaze was distant. She was still toying with her necklace and her hand had started to shake. 'Autumn said it was Easter. Easter said it was Autumn.' She looked at Nell and her eyes were pleading, as though she wanted Nell to confirm the truth for her. But all Mrs Hamblin said was, 'I didn't know which one to believe.'

# 8
# NOW

Some mothers know what sort of person their child will grow up to be.

Nell saw the harried mothers outside of PS 198 on weekday afternoons at 2:15. It was the best public school in the tri-state area, its alumna moving on to Harvard, Juilliard or sometimes straight to Broadway. The children were barely children at all, Nell thought. They had schedules and tutors and they knew words like 'deadline' and 'transcript'.

These miniature adults, dressed like flight attendant Barbies and I-need-to-speak-with-your-manager Kens, were trains on a set track. Nell would have liked to meet up with those children in ten years, in twenty. She would like to ask them if they were still stuck to that track, with all of the world's tragedies blurring by like trees past the windows of their lives. Maybe there was something to that. Maybe it was a better way to live, only vaguely aware of how terrible life could be.

Reina was in preschool before she disappeared, and already Mrs Eddleton had prepared her for this sort of mini-adulthood. *She wouldn't have done well in this world*, Nell thought.

Nell was sitting in a traffic jam caused by all the au pairs and mothers and full-time dads collecting their prodigies from school. There was a comforting efficacy to it, little wooden dolls in an old cuckoo clock.

But Reina had been the chaotic child, and given time, she would have been the one teachers called meetings about. She would have set fires and pushed and stolen little trophies she didn't even really want.

Nell never said it out loud, but she had known her little girl. She had known the sort of person she would have grown up to be.

Her phone rang. Stopped in the gridlock anyway, Nell answered it. She set it to speaker and rested it in the cup holder. 'I'm on my way,' she said.

'Drive faster,' Lindsay said.

'How'd it go with the insurance?'

'They're calling it theft and arson. I'm getting a new coupe. If you're nice, I'll let you drive it.'

'Liar,' Nell said.

'Well, I'll let you sit in it, even though you *abandoned* me to go on your ill-advised mission.'

Nell rolled her eyes. 'I'm through the school traffic now. I'll be there in two minutes.' She pressed 'end call' before Lindsay could reply. She had resolved not to argue with her sister today, not even in the form of their playful bickering. She had barely slept, and there was still so much to untangle about what the mannequin in the car meant.

She was thinking about Matthew Cranlin, whose

name hadn't been a part of their lives for nearly seven years. Much like Reina and the Eddletons, he had been left behind in suburban Missouri. On the surface, it was easy to see why he had caught Lindsay's eye. He was pretty in all the same ways that she was: sparkly-eyed and well-groomed.

Lindsay, twenty-one at the time, had constructed her appearance to give the impression of wealth. Matthew Cranlin had not only the appearance, he was the real deal. His parents had made some solid stock investments in IBM in the early nineties, and now they had more money than their multiple homes could contain.

It had been a Venus flytrap of a marriage, Lindsay's first love. The first time she had felt glamorous and important. From Nell's perspective, 'love' had been the wrong word. It had been an addiction. A foreign substance flooding her veins, making her hazy and heavy-lidded with lust until it all crashed to punishing wave after wave of pain.

Years later, when Robert came about, Nell had her suspicions about him as well. He was also pretty, also rich. It was clear that Lindsay had a type. But where Matthew had hidden Lindsay away, Robert had been an open book. He was from a large family, parents and siblings coming and going, carrying little nieces and nephews, kissing each other on the cheeks and planning Dirty Santa swaps for Christmas parties.

He never seemed impatient or angered by Nell's presence, not even when she came to steal her sister away for entire afternoons. If it was late, and the sisters had downed one too many glasses of wine by the fire, he would get the spare blankets from the hall closet and make up one of the guest beds for Nell without being asked.

Those guest bedrooms were ultimately what undid the marriage. Not only was Robert a man who valued family, he also wanted to cultivate one of his own, little babies popping out of Lindsay like garden blossoms. They would attend private school, of course. Summers at the Cape (memories are important), non-GMO baby foods (no cancer and reproductive issues down the line for little Susie or Robert Jr.), BPA-free bottles and white-noise machines to ease the transition from womb to world.

Lindsay played along. Who knew, maybe she meant to go through with it. For a short while, he sold her on the idea of being one of those helicopter mommies you see at every dress rehearsal, mouthing the words and throwing jazz hands to their mortified child. She'd even gone so far as to let him assemble the crib.

But then, faced with the prospect of Diaper Genies and Pedialyte, she panicked.

Nell blamed herself for this. Because of what had happened to Reina, Lindsay knew that children were fleeting little things, like rainbows cast on the wall in a beam of late afternoon sun. She couldn't sign on for that.

When Nell pulled up in front of the insurance agency, Lindsay was kerbside and she got into the car before Nell could put it in park. 'How was your murder interview?' she asked.

'Fine,' Nell said. 'I have enough to draw up an outline. I'm going to email it to Jasper by the weekend.' Outlines were the only organised thing Nell could produce. The rest of her life – her first drafts, her notes, her dresser and closet and kitchen sink – were all a helpless mess.

'I googled myself last night,' Nell confessed. She wasn't sure why she blurted that out. She was tired and the loneliness of last night's thoughts had grown unbearable.

'Like your book reviews?' Lindsay was rummaging through the glove box for a tissue. The late fall chill left her face perpetually leaking.

'No,' Nell said. 'Like from before.'

Lindsay blew her nose. 'From Missouri?' Her voice was incredulous.

'I wanted to see if there was anything new. There wasn't.'

'I've been thinking since yesterday,' Lindsay said. 'Maybe it would be cathartic to just tell Sebastian.'

'Were they serving alcohol at the insurance agency?'

93

'I'm serious. He loves you, Nell. And I don't mean Hallmark card and flowers on your anniversary love. I mean he's deliriously, stupidly, borderline psychotic in love with you. He might understand.'

'That's what I'm afraid of,' Nell said. 'He'll understand. He'll understand that I'm not what he thought.'

'Yes you are,' Lindsay said. 'You're way more honest with each other than I ever was with Robert. It's a little disgusting how much you respect each other.'

It hurt to breathe. Nell was imagining what would happen if she told him. She didn't expect that he would yell or even say something truthful about how heartless she was. Rather, she would wake up in the morning and find that he'd left her. All of his things removed from the closet and the bathroom vanity. Even the bougie espresso mugs he kept stacked by the Keurig – gone.

'If this Easter lunatic gets out ahead of you and tells him, that's worse. There's something redemptive about telling him yourself,' Lindsay said. 'Nell, you have a good thing with him. I don't want to see you fuck it up.'

But Nell had already fucked it up. She fucked it up when she was eighteen years old, long before she even knew Sebastian. Long before she believed it was possible that someone would love her.

On particular sleepless nights, she tried to imagine Reina walking through the door of her

94

apartment one day as though she'd always been there. But the image could never form. It fell apart, like the moment you realise you're dreaming and wake yourself up.

Nell didn't say anything for the rest of the drive, and Lindsay wisely decided not to push it.

✹

There was a van parked outside of Lindsay's house when they pulled up. Lindsay looked at her watch. 'They're early,' she said.

'Who?' Nell asked.

'I'm having security cameras installed. The insurance agent gave me a number and whoever stole my car is crazy if they think they're pulling that shit twice.'

Lindsay sashayed to the van while Nell pulled into the driveway. Lindsay lived in a white-collar castle of a house, with high ceilings and skylights and a coffee maker that came to life when someone said the word 'brew'.

It wasn't Lindsay's usual taste. Growing up in foster homes had left her rather like a cat; she favoured small, quiet spaces, all of her valuables in one place where she could see them.

While Lindsay dealt with the installation, Nell called Sebastian at work. He answered on the first ring.

'Hey,' he said. 'How'd everything go?'

'Lindsay's fine. She's getting a new car out of this, so she's happy,' Nell said. She hesitated to say much more than that. While she had given Bas *nearly* all of her secrets, she hadn't been so generous with Lindsay's. All Sebastian knew of Matthew Cranlin was that he was an asshole with no redeeming qualities, and the only acceptable thing to do was hope he contracted a venereal disease involving microscopic crawling things.

'What about the mannequin?' he asked.

'I don't know,' Nell said. 'She's being really cagey about it, but she's installing security cameras so at least she's taking it seriously.'

'Maybe we should do the same thing,' Bas said. 'This new book you've just finished – it's going to be big, Nell. And there are a lot of weirdos out there. I worry.'

There were cameras in the apartment lobby, in addition to twenty-four-hour security, but Nell was still touched by his concern.

'Lindsay is going to shoo me away if she suspects I'm staying over to babysit her, so I'm going to tell her you insisted on coming over for dinner tonight and making your famous lobster bisque. You won't take no for an answer.'

'Sounds like I'm being pretty obstinate,' Bas said.

'Very. I'm certainly not going to argue with you.'

'I'll be there at seven. I guess I'm going to swing by the store for lobster after work.'

'Can't wait,' Nell said.

'Gotta go, Nells. Love you.'

'Love you.'

She'd been ending their phone calls with those two words for more than a year now, and they still felt alien to her. Like she was reading from a script, even though she happened to agree with her lines. She was still waiting for the day she could believe that this was her life. That her social worker wasn't going to show up one morning without warning and tell her to go pack a bag, it's over, there's another family with a vacancy.

❋

Sebastian showed up at exactly 7:00, a bag of groceries in each hand. Lindsay, curled on the leather sofa in front of the modular electric fireplace, lifted her iPad. She tapped the purple SECURITY ASSURE+ app. Ten squares appeared on the screen, with live views of her house. The driveway. The brick walkway framed by rose hedges and Japanese maples. The in-ground pool whose vinyl cover was filled with old rainwater and leaves. There was an aerial view of Sebastian on the landing with a grocery bag in either hand. He was in grey night vision, and when he glanced up at the camera his eyes flashed white, an animal in headlights.

'It's pretty fancy, right?' Lindsay said, holding it up for Nell to see.

'Very,' Nell said, standing to answer the door. 'You should angle one to spy on the neighbours.'

'If I wanted to see white women get day drunk, I'd stand in front of a mirror,' Lindsay said.

Nell was grateful for Sebastian's presence. He had a congenial spirit. He knew how to be engaging without being overbearing, just the right amount of cringeworthy and witty. Nell and Lindsay sat on the counter on either side of the stove, watching him dump the lobsters into the boiling water. They waved their claws in languid panic. He closed the lid.

He was telling a story about his boss, Gerald, whose teenage daughter had recently gotten her driver's licence. She took a turn with too much zeal and hit the bumper of a delivery truck. That truck, it turned out, was delivering printer supplies to Gerald's office. Some comical kismet.

Lindsay smirked into her lime and seltzer. She was trying not to look troubled, but she couldn't manage her usual boisterousness. Normally Lindsay loved to entertain. Two dinner guests or two hundred, her grandeur was always the same. But not tonight.

Nell knew it was because she'd brought up Matthew that afternoon. Even if Lindsay didn't believe he had anything to do with this, just saying his name brought him back, like Bloody Mary in a bathroom mirror.

'Show him the cameras,' Nell said. New toys always improved Lindsay's mood at least marginally. Though Lindsay never grew a sentimental attachment to inanimate objects – she could move without packing her old clothes and easily replace anything she broke – she was the upscale version of a hoarder. Instead of those emotionally damaged people surrounded by labyrinths of newspapers and coffee makers, she was emotionally damaged with six sets of hand-painted dishes, bathroom drawers filled with earrings and about a billion Swarovski figurines. God, those things were everywhere, casting rainbows all over the house. Cats, couples kissing, martini glasses filled with mini crystals meant to look like water.

This wasn't even Lindsay's only iPad. She had another upstairs in a desk drawer. She couldn't find it one day and thought she might have left it at the yoga studio or in the park where she'd been using it to read one of her torrid romance novels. She drove to the Apple store that same day to replace it. Later, she found the old one where it had fallen behind the claw-foot tub when she fell asleep in the bath. She could have returned the new iPad, but, well, it was newer. Just like the old one, but rose gold rather than silver, and a clean slate with 128 gigabytes of internal flash memory.

That was the most beautiful thing about new electronic gadgets: the clean slate. A virtual world in which nothing had happened yet, like the first day of Earth.

Lindsay tapped at the screen now, and Sebastian leaned against the counter to look.

Nell drew her knee to her chin, watching them. There were many things she appreciated about Bas, not least of which being that even Lindsay could get along with him.

His finger hovered over the screen. 'What's that?'

'The back yard.'

'No. On that tree. Is that a – what is that?'

Nell squished between them to look at the screen. There in crisp black and white was the row of trees that sectioned Lindsay's house from the house to her left. The night vision cast an oval of brightness that receded to black at the edges. One of the trees had something hanging from a branch, heavy and limp, rocking against the trunk on the next gust of wind.

They all seemed to realise what they were looking at in the same instant. They didn't react. Not at first. Reactions made things true. Two women from a troubled upbringing and one man from a stable loving home still had that belief in common.

Lindsay was the first one to speak. 'That wasn't there the last time I checked the cameras.'

'Are you sure?' Nell said.

'Yes I'm fucking sure,' Lindsay exploded.

'Okay,' Sebastian said. 'Okay. I'll go look. Just turn on the floodlights and stay inside.'

They all should have stayed inside, in fact. Nell thought this, and yet she and Lindsay still followed him to the sliding glass doors that led to the back porch. A bamboo wind chime clacked and clattered like a round of applause in the darkness.

Lindsay switched on the light. On her iPad, the night vision switched to day for the little square of the back yard. They all looked at the screen rather than through the door at first. Hanging from the tree was a body, bound by the neck with a length of rope.

Lindsay let go of the iPad with a gasp and Sebastian reflexively caught it.

Nell made herself look away from the digital image and outside at the real thing.

'It's a mannequin.' She said it even before she was sure. Her brain wasn't completely allowing her to see the thing hanging from the tree, but once she'd said those words, her brain decided that it would be all right to go ahead and register it.

Nell slid the door open and marched across the deck and down the steps.

'Nell!' Bas was calling after her, but she didn't stop walking. She didn't stop because her true instinct was to run back inside and hide from this thing, and she knew that she couldn't. She knew that this was some sort of message. That it was important and she couldn't afford the luxury of fear.

The mannequin looked different to the one that had been pulled from Lindsay's car. This one had a plastic gleam. A toothy smile was drawn in Sharpie over the red lips, forcing a gruesome grin onto a benign expression.

This one had a dark brown wig, cut to the shoulder in a mimicry of Nell's hair. The eyes were dark and dead, staring into the city lights far in the distance.

Lindsay came up behind Nell and grabbed the thing, pulling at it. The rope had been loosely tied, and the mannequin fell to the ground, rigid, its arms bent as though receiving a gift.

'Don't touch anything,' Bas said. 'I'm calling the police.'

'No.' Lindsay shook her head. Her breaths were coming in hitches. Her eyes glistened, and she looked like she was about to cry. 'No, we're not calling the police.'

Nell grabbed her sister by the hands and reeled her a step closer. 'Look at me,' she said. 'We have to.'

Lindsay didn't say anything more. She only shook her head. Her entire body was trembling. It was so rare for her to be the one who came undone. It was a rule that one had to hold it together when the other couldn't, and so Nell was the calm one. The practical one. 'Let Sebastian call them,' she said. 'We'll go and look at the security footage, okay? It must have picked something up.'

An alarm wailed from inside the house. Nell's heart leapt. She remembered the lobster pot on the stove, and ran for the kitchen. The pot had boiled over, angry steam rising up from the burners as they were doused with water. She clicked the burner off and waved an oven mitt in front of the smoke detector until the shrill beeping stopped.

She heard Sebastian talking on the phone, still out on the porch.

Lindsay was in the kitchen now too. She opened the cabinet doors and grabbed the wrench she kept between the dishes, brandishing it. Anywhere Lindsay had ever lived was filled with weapons. Hammers under the mattress, bread knives behind the toilet tank.

'Linds?' Nell moved closer to her. 'Is this something Matthew could be doing?'

Lindsay wiped a tear from her eye with her trembling palm. 'No,' she said.

'You're sure?'

She nodded.

'Because you never let me call the police when he—'

'It's not fucking him, okay?' Lindsay said.

'Okay,' Nell said. 'Okay.'

Nell trusted her sister more than anyone. More than Sebastian, more than herself. They both understood the importance of being honest with each other.

Still, Nell recalled a time when Lindsay had not been honest. When she'd covered for her husband. When she'd lied for him.

# 9
# NOW

Police lights flashed through the cream-coloured curtains, flooding the living room in red and blue.

Lindsay squirmed as though her grey yoga pants were filled with bees. She hated the police almost as much as Nell did. When Reina disappeared ten years ago, the entire family fell prey to the constant scrutiny of police. Even Lindsay, sequestered as she was on the island of her marriage. They were all interrogated over and over again. When a child disappears, someone has to be the villain. With the world watching, the police can't step up to a podium empty-handed.

The police could have written novels themselves, Nell thought, the way they came up with wild retellings of what had happened that day. The sister kidnapped her niece and sold her to sex traders. The mother got overzealous with corporal punishment and was too afraid to call for help, so she let her child die. Maybe she buried her alive. It was the father; he had a new girlfriend and he didn't want to be tied down. It was the grandparents.

It didn't matter whether any of this was true. If

someone in a police uniform says it, enough people will believe.

While Lindsay was showing the officer the footage on her iPad, the doorbell rang. Nell answered the door before it occurred to her that she should be more cautious. Whoever hanged the mannequin in the back yard had done so recently; Lindsay had been happily toying with her new surveillance system before Sebastian arrived, and it would have been hard to miss a life-sized mannequin hanging from a tree if it had been there.

Only now was Nell thinking of this: someone had done this. Someone was still out there. Someone knew where both she and Lindsay lived. Given Nell's profession, this should have occurred to her much sooner, but the backyard discovery had robbed her of the clarity she possessed when facing her laptop. Her mind was scattered, chipped and cracked.

There was a middle-aged woman standing on the doorstep, a manicured hand to her chest. She reeked of perfume; something that cost three figures but smelled like it had been rubbed onto her pulse points from a magazine sample. She wore a lemon-yellow cardigan and a string of pearls around her neck.

'Oh, hello.' She blinked at Nell. 'I've seen you here and there, but I don't think we've been properly introduced.' She held out a hand. 'I'm Lindsay's neighbour, Mrs Porter. I live just over there.' She pointed across the street, to yet another in the valley of identical McMansions.

While it was true they hadn't formally met, Nell knew all about this neighbour – and many others. Mrs Porter was the one with all the birdfeeders and the binoculars that she insisted were strictly for birdwatching. And she hated cats, especially the Sellers' tabby, who waited in her hedges to pounce on the sparrows at the feeders.

'I saw the police cars and I just wanted to make sure everything was all right.' Mrs Porter pushed past Nell and glided into the foyer with all the poise of a Disney princess meeting her prince at the ball.

Lindsay was rubbing her brow with her thumb and forefinger. 'Yeah.' Her tone was snappy. 'Everything is fine, Mrs Porter.'

'Ma'am, it would be best if you left and let us do our job,' one of the officers said.

'Of course, of course.' Mrs Porter waggled her fingers at Lindsay in goodbye. 'I'll call you tomorrow, sweetie. So glad you're safe.'

Nell watched the woman leave. She returned to a small crowd of neighbours who had gathered on her own lawn; she greeted them with her arms out, a gesture that said, 'I tried.'

A third officer descended the staircase. 'The house is clear,' he said. 'No evidence that anyone's tried to break in. Anything on the security cameras?'

'It's supposed to start recording when it detects

motion,' Lindsay said. She was scrolling through the list of recorded incidents – Sebastian arriving with dinner at 7:00, Nell opening the door. An aggressive gust of wind bending the branches at 7:15. The camera did pick up the mannequin at 7:45, swaying when the wind blew, but there was nothing before that. Nell had already gone through the footage while they were waiting for the police to arrive.

There had to be something. Nell had even tapped the recycle bin option to make sure nothing had been accidentally deleted. But there was a solid thirty minutes in which nothing had tripped the motion sensors on any of the cameras. There was no evidence of anyone fleeing the property either.

'We'll need to take this.' The officer who had been speaking to Lindsay was now taking the iPad from her hands. 'We'll be in touch tomorrow. If you feel unsafe in the house, is there someplace you can stay tonight?'

'She'll stay with us,' Nell said.

Lindsay didn't argue. She had regained some of her composure now, but even if she didn't look frightened, Nell knew that she was. She had the sudden thought that she was never going to let Lindsay out of her sight again. They would live the rest of their lives sitting in the same chairs, riding in the same cars, going to the same places, just like Easter and Autumn before a surgeon tore their single life into two separate ones.

After the police had gone, the first thing Lindsay did was reach under the couch cushions, fishing around until she found what she was looking for. She held up an old hammer, rust-worn with splotches of white and blue paint on its handle. 'Here.' She handed it to Nell. 'Keep this in your purse. You never know.' She was all at once too busy to keep still. 'I guess I should pack a few things, huh?' She breezed through the foyer, under the gaudy copper chandelier with Swarovski drippings, up the staircase and towards her bedroom. Nell followed, and she sat on the bed as Lindsay opened the double doors of her massive closet.

Robert's alimony checks paid for all of these things. Lindsay had become a serial divorcer by trade. She had never worked a day in her life, and yet somehow she'd always found money. In foster care she stole or connived, hoarding singles and fives in her bra and underwear, never letting it out of her reach. She was so afraid of being left with nothing, no way to care for herself or the sister who had been left in her charge. This was how she survived.

'Don't start with me,' Lindsay said, and knelt to pull the suitcase out from under the bed. 'I already told you, this isn't the sort of thing Matthew would do. And anyway, he's in Missouri. What's he going to do – drive all the way up to the Rockhollow suburbs with a trunk full of shop mannequins just to scare me? For what?'

Nell had to admit that it didn't make sense. Matthew was an impulsive sort of monster. He didn't run a long game with his rage. One minute he was taciturn and the next his face was red and the veins bulged out of his neck. He didn't have the patience or the attention span to plan his attacks. They just came before you could duck.

'What about Robert?' Nell said.

'He wouldn't be able to come up with something like this,' Lindsay said. 'He didn't even watch scary movies.'

'Well, there has to be someone who's pissed off at you,' Nell said, exasperated. 'Mannequins don't drive cars or hang themselves.'

'Why does it have to be my fault?' Lindsay said. 'What about you? You're the one who just made a million dollars trying to humanise a baby killer. How many people read that press release? That's bound to piss a few people off.'

Lindsay had a point and Nell knew it, no matter how she wished it weren't so. Nell wanted to believe that this was some sort of vicious prank. A spurned ex-lover from Lindsay's substantial list, or an uppity yoga wife whom Lindsay had flipped off in traffic. Anything that could be solved by drawing up a flowchart of possible suspects.

But if whoever was doing this was trying to prove something to Nell, that opened an ugly chasm of possibilities. Strangers she had never met, people who had seen the swamp. There was no telling how many people had read it, or who they were, or what they were capable of.

# 10
# THEN

Five months after Reina was born, the Eddletons came to see her for the first time. It was December, and the hiss of the radiator had lulled the baby to sleep, for which Lindsay's neighbours were undoubtedly grateful.

Nell had been trying to take a nap herself, but when Lindsay opened the door to let the Eddletons in, Nell sat upright and attempted to fix her hair, combing her fingers through a crusty substance that was probably baby vomit. Lindsay had taken to calling the baby 'Demon', spoken without affection. Worse than the havoc her new niece brought to the apartment was the effect she had on her sister. 'Little Demon tried to kill you on her way out, and she won't rest until she's finished the job,' Lindsay had muttered that very morning when she found Nell huddled on the bathroom floor, too spent even to cry.

Ethan stood a pace behind his parents with his eyes downcast. His dark scraggly hair covered the top half of his eyes, but he gave Nell an apologetic frown.

Nell had only met Mr and Mrs Eddleton once

before, in the early morning hours. She'd been hopping down the stairs of their five thousand square foot home, wrestling to get into her left shoe. They hadn't been horribly impressed with her then, but at least she had looked pretty, and her clothes and hair had been clean.

Mrs Eddleton floated into Lindsay's apartment like an apparition, her violet crepe skirts rustling and full of whispers. Her matching coat was trimmed in a soft grey fur that Nell knew to be wolf. Mr Eddleton was a hunter, Ethan had said, and he had the pelts fashioned into presents for his wife.

With one look around the tiny apartment, Mrs Eddleton's wrinkled nose said what her mouth didn't: that her son had ruined his life by merging his DNA with such an unfortunate specimen. Newly fifteen, Nell was no wiser, no more assured and no more employable than she had been when she first peed on the stick.

But Mrs Eddleton's disdain lessened when she peered over the crib. Nell imagined this was the face she would make when considering melons in the grocery store. 'May I?' Mrs Eddleton asked. Without waiting for permission, she lifted the sleeping infant into her arms.

The baby awoke with a screech, but when Mrs Eddleton stuck her acrylic French-manicured nail in the baby's mouth, the baby stopped and looked at her curiously.

Nell hadn't seen Ethan since that day at the hospital, but now she was reminded of how much the baby looked like him. The same dark eyes, with heavy lashes and just a bit of a blue undertone in the irises. The black hair and pale skin.

Nell hated the way Mr and Mrs Eddleton looked at her, but Mrs Eddleton in particular. She hated that she was better than her circumstance, that she was smart and that she had been reading Voltaire before this baby stole every moment of silence from her life, and that there was nothing she could do or say to prove it. Nobody would see her mind – much less that she had one. They would see her carting around this screaming little thing she had brought into her life and the mess it had made of everything.

'Reina is an unusual name,' Mrs Eddleton said.

Reina. It meant 'queen'. The baby had looked like a queen when it came out of her, Nell had thought. Bloody and thrashing and fierce. She had wanted for her daughter to always have that ferocity; she was going to need it in a world that didn't hand her any certainties.

'We'd like to take her,' Mrs Eddleton burst out.

'Mindy—' Mr Eddleton said.

'It's a bit late, but if we apply now we could reserve a spot at a good preschool.'

Nell did not know why the Eddletons had come around after so much time and were now making such a demand. A good mother would be outraged.

A good mother would take her baby out of those meddlesome arms and say that her child's place was with her, that anything her baby needed she would provide.

But she also saw the bubble in the ceiling where water from the upstairs apartment was leaking. She heard what could have been a car backfiring or a gunshot outside, a sound that had become so familiar she never flinched. And she felt the drought of days without sleep. She saw a little queen being offered the promise of something better. And she heard the silence the baby's absence would bring. All the books she could read in that silence. The writing she could do. The uninterrupted thinking.

For just a moment she could imagine it. A glorious, perfect silence, in which she could be something – anything – but somebody's mother.

'You're welcome to stay overnight as well,' Mrs Eddleton said, with obvious difficulty. 'I understand—'

'It's all right,' Nell said. 'It's all right. You can take her.'

# 11
# NOW

When Oleg met Nell that afternoon at a downtown café, he was wearing a brown mohair sweater with a red scarf. The perfect image of a gloomy autumn day.

Nell's stomach was in knots, fluttering in that frantic way she experienced whenever she googled old news clips from her past. This was only her second time meeting the twins' brother, and she was embarrassed to look such a mess.

'You look tired,' Oleg said. 'You haven't slept?'

She steeped her tea, dark amber blooming in the steamy water. 'My sister would say it's rude to comment on a lady's appearance.'

'Is it?' he said. 'My apologies. You should say something about mine to make it even.'

Nell smirked. He pointed at himself with both hands to emphasise that he was serious. 'Go on. One thing.'

*You look like your sisters*, Nell thought. Though he was five years their senior, his face had less of an edge. He appeared more youthful, and his eyes had a starry quality to them. He had enviably soft-looking skin, and a flush across his cheeks and nose where the wind had bitten him.

Still, Nell felt obligated to say something critical. It clearly meant a lot to him. 'You're very tall,' she said.

'Ah, yes.' He took a sip of his latte, holding the cup by the brim with the fingertips of either hand. 'Like a telephone pole, I suppose.'

People had often remarked that Nell and Lindsay were nothing like sisters. When they went out together, they would hear things like 'When your friend returns from the restroom, will she be ordering more wine?' or 'Is your friend single?'

Now that Nell had met Easter, despite their resemblance she wouldn't have assumed that Oleg was her brother.

'So you've met Mom Esther,' he said.

He was referring to Mrs Hamblin. Nell nodded.

'I think she liked you,' he said.

'Did she?' Nell let out a nervous laugh. 'I was worried I'd scared her off.'

'She called me last night. She wanted to know if you were going ahead with the book.'

'I'd like to,' Nell said. A pause. 'I'm going to be honest in what I write about your family, but you may not like everything I have to say.'

'I would go along with whatever Easter decided to do. It's her story, after all,' he said. 'I'm glad that she picked you. You're…' he paused, trying to find the right word. 'Objective.'

'That's important to me, yes.'

Easter was going to be a challenge, not because she was delusional, but because she was clearly a liar. She judged people on whether they believed her stories. Oleg would be Nell's way to fill in the gaps. And there was another obvious gap.

'Oleg.' Nell met his gaze. 'You've said a lot about Easter, but not very much about Autumn.'

'Haven't I?' he said. 'I suppose I spend so much time thinking about her, I don't keep track of what I say out loud. She's just always there.'

'I'd love it if you could tell me about her,' Nell said.

He nodded. 'She loved the music here. Red Hot Chili Peppers and Metallica. I don't know how she could stand it. It's all noise to me. And she loved going to the cinema. She loved dance clubs, too – anything loud.'

Nell knew the journalistic stages of a murdered woman. First, newspapers sought to appease the morbid curiosity. There were grim details about where the body was found, whether it had been wearing clothes, whether there were signs of sexual assault, if she had any suspicious lovers. Later, when all of this had been exhausted, the desperate public wanted to be taken back in time. Who had she been? What were her dreams? How did she fill her days? Was she anything like me?

It was always the women who drew this sort of

curiosity, to the point of obsession. Men were murdered too, of course; in fact, more men were killed than women. But only the women and girls moved papers and generated ad revenue online. And female murderers garnered just as much attention. The only difference was that the latter generated more outrage.

Oleg's response was the sort of thing Nell had read in YouTube tribute videos and on findagrave. com.

Oleg caught her pensive expression. 'It sounds like you were hoping for something specific,' he said. 'Maybe if you tell me, I can help.'

'Easter didn't have anything kind to say about Autumn,' Nell said. 'It sounded like she was trying to paint her as a psychopath.'

One thing Oleg did have in common with Easter was that he could hide what he was thinking. He looked out the window, where cars were gridlocked in afternoon traffic. Nell's car was parallel parked between two fuel-efficient hybrids. She'd offered the car to Lindsay that morning, to which Lindsay said 'ew' and hounded her insurance agency for a rental.

'Nobody is entirely one thing.' Oleg turned to look at her. 'Would you agree with that?'

'Sure I would.'

'Love isn't an easy thing,' he said. 'We think it's natural to love, but it's a learned behaviour. Nobody loved Iskra and Klavdiya.' He used his sisters' birth names now. 'They came out sickly. The doctor told my parents that the twins were going to die. He said it would be best to give them to an orphanage. Maybe someone with money would adopt them. My parents kept the girls for as long as they could, but my sisters grew up knowing they were a burden.'

Oleg didn't speak on his own behalf, and Nell wondered what abuse he also endured at the hands of his parents. A part of her wanted to ask him. More than that – she wanted to reach across the table and touch his hand to offer comfort. The foster system in which she had grown up was surely different than the orphanages in Russia, but at the heart of both worlds was the deep-rooted feeling of being unwanted. Nell knew something about that, at least. Bonnie had never tried to parent her from behind bars; she said things like 'do your homework, don't grow up to be stupid' on a recorded line, and Nell never knew who might be listening in. Her father hadn't tried to regain custody; he didn't even call unless it was Christmas or he was in an emotional drunken stupor, and sometimes not even then.

Maybe things would have turned out differently for her and Lindsay if they'd been wanted.

She resisted her impulse to reach out. But she couldn't help saying, 'It must have been difficult for you to watch them leave you behind.'

Something changed in Oleg's eyes. His usual

tranquillity was betrayed by a sudden, stabbing coldness, and Nell could see him as a little boy watching the airplane flying overhead. She could see him left destitute, bereft and loveless as his only allies were swept away.

In a blink it was gone.

'I was happy for my sisters. I believed they would be better off somewhere else,' Oleg said. 'Autumn was like – how do I put it? She was like a drawing, and underneath that drawing you could see the erased pencil lines from who she was supposed to be. She played a part because she wanted it to be real.'

Playing a part, Nell understood.

'But was she a psychopath? No,' Oleg went on. 'She was just trying to be normal. She always covered up her surgery scars. If someone saw them, she would lie about where they were from.'

'What would she say?' Nell asked.

'That depended on the person. If it was a man she liked, she would say she fell while climbing rocks. Something like that; it made her sound interesting. To someone else, she would make up a childhood injury.' He nodded to the pad jutting out from Nell's purse. 'Aren't you going to take notes?'

'It's easier for me to remember things if I don't stop to write them down.'

He raised his drink to her in a salute. 'You're a strange one. I suppose that's why you're good at what you do.'

Nell laughed. It surprised her how much Oleg, practically a stranger, was able to put her at ease. She wanted to make the interview last, because she knew that once it was over, she would be going back to her apartment. Back to checking her phone in case Lindsay called. Lindsay had told Nell her schedule: hot yoga at ten, lunch at twelve with a friend from spin class she would otherwise avoid, then a quick trip to the bodega for something without artificial dyes and flavourings, because she swore all the food in Nell's fridge was poison.

'What about your parents?' Nell asked Oleg. 'Do they come to visit Easter? What do they make of all this?'

'They're dead,' Oleg said, unsentimental.

Nell wanted to tell him that she was sorry for his loss, but something about his demeanour said that wasn't necessary. He didn't like to dwell. She let him continue.

'My mother and father were unhappy when I first connected with the twins. My mother especially. They wanted it to be as though the twins had never been born.'

Oleg told her about their reunion at the airport, how Easter was in charge of decorating their tiny apartment and preferred never to leave. He had a lot to say, for which Nell was grateful. The men she interviewed usually didn't want to talk; it hadn't surprised her to hear that Mr Hamblin disapproved of the interview. It was the wives and sisters and mothers who wrote little stories in their heads each day, turning them over until they were polished and beautiful. They could begin mid-sentence, out of nowhere, but they were well-tended.

Oleg proved that men could be this way too. In his stories, Easter wasn't a murderer and Autumn was still alive; Nell could almost believe that both sisters were still at their apartment, arguing over the TV being too loud or whose turn it was to take out the trash. Autumn had been nearly deaf in her left ear after a childhood bout of swimmer's ear. She had suffered in silence, covering the inflamed ear with her hair, afraid that her adoptive parents would abandon her for being a burden, the way her birth parents had. By the time anyone noticed, it was too late to repair all of the damage.

'What about Easter?' Nell asked.

Oleg blinked. 'What about her?'

'Swimmer's ear is very painful. She must have noticed something was up, especially when Autumn started wearing her hair differently.'

'I don't know about that,' Oleg said. 'I wanted to understand my sisters. Their adoptive parents paid for me to fly out and visit them every Christmas and summer, and as their older brother, I wanted to be their mentor. Their protector. But I had to accept that I'll never know what sort of bond they had. I don't think anyone can.'

*He's right about that*, Nell thought. She didn't need to understand the Hamblin sisters in order to tell their story. She only needed to report the facts, and leave the readers to draw their own conclusions. But she would humanise Easter even after Easter had murdered her own sister, and there was the true challenge.

Oleg drew his phone from his pocket and checked the time. 'I have to go,' he said. He didn't offer an explanation. He downed the last of his drink and said, 'You'll be in touch when you need more, yes?'

'This should last me a while. Thank you.'

'Thank *you*.' He emphasised the last word.

He moved to stand, but then paused. 'You said that you thought you'd scared Mom Esther off. What happened?'

'She told me she'd found a dead rabbit in the garden. I – don't think she meant to tell me, but it just slipped out.'

Oleg settled back in his seat. 'Oh.'

Nell looked at him expectantly but she said nothing.

'There are quite a few stories like that. One would blame the other.'

'You're their brother,' Nell said. 'Who did you believe?'

Oleg took a deep breath, and she could see that this was painful for him. Losing a sister was already an impossible grief, but perhaps knowing your sister was a monster was just as terrible.

'The girls didn't have an easy life in Russia,' he finally said. 'When they came to America they had a perfect life, but it came too late. My parents resented them. There was no love in our house, and Easter was desperate for it. Like a kicked dog. Even as a baby, she learned that there was no use crying, so all of that desperation built up in her. It swelled up and burst, like a boil.'

Nell understood what it was like to grow up without much comfort. If she subtracted Lindsay from the equation, she could imagine Easter's desperation perfectly.

'There was a little boy in their school who nearly lost his eye when one of the twins threw a rock at him. Even he wouldn't say which one of them it was.'

'But you have your suspicions,' Nell ventured.

'All I have are guesses,' Oleg said. 'But he wasn't the only kid with a similar story. Like I said, they handled things in their own way. But here's what I do know: Autumn *thrived* in this country. She was loved by everyone she met. Easter lived in the shadows.'

Nell tried to imagine Easter holding a rock over a fledgling baby bird. Her blood went cold.

●

Once she was back in her car, Nell took out her phone. Three texts from Sebastian:

*Just checking in*
*Love you*
*Are you working?*

She typed out a reply: *Heading home. Love you too.*
Then a text to Lindsay: *Confirm you're alive please.*

The harsh November wind shook the car. Cold stole in through the seam in the window, and Nell could see her breath. Weather like this always left her feeling tumultuous. The chill wasn't a problem, but sometimes she couldn't help shivering.

This was one thing she and Reina had had in common. Reina never seemed bothered by the cold. When she pulled her escape stunts – scaling from first-storey windows or creeping out through back doors – she never took a coat. Sometimes she would be missing for hours and they'd find her hiding under the porch, peeking out at them through the wood slats, or standing behind a tree, or on the floor in the back seat of a parked car. Even on days so cold you could see your breath, even when she was shivering and chattering her teeth, she never seemed to mind.

*Reina.* When Nell first blurted out that name in the delivery room, she didn't know that it would haunt her for the rest of her life.

# 12

# THEN

The Eddletons turned Reina's first birthday into an affair. Their manicured lawn was obscured by tables of catered food, and a bouncy castle jostled with the rambunctious flips and spins of children from the country club.

It seemed like a waste to Nell. The baby was only one. She wasn't going to remember any of this. More ridiculous still were the gifts accumulating by Mrs Eddleton's prize rose bushes, Reina beside the mound of bright wrappings, staring at the display as though it were a pile of horse droppings.

'Hey, Demon.' Lindsay knelt beside her, her white heels sinking into the grass. 'I hear you've become an expert on blowing kisses. Do I get one? Especially seeing as that big box with the sparkly bow is from me?'

The baby tore up a fistful of grass.

'Do you want to open your present? It cost a million dollars.'

The baby glanced at Lindsay and then returned to tearing the grass.

'Mrs Eddleton says she's blowing kisses, but I've

yet to see it,' Nell said. She slept most nights in the guest bedroom adjacent to the nursery in the Eddletons' house. She had hoped that being the one to take care of the baby in the mornings and put her down at night would turn her into something that resembled a mother.

'I think Mrs E is making it up,' Lindsay agreed. 'So she doesn't have to explain to her snobby friends that her grandchild is – well, look at her.'

Nell bristled. She wanted to say that nothing was wrong with the baby, but Lindsay would see that she was lying. For the first six months, Reina had done nothing but cry, until her skin was so red and hot that Nell thought she was running a fever.

And then, one day, miraculously, the crying stopped. Nell would find the baby in her crib each morning, staring at the ceiling. But staring was all she did. She did not care for Mrs Eddleton's incessant coddling or the musical stuffed toys Mr Eddleton gave her. She didn't bounce in her swing or hold on when she was scooped up from her crib.

'Mrs Eddleton says this is normal,' Nell said. 'She says this is how babies act.'

'It's not how you acted,' Lindsay said. 'You were annoying as hell, but at least you smiled once in a while.'

'There she is,' Mrs Eddleton sang. She had a way of emerging from nowhere, her arms outstretched. 'There's my Rainy-Day. Do you like your party?'

The baby deflated with a sigh.

'I think someone has a full diaper,' Mrs Eddleton said, and tapped the baby on the nose.

'I'll take her,' Nell said, mustering the beaming, toothy smile the Eddletons had come to expect from her. At least then on the surface she could look like she belonged.

'Would you?' Mrs Eddleton said. 'I've got to check in with the caterers.'

Reina was heavy when Nell took her; she sat against her hip unceremoniously. The stench from her diaper was overwhelming. This was a challenge ever since Reina had stopped crying – she would sit in her own filth until someone discovered it. She'd already suffered from diaper rash so many times that Nell had lost count – just more tallies in her shortcomings as a mother.

Lindsay followed her into the house. Though she knew how to dress like these socialites, she hated everything about them. 'I don't know how you can stand to sleep here,' she muttered as they ascended the grand staircase that led to the nursery. 'I will never have a rich boyfriend, mark my words.'

'Ethan isn't my boyfriend,' Nell said.

'Uh huh. I hope you're remembering to take the pill while you're having sex with your not-boy-friend, Ms Capulet. And that he's remembering to bag it. Can't be too careful.'

'Would you shut up?' Though it was true that

Ethan and Nell had been together as recently as that morning, there was no word for what it was, or what they were to each other. Much like their baby's silence, there was something to it that couldn't be pinned down. There was an inherent desperation. Each touch a signal of light spread out across the ocean during a deadly storm in search for survivors. Each kiss a confirmation of breath. They were trying to keep each other afloat, or else drown the other so they wouldn't have to sink alone.

Just as they reached the top step, the baby rested against Nell's shoulder. Her soft, dark, baby-bird hair brushed her neck, and Nell could feel the full weight of her head. There was something foreign about this small gesture of affection; Nell had never witnessed it before. At last, in being held, the baby understood who her mother was, and that they were meant to love each other.

In that moment, Nell hated herself for the thousand spiteful thoughts she'd had about her own daughter. The baby was only a baby still. It wasn't her fault if she was difficult. She didn't mean to be cruel.

Nell stroked the baby's forehead, melting.

Lindsay hesitated. 'What's wrong with her?'

'She's just being sweet,' Nell said, pretending this was normal behaviour, indulging in such a beautiful idea.

'No. Nell, her cheeks are swollen.'

The flimsy moment of indulgence was gone as quickly as it had arrived. Nell drew back and saw what Lindsay saw. The baby's eyes were sleepy and glazed. Her face had started to swell. Her breathing had taken on a feeble rattle. Frantic, Nell saw the swelling in the left arm, the fingers bloated and stiff.

The rosebush by the presents had been buzzing with bees.

She was down the stairs and through the door before she knew she had moved. The sun was blinding, suddenly, and the line of shining cars parked along the cul-de-sac registered as a colourful blur.

'Here.' Lindsay was beside her, and she steered Nell towards her car. It was the only one here with a dull finish and a passenger-side mirror that was held in place by black electrical tape.

'The car seat is in Ethan's car.' Nell's voice floated away from her as she spoke.

'The hospital is only a few blocks. Just hold her.'

Nell's eyes were filling with tears. 'I need to get Mrs Eddleton. I won't know what to do, I—'

'There isn't time, Nell, pull your shit together.' Lindsay opened the passenger door and pushed her into the seat.

Lindsay started the car, and the radio came on with it, full blast. The burst of sound prompted no reaction from the baby, whose close proximity felt nothing like affection and everything like exhaustion, now that Nell was really paying attention.

'Reina?' Nell cupped the baby's chin in her hand. 'Does it hurt? Can you show me where the nasty bee stung you?'

The baby's chest heaved with laboured breaths, but her eyes were calm even as they began to dull. She was staring at Nell. Observing her, Nell thought. She found Nell's panic interesting.

Lindsay drove recklessly and without fear, and pulled to a screeching stop in an ambulance zone. 'Go,' she told Nell. 'I'll park and then I'll come find you inside.'

It had been a year since Nell was in a hospital holding her baby. That year felt like a lifetime. Everything had changed. But to the nurses she was still a bumbling teenage mother who was entirely to blame for whatever situation she and her baby were in.

Someone took Reina away from her, without kindness or explanation, leaving her to sit in a crowded waiting room.

By the time Lindsay found her, Nell was hugging her own stomach and sobbing.

'Oh, Nell.' Lindsay dropped into the chair beside her and pulled her into her arms. 'It's going to be okay. Things like this happen all the time.'

The rarity of such a sincere comfort, untainted by Lindsay's usual sarcasm, only made her cry that much harder. Because Nell knew the truth. She would have given anything to be frightened about the bee sting, but she wasn't. There was no shot that could be given to the baby, no remedy that would fix her. The baby was broken in some other way, and Nell was tired, so tired, of pretending she wasn't.

To the strangers in the room, she looked like a frightened mother who wanted to take her baby home. But she wasn't like them, and she didn't want to take her baby home.

She had always told Lindsay all her secrets. But in the year since the baby had been born, Nell had become a collector of silent fears and thoughts. Ugly thoughts. Cruel ones. And she didn't dare say them out loud. Even Lindsay wouldn't be able to understand. She would be disgusted. Nell could see it. She would surely not be sitting beside her now, petting her hair and telling her not to worry.

It was more than an hour before the doctor came to find her. By then, Nell had exhausted herself and was staring at the muted episode of *Ricki Lake* and trying to follow the captions.

'Do you want me to go with you?' Lindsay asked.

Nell shook her head. All the crying had made her tired, and as she followed the doctor down the bright hallway, his chattering barely registered. So rare to have a doctor that bothered to explain things, much less try to console her. She knew that she should be grateful.

He led her to the room where the baby was sitting up on a neatly made bed, beside a nurse who was trying to entice her with a stuffed bear.

She was wearing a clean diaper, and Nell remembered, with humiliation, the baby's full diaper when she brought her in.

'Quite a brave girl you've got,' the doctor said. 'Most of them cry when they get a shot.'

'She won't cry,' Nell said.

'The epinephrine may leave her with a little bit of a headache, but she should be back to normal by tomorrow.'

'This is normal for her,' Nell said, nodding to the baby's dark and heavy-lidded eyes. 'I think maybe she's hard of hearing, or – well, I read an article about children with autism.'

The doctor grabbed the clipboard from a nearby cart and hit it against the wall. The loud *crack* made Nell jump. The baby whipped her head in the direction of the sound, her eyes fierce.

'Nothing wrong with her hearing.' The doctor laughed. He patted Nell's shoulder reassuringly. 'You have a perfectly healthy little girl. I always tell first-time mothers not to turn to books for parenting advice. It'll only put worries in your head.'

'She doesn't cry,' Nell insisted. 'She got stung by a bee and it almost killed her, and she never cried once.'

'Shock is a common symptom of anaphylaxis. She's allergic to bees, so you're going to want to limit her time outdoors. As to the not crying, I see about a dozen mothers a day who would envy you.' He put his hands on his knees and leaned towards the baby. 'Do you want Mom to take you home now?'

Reina stared at the doctor for a long moment. And then without a sound she held her arms out to Nell with the militaristic rhythm of a soldier giving a salute.

'There, see?' the doctor said. 'There's nothing to be concerned about.'

Looking back later, Nell would see this moment as a turning point in her life. The memory of this day would find her in every city, in every bed she would ever sleep in, from the Eddletons' mansion to Lindsay's couch, to her studio apartment in Rock-hollow with Sebastian's leg hooked over her thigh.

*Don't tell anyone the truth*, the memory would whisper. *No one will ever believe you.*

## 13
## NOW

As proof that she was still alive, Lindsay texted Nell a photo of her newly pedicured toes, wearing spongy green toe spacers.

Nell stuffed her phone back into her purse as she crossed the apartment lobby. She was glad to be home, where there were multiple surveillance cameras, locked access to the elevators and security guards at all hours.

It also helped that the penthouse was thirty stories up. Still, Nell felt a sense of unease as she worked her key into the door.

Nobody could be here. She knew that. And yet, there was part of the imagination that never turned into logic. She checked all the windows, behind every door. She even pulled back the shower curtain.

At last convinced she was alone, she microwaved a mug of potato soup and heaped on a handful of shredded cheese. It was the first time she had had an appetite since last night's ill-fated dinner, and just the smell of the food made her feel better. It was amazing how worry and optimism shifted like twists in a kaleidoscope. *Nobody's dead*, she reminded herself. Nobody was even hurt. Matthew Cranlin was far away. The Eddletons were far away. The police would check the surveillance for the shop and find out who stole the mannequin. It would be neighbourhood kids, like Lindsay had said. If anyone had wanted to kill them, they would have tried by now.

Lindsay wasn't entirely liberal with details sometimes; she had probably pissed someone off, complaining that they'd parked too close to her flowers or their dog barked too much. That's all this was. Or bored privileged children mimicking a horror film for laughs.

Nell took her soup to her desk and opened her laptop.

The first paragraph of Easter and Autumn's story sat half-written on the screen. Nell stared at the unfinished sentence. She was always doing that – leaving little messes for herself to sort out later.

*Easter thought Autumn was*

What? What had Easter thought about the sister she'd murdered? Nell had been confident enough to begin the sentence, but now without its conclusion the words were meaningless.

This was the first time Nell had written about sisters. As with all things relating to Easter Hamblin, she felt at a loss for where to begin. Nell's only experience was Lindsay. Complicated, abrasive, beautiful Lindsay, who was every bit as fucked up as Nell. Perhaps more fucked up, in fact, because she was the oldest and had understood more of what was happening to them as children. But the story of Easter and Autumn Hamblin managed to surpass anything Nell and Lindsay had lived through, because Nell and Lindsay were still alive. That was more than could be said for Autumn, who was buried in East Rock cemetery in an unmarked grave so that the family could mourn her privately.

Nell tried to imagine Easter as a teenager, bearing the scars from where her sister had been built into her hip and forearm. The co-dependency mixed with resentment. Jealousy. Easter had been so bitter when she talked about Autumn socialising with the neighbours.

Nell finished the sentence.

*Easter thought Autumn was hers.*

She spent the next hour writing furiously, deleting and rewriting descriptions of Easter Hamblin as she had looked through the glass at Royal King's State Penitentiary. She wrote of Easter's green eyes, which sparked brightly – even flirtatiously – when she was about to say something wicked.

Nell didn't stop until she'd completed five pages, at the end of which she knew this would not be a story with a sympathetic villain. Easter Hamblin was interesting, as was her dead sister, but there was nothing for an audience to love but her mystery.

The first chapter was done. Her audience would

now have a clear picture of Royal King's State Penitentiary, sitting on a flat expanse of concrete like the final castle in a perilous conquest. Within that prison is Easter, a twinless twin, still muttering with mad conviction that her sister isn't really dead.

*Easter Hamblin is a Mariana Trench*, Nell wrote. *She is the darkest wave in the deepest ocean. We don't need to see what's swimming inside her to know that there are frightening things.*

Nell began the next chapter; Autumn's chapter, she decided. First the murderer and then the prey. She forgot all the private browser tabs of searches into her own sordid past. As long as she kept writing, she had focus and drive. She had a puzzle that could be neatly assembled using evidence filed in court records. She had grisly crime scene photos that revealed exactly where Autumn Hamblin's body had turned up and forensic reports that explained what had happened to her. The hyoid bone had been crushed: clear evidence of manual strangulation. It was a tragedy for the Hamblins; but it was also a relief, because there would be no more wondering. No more hoping. No private browsers opened so that they could search for traces of their missing daughter and all the secrets she kept.

A key turned in the lock and Nell flinched.

'Oh my God.' Lindsay burst into the apartment, dragging the lone syllable of that last word. 'It took

142

me like an hour to drive three blocks. What is with the constant construction in this fucking city?'

Nell clicked save on her Word doc and then spun in her chair. Lindsay was her usual state of flustered and still somehow magically put together. She held up an engorged plastic bag. 'I bought Chinese for dinner. Never let it be said that I don't contribute.'

Lindsay moved into the kitchen and began dismantling the contents of the bag, still rambling about her afternoon. The blood drawn by her zealous manicurist, and the woman getting a pedicure, whom Lindsay had affectionately nicknamed The Cunt Rocket.

Nell hadn't said a word, and Lindsay scarcely seemed to notice when Nell slid onto a barstool to watch her. Lindsay kept busy when she was nervous.

It hadn't always been this way. When they were children, worry made her stoic and mean – especially to their foster parents and the other children in their group homes. After they'd visit their mother in prison, Lindsay could go entire days without uttering a word, and she would tug aggressively at the buttons of Nell's coat, tear out strands of hair with her aggressive brushing.

She only began busying herself after she married Matthew. Lindsay seemed to believe that if she moved fast enough, nobody would notice the bruises under her concealer, or her limp, or the new cap on a chipped tooth.

Nell was checking her sister for bruises now, out of habit. But nothing had outwardly changed.

Finally Lindsay looked up and said, 'Why are you looking at me like that?'

Nell knew she had to handle this delicately. Lindsay hated when Nell worried about her, and even more than that, she hated being vulnerable.

'I've been thinking about the mannequins is all,' Nell said.

Lindsay rolled her eyes as she opened a cabinet to retrieve the plates. 'I meant to tell you, I have a lead on that. It was Lena Alway.'

'Who?' Nell reached for a fortune cookie, then thought better of it.

'Stick-up-the-butt Botox Barbie,' Lindsay said. 'With the tacky long nails and neon bleached hair. She's that blue house on the corner with the big fountain in her driveway, to give you an idea of what we're dealing with.'

Nell was sure she'd passed the house a thousand times, but all the McMansions in Lindsay's neighbourhood looked the same to her, just like every city block in Rockhollow looked the same to Lindsay.

'She came forward?' Nell asked.

Lindsay snorted. 'No. But back in January she accused me of trying to steal her husband. Like I want that greasy douchebag.'

Nell's gaze went flat. 'You slept with him, didn't you?'

144

Lindsay batted her lashes, and Nell burst out with a laugh.

'It was one time,' Lindsay said. 'Two.'

Nell's laughter was born of relief more than anything. Lindsay. Abrasive Lindsay, who made herself impossible to like by her own design. At last there was an explanation.

'I've gone to the police, since I know that's your next question,' Lindsay said. 'That Officer Rayburn guy we met with at the station. He said it's hard to do anything without evidence, but we'll get her.' She grabbed her phone off of the counter and held it up. 'I've been checking the cameras all day. We'll get her.'

'You're staying here until then,' Nell said.

'She's not going to hurt me,' Lindsay said. 'She's rich lady nuts, not psycho nuts.'

'Linds.'

'You don't want me here,' Lindsay said. She gestured towards Nell's laptop. 'You've got your book, and Sebastian.'

'Sebastian doesn't mind,' Nell said. 'He likes you.' Bas's hesitant affection for Lindsay was a testament to his kindness. She wasn't an easy person to take in large doses, and Nell knew it.

As though on cue, Sebastian's key turned in the lock. He saw Lindsay dumping a carton of shrimp fried rice onto a plate and a dreaminess overtook his gaze. 'I could smell that all the way from the elevator. I was hoping it was coming from here.'

Lindsay preened. 'This is my way of thanking you for letting me sleep here last night, but I was just telling Nell that I'll be going back home tonight.'

Sebastian took his usual barstool beside Nell and accepted the plate Lindsay slid towards him.

Nell was going to argue, but suddenly all she could think about was Easter, who believed Autumn belonged to her. Who held on so tightly that it broke her.

When she was researching the Widow Thompson's story, Nell had been especially clingy towards Lindsay. She had nightmares of their mother getting paroled out of prison, climbing the trellis outside of Lindsay's bedroom and then drowning her in the bathtub. One nightmare was so vivid that Nell drove to Lindsay's house at three in the morning and stood outside ringing the buzzer to the security gate until Lindsay appeared, half asleep with murder in her eyes.

Was it happening again? Had Nell taken a petty feud between neighbours and turned it into a crime scene in her own head?

'Hey.' Bas bumped his shoulder against hers. 'You okay?'

Nell forced a smile. 'I've been writing about the Hamblins all afternoon. It's made me feel gross is all.'

After dinner, the three of them settled in front of the TV. Lindsay stayed for *Jeopardy*, during which she got virtually none of the questions right. Then she stood and grabbed her coat off of the hook. Nell could see that there was no sense arguing.

'I'll be fine,' Lindsay said, catching the look on Nell's face. 'Officer Whatsit said he'd send a patrol car to sit outside of my house all night if I ask.'

'Rayburn,' Nell said.

'Yeah, him.'

'Please take him up on it,' Nell said.

Lindsay winked as she opened the door. 'I'll send you proof of life when I get home.'

As promised, Lindsay texted a picture of herself lying in bed. Nell told herself not to worry. Everything was all right. The entire world was not as dark and cruel as the cases Nell researched.

Autumn Hamblin and the Widow Thompson's children were the unlucky ones. But they were the exception, not the rule.

# 14

# NOW

For the next week, there were no further incidents. There was still no evidence of Lindsay's neighbour staging the mannequins, but there had been no threats either. Lindsay said the cop car parked outside her house had been enough to scare her off – and probably embarrass her into minding her own business.

Still, Nell woke every night worrying, resisting the urge to speed to Lindsay's house. Sebastian stirred beside her and she knew that she had woken him, though he never let on.

On Friday at three in the morning, Nell decided to turn her insomnia into something productive.

She slid from the bed, made herself a cup of hibiscus tea and sat at her computer. Her latest unfinished chapter was about Oleg, the young man with the impish grin in the photo with the twins. Nell stared at it now, lit up by the cool glow of her screen. His blond hair was parted on one side, laid flat and caramelised against his head. It was 2010, and he was standing in front of a mall entrance with his hands in his pockets.

One of his sisters stood beside him; the other had presumably taken the photo. 'That's Autumn,' Oleg had said, tapping the photo with his groomed fingernail.

'You're sure?' Nell had asked.

He'd nodded. 'Easter hated to be photographed alone.'

'She wouldn't have been alone. You were there.'

He'd met her gaze. 'Her definition of alone meant not with Autumn.'

Nell stared at Oleg and Autumn now. A well-meaning brother and a sister with less than a decade left to live. If what he'd said about Easter was true, then she would always be alone now.

A shuffling behind her alerted Nell to Sebastian's presence. It was the friction of his socks against the hardwood floor. He was always cold in the winter, unhooking his robe from the bedpost even when he went to the bathroom at night. It was Nell's fault; she never set the thermostat above 65, even as she padded around barefoot in nothing but a baggy t-shirt.

Sebastian leaned over her chair, his weight tilting it back on its axis just slightly. He hadn't been in bed long enough for sleep to sour his breath; he still smelled like mint Listerine and dryer sheets. He kissed the back of her neck and Nell canted her head towards him.

She didn't let on how uneasy she felt to have him

near her. There was something unnerving about him seeing her unfinished manuscript, the story messy and incomplete and fraught with errors. She rarely allowed it, the same way she turned her back to conceal her caesarean scar from him when she was getting dressed.

Nell slammed the laptop shut and spun in her chair to face Sebastian.

He sat on the edge of the coffee table, putting them at eye level. Nell realised that all week he'd pretended to be asleep as she tossed and fretted about Lindsay, but his quiet patience had worn thin.

'Are you going to tell me what's bothering you?' he asked.

*No*, Nell thought. All she could ever afford him was a fraction of the story. She told him about her pregnancy, but not about Reina. Her childhood in foster care, but never the ugliest parts. She told him about the cases she researched and the toll they took on her, but never the real reason – the memories they triggered.

'I can't figure Easter Hamblin out,' Nell said, by way of an answer. 'Either she's manic, or she's playing a game with me.'

Nell curled her legs up onto the chair, hugging her knees, instinctively covering the scar hidden by her t-shirt. Starting at the beginning, she told Sebastian everything Easter had said about her sister during their interview.

Sebastian betrayed no shock in his expression. He looked thoughtful. 'Did you humour her?'

'I didn't say whether I believed that Autumn was still alive,' Nell said.

'What if you played along?' Sebastian asked. 'What if you had a chapter entertaining Easter's fantasy that Autumn is still out there, plotting her next attack?' At Nell's blank expression, he exhaled. 'That sounds stupid now that I've said it.'

'No,' Nell said. 'No, that might be a good idea.'

Sebastian raised his shoulders haughtily. 'In that case, glad my genius could be of help.'

❉

In the morning it snowed. A flurry that looked like pieces of the sky's paint flaking down. Nell sat in her car, staring at Royal King's State Penitentiary, whose image was sliced over and over by the windshield wipers. Despite the warmth from the vents, a chill had stolen into Nell's bones.

Nell was never remanded after Reina's disappearance, even after her arrest. The only good thing that came from Lindsay's marriage to Matthew had been his money, which paid her bail, and for the top lawyer in western Missouri. The lawyer staunchly maintained Nell's innocence, creating such a vivid account of what happened that day that Nell almost believed it herself.

She checked her reflection in the visor mirror. She wasn't wearing makeup. Makeup was a type of mask, and Easter Hamblin saw right through those. Nell needed to be straightforward, speak clearly, and show no trace of the secrets she kept. That way she could get Easter to focus on herself. That way the book could get written.

By the time Nell sat at the visitor's window and took the phone from the receiver, she was ready.

Easter Hamblin sat before her in her grey jump-suit, a wry smirk on her face.

'You spoke to my mother,' Easter said. Her Russian accent teased her words just slightly today.

'You've been in touch with her?' Nell guessed.

'No,' Easter said. 'But I can tell when someone has spoken to her. My lawyer looked the same way you do. My mother's pity for me is contagious.'

'You think that I pity you?' Nell asked. Her note-book sat open before her. Easter looked at it, then at Nell.

'Isn't that why you're here? Because you want to paint me as a victim?'

'I'm here to tell your story,' Nell said, not letting her emotions show. She wasn't even sure that she had any emotions in that moment. She was never sure how to feel about Easter. 'I'm here to tell your side of things, because you're trapped in a cell for the rest of your life, but I can make sure your words slip through the bars.'

Easter smiled at that. She pointed a finger and tapped it against the glass, as though Nell were the one in a terrarium. 'You're good,' she said.

Nell went on. 'The last time we spoke, you told me that Autumn hated everyone but pretended to like them.'

'She does.' Easter shrugged, with the resigned nonchalance of a suffering sister. 'You have no idea how infuriating it is to know someone is full of shit, but there's no way to make anyone else see it.'

Nell knew the feeling very well. Matthew had been cut from the cover of a romance novel: he had money and abs; he called his mother every Sunday; he taught his nephews how to pitch a baseball; he treated Lindsay like a princess. Except for when he didn't. Nell had seen through all of it, and it hadn't mattered. For all the words she could write, there had been nothing she could say about Matthew that would convince Lindsay.

'I read the papers,' Easter said. 'They want to make my sister out to be a saint. And people just eat it up.'

Easter was getting agitated, and Nell could sense a tangent brewing.

'I don't write for a newspaper. I'd like to write the truth about Autumn. I'm here for your side, remember. As long as you tell me the truth, it'll go into the book.'

This was mostly an appeal on Nell's part. She

154

knew that Easter Hamblin was not going to tell her the truth. But it didn't matter, so long as what Easter had to say was different and more substantial than what the papers said.

Easter was quiet for a full minute. Nell had been counting the seconds in her head, and when Easter at last drew a breath to speak, Nell grabbed her pad and made a note of the lengthy pause. A suspenseful silence was a great way to begin a chapter.

'Autumn was born first,' Easter said, favouring her Russian accent. 'I was plucked out alongside her. That's the way it was from the start: she led the charge and I was a tumour with an identical face.

'You've had roommates, yes? Maybe you've shared a bed with your sibling during a thunderstorm. But sharing a body with someone is the most intimate hell. She didn't end at this scar' – Easter rolled up the sleeve of her jumpsuit, revealing the deep, shining purple line that ran up her forearm – 'and this isn't where I began. There was no beginning or end to either of us, and there never will be. Autumn could hide from everyone, but not from me. For this, I loved her, even though she was a monster. I took the blame for her. I took the blame when she caught the rats in the garden at the orphanage. She carried them by their tails, biting at the air while she laughed and then tossed them into the fire. When we were found out, she blamed me for it. She burst into tears and said I had frightened her.'

She paused here, waiting for Nell's reaction. But if Nell could hear the Widow Thompson describe how she'd drowned her children without flinching, she could stomach a few rats.

'You took the blame,' Nell said. 'Why?'

'I asked myself: is there any difference? It was two pairs of shoes walking through the garden. Hers and mine.'

'You must have been frightened,' Nell said.

Easter shook her head. 'When I was attached to Autumn, I was safe. We didn't share any organs, but that didn't matter. Autumn used to say that there were rivers running through both of us. She said the rivers were polluted, all of our secrets and sins flowing from one heart to the next. She was afraid that if I were to die, the doctor would cut us apart and all of those things would come spilling out onto the operating table.'

'You were ten when you were separated,' Nell said. 'What was that like?'

Easter closed her eyes. She drew in a deep breath through her nostrils, and her shoulders rose, and it was as though she were standing outside in the free air inhaling the crescendo of a breeze.

It was the first genuine emotion Nell had seen from Easter. It was the very first thing about Easter Hamblin that she believed.

'We went under that knife as Russian orphans,' Easter said, when she at last spoke. 'But when we woke up, we were little American children. If we wore long sleeves and learned the language, we could be anybody.'

It was frightening the way that Easter could switch between her Russian and American accents. It reminded Nell of the Magic Eye book in one of her foster homes. At a glance, it was a page of white and blue lines, but if you fixed your gaze just right, there was a tiger poised to leap out and claw you to shreds.

Easter's eyes flitted to the clock on the wall behind Nell. 'Our hour's up. The phone will cut off in a minute.'

Nell had never been very good at keeping track of time, but even so, she was surprised how quickly the hour had disappeared. She had been so immersed in the twins' childhood. 'You're right,' she said, and held up her pad before tucking it into her purse. 'This was very helpful.'

'You'll come back?' Easter asked.

'Next week,' Nell said. The phone clicked, and then went silent. She averted her eyes as she stood, not watching as the corrections officer led Easter back to her cell in solitary confinement.

## 15
# THEN

'Sharing a body with someone is the most intimate hell.' That's what Easter had said. It was easy for Nell to understand. She and Lindsay had been inseparable in their own way, out of necessity, not choice. It was a love sometimes indiscernible from hate.

When Nell was nine and Lindsay thirteen, Nell saw her first glimpse of a normal life. They were fostered to a couple that were only looking to take on one child, but they would make allowances for two. 'Everything is set up for a single child,' the social worker said as they drove between rows of brick-front houses. 'So try not to eat them out of house and home.'

This was a privilege, Nell and Lindsay knew.

No more group homes. No more stomach bug outbreaks. Though Lindsay was adamant that she would continue to sleep with a pocketknife in hand.

The couple even had a normal last name: Smith. And a house with a white fence that was only a bit dilapidated, and beds of roses that were only a little wilted and brown.

The Smiths preferred girls after too many violent outbursts from the troubled boys who had passed through their doors. Especially around puberty, boys were crude, reclusive and what Mr Smith called 'stormy'. He had winked at Nell in the rear-view mirror as he drove. 'And they smell pretty bad, don't they?'

Nell liked him the moment he said that, because it was true. At their last group home, Nell and Lindsay slept like sardines in the bottom bunk, below an overweight boy who farted in his sleep.

But Lindsay didn't like the Smiths. She didn't like anyone, and she stared out of her window with her jaw set. *Don't ruin this for us*; Nell had tried to project the thought into her sister's head. Already she was fantasising about the adoption papers. She wouldn't have to visit Bonnie in prison again. She wouldn't have to endure another drunken phone call from her father when he managed to track his daughters down so that he could apologise. The sloppy weeping only churned Nell's stomach, and she would listen to it in frozen silence until Lindsay said 'for fuck's sake' and hung up.

This was their chance to have a real family.

The Smiths had a small, tidy house, with a full-sized bed in the spare room for Nell and Lindsay to share. But when it rained, a leak came in through the ceiling and doused the left side of the bed. It rained a lot that spring, so one night Nell would sleep on the dry side of the bed and Lindsay would take her pillow and blanket and sleep on the floor. The next time it rained, they would switch.

This was the only flaw in an otherwise comfortable setup. The public school wasn't terrible. Mrs Smith was a decent enough cook. Mr Smith invited them to watch football in the evenings and taught them how the game worked.

Slowly, even Lindsay began to warm to the idea of this beige split-level house and the sound of crickets serenading them to sleep.

Less than a month in, it was once again Nell's turn to sleep on the floor as rain pounded the roof. She didn't know what woke her, but it was loud, like a clap of thunder. And yet she didn't move. She didn't open her eyes.

She heard Lindsay whisper something. The creaking of the mattress coils like a hundred groaning ghosts.

This was what had woken her, Nell realised. The mattress creaking, and then the slam of the rickety headboard against the wall.

A hard breath.

A groan that wasn't quite pain, but some other sort of agony. It was vulnerable and strange, like a little boy trapped inside a man's body. It terrified her.

More whispering. Nell opened her eyes without meaning to. Without wanting to.

She saw Mr Smith's outline in the darkness as he retreated into the darkness of the hall. His bare back showed a single dark mole at the hip.

The sheets rustled in the bed, and when Nell sat up, she saw that Lindsay was curled away from her with the blankets pulled over her head.

Nell wanted to speak, but just as she had opened her eyes without wanting to look, she was now silent without wanting to be silent.

A week later, Nell and Lindsay were rounding the block on their walk home from school when they saw the social worker's car in the driveway.

'She wasn't supposed to come back,' Nell said, already sounding hysterical, her eyes filling with tears. 'We were supposed to live here.'

'We can't,' Lindsay said. There was no emotion in her voice.

'This is your fault,' Nell spat out.

'Wait,' Lindsay said. But Nell was already running ahead of her, her backpack hitting hard against her shoulders.

'I hate you!' Nell screamed back at her sister. It echoed off the pristine houses and the freshly paved cul-de-sac. 'You ruin everything. I hate you. I hate you!'

✻

# NOW

'It's fascinating,' Nell said, as Sebastian poured them each a glass of wine. There was chicken roasting in the oven, and the apartment was warm with the smell of it. 'I can't work out how much of what she's saying is true.'

'It's probably all true,' Bas ventured. 'But maybe not in the way she says. Maybe she's saying Autumn killed the rats and that rabbit, but it was really her.'

Nell considered this. 'Their mother told me a story about Easter trying to catch a kitchen mouse and Autumn killing it.'

Sebastian sipped his wine. 'Maybe she has it backwards too.'

'What makes you so sure?' Nell asked.

'Let's look at what we know for a fact,' he said. 'Easter murdered her sister and pretended to be her for weeks—'

'A year,' Nell corrected.

'She's clearly delusional,' Sebastian said. 'Plus those stories of kids accusing one of the twins of hurting them. It must have been Easter, but they were too scared to say so.'

'Her own family doesn't even have it sorted out,' Nell said. But she wasn't discouraged. 'The manuscript is turning out very noir. It's not what I expected, but I think it'll work out better. All the articles and TV specials have been speculation, but this book will be what Easter tells us. Believe it at your own peril.'

It wasn't rare for Sebastian to take an interest in her work, but it was rare for Nell to be so eager to discuss it. They spent dinner going over the interview, making a game of guessing what was real and what was Easter's warped sense of reality.

By her fourth glass of wine, she was sleepy and giddy and her head was filled with words. Not that any of them would do her much good now. She rested her chin on her fist. 'I'm not going to get anything done tonight.'

His hand was on her knee now. 'You've given this book enough of your time today,' Bas said. His thumb traced a crescent moon on her skin. 'Don't let it swallow you up like the last one did.'

Nell stared at him. His nose and forehead were flushed. The dim kitchen light caught the grey flecks in his eyes, like little stars.

Sebastian was the only one who had ever made her feel human. She wanted to tell him that, but she was only good with words when they were ugly. When she was talking about congealed blood, or how long it takes for post-partum depression to manifest into a delusional psychosis. Or before any of that, before she had written a single book, when she tried to tell Ethan Eddleton the truth about their child.

But with Sebastian, she said almost nothing and felt everything. She gave a little smile, and his hand slid up her thigh.

'I love you, you know,' he said.

'Even though I'm fucked up?'

'Don't do that tonight, Nell.'

'Okay.'

He kissed her before she could say anything else. When he drew back, her head lolled sleepily so that her forehead pressed to his.

*I love you too.* She wanted to say it, but she never could when it mattered. Her arms coiled around his shoulders. He tried to carry her to the bedroom, but he stumbled back against the counter and a barstool toppled over. Nell giggled into his mouth as it clattered to the ground.

They fell into bed as though they'd been dropped from the sky, flushed and laughing as they wriggled out of their clothes.

The curtain was open, and Nell looked out at the city lights, glittering, the cars like the eyes of slithering snakes. The view was only of Rockhollow, but from here it might as well have been the world. The whole ugly, strange, beautiful place that only made sense when Sebastian was inside of her.

'Nell,' he murmured. His heat warmed her skin. 'Look at me.'

She looked away from the window. His eyes were dark and moonless. His back was to the window, so that none of its lights reflected in his gaze. But she could still see the city in him. She could see everything that was ugly, and everything that was good.

# 16
# NOW

Nell woke to her phone vibrating on the nightstand.

Her heart was hammering in her chest, and there was the dizzying sense that the world had ended while she'd been asleep.

Her phone gave another angry buzz. She stretched across the mattress to reach it. She was alone in bed, she realised. The shower was running, and water rushed through the exposed pipes in the ceiling. Her sweat and Sebastian's being washed from his skin and floating off into the river.

A subtle headache was forming behind her eyes, and she suspected that she was still a little drunk. It wasn't even 4AM, too early for the sun to rise yet, which meant Sebastian had hours before he needed to get ready for work. His insomnia was back, Nell thought. It only ever came about after sex, when his mind was so frenzied that it prompted him to worry. Like Nell, there were things that Sebastian kept hidden. But this didn't mean that they were the same. While Nell worried about her past, Sebastian worried about their future.

The phone buzzed again. The light from the

screen burned Nell's eyes as she read the texts. They were from Lindsay:

*Nell? Are you awake?*

*Please be awake.*

*I need you to come get me. Don't freak out. Everything's fine*

*Drank too much*

*Woke up next to some rando*

*His whole house smells like ham*

*2 W Lazarus Road*

Nell quickly typed out a reply:

*Jesus Linds*

*On my way*

Nell tried calling, but it went straight to voicemail. She tugged on a pair of jeans and a sweatshirt. It had been years since she'd had to clean up the mess of this particular version of Lindsay. Following her divorce from Matthew, Lindsay had been an unapologetic party girl. Alcohol, ecstasy, whatever was handed to her in a nightclub bathroom. The unspoken agreement was that Nell would always come get her. She would scoop her up from the bathroom floor, or from the apartment of whatever man she'd gone home with, set her up on the couch with a vomit bowl and a blanket, and never speak of it again. Nell had no business judging even the worst of her sister's decisions; she had them all beat.

'Bas.' Nell drew back the shower curtain. The shower steam smelled like him, warm and heady

168

with the scent of the green bar of soap he was rubbing over his chest.

He met her eyes with a sleepy, suggestive grin. 'Hey. I didn't think you were up.'

'I have to go rescue Lindsay,' Nell said, after breaking apart from his kiss. 'She got herself into some bullshit with a date.'

'She's dating again?' He smeared a blob of suds on Nell's nose. 'Good for her.'

'Yeah, it's fantastic,' Nell said caustically. 'I'll be back in a couple of hours. Of course she had to pick a guy who lives out in the sticks.'

'Want me to come with?' Sebastian asked.

Nell leaned into the shower to kiss him again. Water soaked her hair and the sleeves of her sweatshirt. 'No. Better if I deal with this myself.'

'Be careful,' was all he said before she pulled the shower curtain closed.

For an hour, Nell drove. She drove beyond the city, past the tidy suburban salad of manicured shrubs shaped like chess pawns and gargoyles. Nell knew West Lazarus Road. It was a serpent's tail between marshlands. Follow it far enough and you'd find yourself on Industrial Highway 95, which would eventually take you to the Royal King's State Penitentiary. It was an alternate route, which Nell and Lindsay sometimes took when visiting their mother on the holidays, to avoid the worst of the highway traffic.

How had Lindsay managed to find a guy all the way out here? There were only a few farmhouses set far back from the road, and more cows and horses than humans.

She slowed, inspecting the numbers on the sparse mailboxes beside dirt-beaten driveways.

Another car emerged from behind her, the high beams so bright their glare blinded her. She squinted. It had been at least twenty minutes since she'd seen another soul aside from a raccoon she'd braked to avoid hitting a mile back.

She pressed the gas, returning to the assumed speed limit of seventy miles per hour. The car kept pace.

In the dark, she couldn't tell what model it was, but the roaring grind of the engine and the sulphurous smell suggested that it was old. Suddenly Nell thought of Nathan Stuart, whose last view of this world had been the inside of the Syracuse Strangler's Cadillac Eldorado.

She pressed on the gas, her heart pounding so she could hear it in her ears, a wet, throbbing series of knocks. The car behind her was not being driven by the Syracuse Strangler. The Syracuse Strangler was dead; lung cancer while waiting on death row. And they'd had to treat him for it, because a state-sanctioned death had protocols. Taxpayers funded doctors to treat a man who would die the following January even if he managed to survive the stage four.

But the Syracuse Strangler was not the only monster on earth. She should have considered this. West Lazarus was a deserted road. A lone car passing through at night was like a fish in a barrel. Someone could have been waiting, headlights off.

It wouldn't be a rapist. That's what Nell was thinking as she pushed the accelerator to ninety and the car behind sped up. Any faster and she'd wear the engine out, but if she kept going, she would hit the interstate. There were gaps in the divider and she'd be able to hang a U-turn and switch directions. It was illegal but she didn't care. Risking a car accident would be preferable to what awaited her if her pursuer caught up to her.

Because she was in a car in the dark, the pursuer would not have been able to identify her as a woman. Would not have seen the colour of her hair, or her shape, or her approximate age. And that was the worst kind of monster, Nell had learned: the kind that lacked any sort of preference or reason. The kind that delighted in killing all things equally. It wasn't about attraction or domination but pure thrill.

If she were caught, she wouldn't live to see the true hell of it. Surely she'd pass out from blood loss or from pain first. She would go limp, play dead if she regained consciousness. But she wouldn't last long. Lindsay and Bas would bear the worst of it, finding her body splayed out like a broken marionette.

That's if she were caught. She would die in a fiery wreck before she allowed that to happen. Let her pursuer drag her body from the flames, still smoking. A broken plaything lost all its appeal.

The car slammed into her bumper, jolting her so hard her face smashed into the steering wheel. She tasted blood, saw stars. She stomped the accelerator, engine be damned. Another crash. She heard something hit the asphalt with a metal clatter.

She fell forward again, and that was all it took for her to lose her grip on the wheel. The car spun in a dizzying, high-speed fury, and Nell saw the night go bright for an instant, as though someone had taken a photo with the flash on. She saw the colour in the trees and the pavement and the autumn sky full of clouds. The entire world was bright and clear and spinning.

Then it stopped. There was a hard slapping sound, and Nell thought the tires must have blown. The car felt weightless, as though it were flying.

No. Not flying. Nell smelled the marsh and heard the rush of water that had already submerged her legs as it filled the car.

# 17
# THEN

When Reina was two and a half, she started walking. Prior to that, she would only sit upright and wait for things to be brought to her without her asking; she would have starved to death rather than let on she was hungry. She had never crawled, and Mrs Eddleton was growing concerned, even taking her to the doctor and researching physical therapists. Nell had known better, though nobody would have believed her if she tried to explain that Reina hadn't walked because she hadn't wanted to. That was the only reason. She could have been toilet trained by then too, but she garnered a smug satisfaction from making Nell and Ethan change her diapers. They were especially heinous, and Nell knew this because she had changed hundreds of diapers in foster care. Reina had learned to hold it in for hours, so that everything came out at once, bubbling down her legs and up her back. The smell lingered throughout the Eddletons' million-dollar rooms, making every-thing rancid.

But only Nell saw it this way.

When Reina gripped the cushioned edge of the

ottoman and pulled herself to her feet, Mrs Eddleton was relieved. Reina was not ill or broken; she was merely a delayed genius, who went from sitting idly to climbing a flight of stairs all in one day. She ordered a cake to celebrate the occasion, with buttercream frosting and real strawberry slices.

The child's sudden mobility unnerved Nell, though she couldn't place why. From that day forward, Reina never asked for things. Rather, she found ways to get them herself – pushing the chair over to the counter and climbing the cabinets like a ladder. At age three, she had worked out the child lock on the medicine cabinet and plucked the little plastic stoppers from the plug sockets. But she never tampered with the forbidden bottles or tried to stick objects in the electrical slots. She just wanted to prove that she could access them.

Nell saw this as a sort of warning, though she never said as much. She and Ethan had enough to argue about, and talking about the child made her feel unbearably alone. What was wrong with her? She had a perfectly healthy little girl who smelled of bath oils and spring wind. Everyone else saw some sort of pouting angel where she saw a little monster whose every move was a challenge meant just for her.

She had no way of explaining her fatigue. It wasn't as though anyone needed her. She worked afternoons at the Eddletons' country club, but it wasn't taxing. Mrs Eddleton and Ethan shouldered the load with Reina. Lindsay, newly married, had forgotten how to answer a phone entirely.

But Nell was constantly exhausted. On that day in July, she slept late, wrapped in her down comforter under the blissfully cold air coming through the ceiling vent. Her own restfulness was what woke her. She opened her eyes and saw that the clock on her bedside table read two in the afternoon.

It was strange that no one had woken her. She made herself presentable and walked into the kitchen, where Mrs Eddleton sat reading one of her particularly thick novels. A love of literature was one of the few things Nell had in common with Mrs Eddleton, and she had hoped, once, that they could bond over it. But she fast learned that they didn't share the same tastes. Mrs Eddleton was a fan of comedies and romances – classic or contemporary would do – and movie tie-ins. She read to feel happy and to fall in love with strangers on a page.

Nell preferred the darkest reaches humanity had to offer. Tragedies, thrillers, biographies of serial killers. She liked the bravery that reading granted her. She liked that she was able to face anything so long as it had been printed.

'Where's the baby?' she asked. Three was hardly a baby, but Reina was the youngest creature in the house and it was habit. Nell rarely said the child's name, despite being the one who gave it to her; it always felt strange on her tongue.

'Napping,' Mrs Eddleton said, and raised her eyebrows without looking up from her book. 'She's due to wake soon. Why don't you go and see about changing her? I'm sure she's wondering where you've been all day.'

This sort of passive aggression made Nell often fantasise about moving, but even if she could afford it, it would mean choosing to take Reina with her or leaving her behind. She knew what she would choose and she hated herself for even entertaining it. So she stayed. She put up with Mrs Eddleton's bullshit and she turned for the stairs.

She switched on the light in the nursery, which was darkened by the sun-blocking shades, and made her way to the crib. It was empty. *That's odd*, Nell thought. Was Ethan home? She never knew where he was in a house this size. She lifted the blanket just to be sure.

She made her way down the hall, peering into empty rooms, and back to the kitchen. 'Who else is home?' she asked.

'Just us,' Mrs Eddleton said. She looked up. 'Where's the baby?'

'She wasn't in her crib,' Nell said.

Mrs Eddleton's face went white, and only then did Nell begin to feel uneasy. 'She couldn't have gotten out of her crib by herself,' Nell said. 'Could she?'

'She's very bright.' Mrs Eddleton said it like an

accusation. She dropped her book and stood. 'I don't know how on earth you can't see that.' She didn't stay to finish the argument she'd started. She threw open the French double doors that led to the porch. Nell followed her outside.

Bright as she might be, Reina would lack the physical strength to open those French doors. But there were about a dozen other doors leading out of the house, and it was easy enough to stand on a chair and turn a lock.

'Reina?' Nell called, in that moment not thinking about how strange it felt to say the name.

The Eddletons had a massive lawn. Acres and acres of land. The grass was ribboned in strips of green and brighter green from a recent mowing. There was a tennis court on the other side of the house and a second patio for hosting outdoor parties. But Nell fixed her gaze on the lake on the horizon.

Only once she started running for it did she realise how far the lake actually was. Reina was ambitious enough to scale cabinets; the next reasonable step for a child like that would be to try walking on water. And the child would never ask for help. She hated help. She covered her ears and screeched if she saw someone opening their mouth to offer it. She threw her dish and refused to eat all day if someone tried to cut up her food.

She *was* bright. Despite Mrs Eddleton's accusation,

Nell had always seen that. But what she often forgot to see was that Reina was only a child. A ferocious thing, maybe, but also a small thing. Something in need of guidance. Nell had made the mistake of seeing her own daughter as a burden, rather than seeing the truth that everyone else saw: Reina needed her mother.

Nell imagined diving into the lake. She imagined feeling the sunken lump of her child's body and pulling her up, white and cold. She imagined never seeing her lovely dark eyes again, with their mischievous tint of blue like a sky gone stormy.

Reina gone. Reina never coming back. Never growing up. It was all Nell's fault. She had decided this even before she reached the water. Would it have killed her to try? Would it have been so awful to wait out her child's tantrums so that she could feel the affection everyone else did? It was a child's job to test her mother. It was a mother's job to love her child regardless.

She reached the water's edge and she froze. Tall grass snaked up her skirt, making her legs itch. The surface was placid, and suddenly Nell couldn't move. She couldn't bear for any of her fears to be true.

A loud crack caught her attention. She turned her head.

Reina was standing several yards away, nearly covered by the towering weeds.

'Reina,' Nell gasped, and ran to her.

The child didn't move. She was staring down at something on the ground before her, and when Nell approached, she saw it too. A bird, a fledgling sparrow, too small to be full-grown, lay mutilated on the ground with a bloody rock beside it.

The mother bird was flitting anxiously several yards away, her surviving children chirping as they followed her about. Nell recognised the panic in the mother bird's cry; a moment ago she had felt the same way. It was all too easy to lose your young in such an endless world.

The child sighed, her shoulders and chest heaving with the weight of it.

Nell looked at the rock. It wasn't very big. A child could have lifted it if she used both hands.

✳

'You have lost your mind. Do you know that?'

That was Ethan's reaction later that night when Nell told him about the bird. He closed the bedroom door behind them.

'I know what I saw,' Nell fired back. 'She killed it, Ethan.'

'She is just—' He paused, rubbing his thumb and index finger against his brow. 'She's a little girl. A baby.'

'Babies can kill things,' Nell said. 'Even foetuses

can absorb their twins in the womb. It happens all the time.'

'Christ, do you hear yourself?'

Nell did hear herself. Of course she did. She was the only one in this house who ever listened to what she had to say. Lindsay had been an ally when it came to Reina, but she hadn't been by for weeks. She had disappeared into her marriage as though Matthew Cranlin's house was a creature that had eaten them both.

'You should be on my side,' Nell fired off at Ethan. She knew it was a weak argument but it was true.

'I *am* on your side.' Ethan's voice still had an edge, but he was softening. 'It isn't just about protecting Reina. I'm trying to protect you, too, Nell. Do you know what can happen to mothers who say these sorts of things? My parents would have you committed.'

Mrs Eddleton might, but Nell had noted Mr Eddleton's scarceness when Reina was nearby. He didn't try to play with her or teach her new words. He never said as much, but Nell liked to believe he saw what she did.

Tears burned in her eyes. She almost never cried, and when she did, it was always out of frustration.

Ethan threw down his arms and sighed. 'Don't do that,' he said. 'You're going to make me feel like an asshole.'

'I'm not crazy,' Nell said, hating how simpering

she sounded. 'Your mother saw the rock too. It had blood and feathers on it. What do you suggest? That rocks have started falling from trees?'

'How would Reina have caught a bird? Do you know how hard that would be? She's smart, but she's no aviatrix.'

'Ornithologist,' Nell corrected. 'And it was a baby. There were a bunch of them. I think the mother was teaching them to fly.'

Ethan gave her a pitying look. Whenever they argued about their child, anger gave way to pity. 'I really think you should speak to someone.'

'Speak to someone,' she echoed. And again, louder. 'Speak to someone? Is that the way rich, civilised people handle things, Ethan? Will that make you more comfortable, having your child mothered by someone just like your own mommy and daddy?'

His glare turned vicious, and Nell saw so much of Reina in him that she took a step back.

He stormed past her, down the hall and into the nursery where Reina was sleeping. The door slammed shut, and that was it. If this was going to be a war, then he had chosen his side.

# 18
# NOW

The water was thick with mud, black in the darkness. It rushed in through the vents and the cracks in the doors. Panicked, Nell tried the handle, though she knew it would be useless. Water pressure welded the doors shut.

This was going to be worse than torture, worse than being strung up naked on a telephone line for police to find. It was going to be a silent death, and it would render her invisible. Nobody would ever think to look for a missing car in a nondescript swamp on the side of the road. Sebastian and Lindsay would never know what had happened to her. Where was Sebastian now? He would be leaving for work in a couple of hours. He wouldn't even realise she was gone until hours later, and then he would call Lindsay and they would both go frantic. There would be posters, public appeals. They would search and search, never knowing that she had been dead even before they knew she was missing at all.

The only evidence she had even gone to this road would sink with her, in the text messages on her phone in her purse.

Her purse. She found it floating as the water reached her chest. She fumbled through the sodden contents until she found the hammer Lindsay had forced into her hands days earlier.

It slipped from her wet grasp and she fumbled in the murky black. The water rose and she drew in a gasp an instant before it filled the car completely.

Immediately the world disappeared. Nell knew that, logically, she was still in a car, in a swamp, off of West Lazarus Road. But in the dark, she was in a parallel universe. The hammer was gone, just as the steering wheel and the seats were gone. Just as Lindsay and Sebastian were gone. Even her drunk, ambling father, who had never been kind but was proud of his daughters in his own way. Even Bonnie, with her raspy smoker's voice and her hardened eyes.

Everything was gone.

Nell's fingers snared something and she grasped at it. She thought it might be the latch of some secret door that she could open, and her entire life would go flooding out of this world and into the next along with the swamp water.

The shape of the object woke her from her trance. The hammer. She spun, weightless in the water. Everything moved slowly, and she couldn't see the window in the darkness, but she felt it. She drew back the hammer and hit the glass. Again, again. The glass didn't shatter as she had somehow expected.

Rather, it cracked. She felt the jagged lines forming when she touched its surface.

She drew back and kicked at the prone glass with the heel of her boot.

Her body floated, light and useless. As the water rushed through her ears, she heard Lindsay screaming at the hospital doctors. They were in the delivery room, the baby tumbling in Nell's womb, and the doctors had anesthetised her so they could cut her open and tear the baby out. Lindsay was saying words that Nell couldn't hear, but what she did hear was how afraid Lindsay was. She didn't trust Nell's life in their gloved hands. She didn't trust that this would all be over soon.

Nell felt something break, just like the skin of her engorged stomach. A piece of glass bit at her ankle.

She forced herself back awake. She forced herself to squeeze through the narrow window frame and then swim. She didn't know what direction was up, but she moved anyway. Her delirium had shattered like the window, and now she felt the burning of her lungs. The desperation came back so that she was full with it. The thought of dying, which had moments ago seemed bearable, was now unthinkable. She would live. She would.

She broke the surface of the water with a painful gasp. Time returned, all its little pieces back above the surface where Nell had left them.

She'd been certain that hours had passed under

water, but logic told her it had only been a few seconds. Still gasping, she swam for the road. Without the car headlights, only the stars lit the way, offering her the faint outline of gravel.

Even as she fought to steady her breathing, she tried to be quiet. She listened for the hum of an engine, footsteps, or any sign of whoever had been chasing her.

There was no one.

Slowly, she crawled onto the wet earth and ambled back up to the road. She looked down it in either direction. Her fists clenched, and she reminded herself to keep a clear head. Panic was useless. Panic made people do stupid things.

She looked down and saw that she was still clutching the hammer. She didn't remember swimming with it. But there it was, slick and wet, still splattered with old paint.

Nell held it up and laughed. It was a desperate, hysterical laugh. No doubt the sort of laugh Bonnie had given before she fired the shot that would land her in prison forever.

※

Nell's phone was in the swamp, along with her car and all the identification and money she'd been carrying. It was nearly dawn by the time she reached a gas station; she could hear birds awakening in the shifting darkness. Before that, she'd gone up and down West Lazarus Road, shivering in her wet clothes, looking for number 2, only to discover that the numbers began in the double digits. From there, she had tried all variations of 2. 12. 20. 21. But the address Lindsay gave her didn't exist. She might have been drunk when she texted; whatever the reason, Nell planned to lay a massive guilt trip on her sister when she saw her next.

The gas station was closed. A sign on the window announced that it would be open at 8 AM. Nell cursed the rural outskirts; had this happened within Rockhollow's city limits, there would have been a dozen twenty-four-hour gas stations to choose from.

But of course, something like this would only happen in a place that slept between the hours of 8 PM and 8 AM. And now that she had reached a destination, Nell realised that she was not only shivering from the cold. She was trembling. Blood had crusted on her arms and cheek where the shattered window had sliced her.

She rooted around in her jeans pockets for change. The only good thing about an antiquated gas station in a nowhere town was that they always had a payphone.

The call to Lindsay went straight to voicemail.

'Jesus, Lindsay, where the hell are you?' Of all the nights for her sister to pull this shit. She dialled

Bas's number but it also went to voicemail. Nell slammed the phone back into the cradle without leaving a message. Of course, Bas always turned his phone off at bedtime, rarely turning it back on until he was halfway through his commute.

She picked up the phone again to dial 911, but hesitated. Burying her head under the damp hood of her sweatshirt, shivering in the middle of nowhere and operating on almost no sleep, her thoughts turned paranoid. She thought of the mannequin smouldering on the street beside Lindsay's car, and the other hanging from a noose in a tree.

Nell had forced herself to be reassured by Lindsay's insistence that the mannequins had been a prank, but now she sensed there was a pattern to this. Or rather there was a puzzle, and the pieces were scattered everywhere.

She dropped a quarter into the payphone and dialled a number she had come to know by heart. It was the number written on a Post-it note stuck to the wall by her desk, along with all the other notes she kept nearby for reference in the Hamblin case. Oleg's cell phone.

He answered on the first ring. She imagined him in bed, his pristine hair tousled, his congenial smile replaced by raw exhaustion. She imagined him without pretence, the way he must be when he was alone.

'Oleg? It's Nell Way. I-I know it's late – or early—'

Too late, she realised she hadn't rehearsed this call, and after the night she'd endured, she couldn't think straight.

He interrupted her. 'What's the matter? Has something happened?'

All Nell could think in that moment was that she had never heard worry in his voice before. She knew he'd been through hell thanks to Easter. But she had never pictured it until now. How had he sounded when he took the call that Autumn was dead? When he first picked up the phone and stared down his sister through the prison glass?

'I'm sorry to call you like this but it is important,' Nell said. 'Can you meet me?'

He was there in twenty minutes, which Nell presumed to be some sort of record. It had taken her at least twice as long to make it this far when she was speeding her way to Lindsay. She recognised his gold Buick Century, which was the first car she'd seen since she'd been run off of the road. They stopped making this model fifteen years ago, but he kept it in remarkably pristine shape. He applied this sort of care to everything. Even during their interviews, he had laid his straw wrapper on the table, pressing it at the crease and then folding it into perfect squares as he spoke. He didn't even seem aware that he was doing it.

He leaned across the passenger seat to open the door for her, and she leapt gratefully inside. The heat was blasting, and it thawed the frozen chunks of hair in her ponytail.

She closed her eyes. For the first time all morning, she allowed herself to believe that she was safe.

'Thank you,' she said.

'What are you doing out here in the freezing cold?' Oleg asked. 'Why are you soaked?'

He hadn't started driving yet, and Nell realised that she hadn't told him where to take her. She didn't know where she was heading. She hadn't thought beyond getting him here, so that she could ask him her next question.

She leaned forward and cupped her hands over one of the vents, and then she turned to him. His hair was neatly combed, although his eyes were weary.

'Oleg,' Nell said. 'I want you to know that I've always been honest in our conversations. That's important, because when people entrust their stories to me, I want to give full transparency about how I'm going to use them.'

'Yes,' Oleg replied slowly. 'I know that.'

'So I need to ask you something about your sisters. Take your time before you answer.'

He raised an eyebrow. 'Nell, what is this about?'

'Is there any possible way,' Nell said, 'that Autumn is still alive?'

# 19
# NOW

They drove in silence. For the first several miles there was only the sound of the engine.

Oleg gripped the steering wheel so tightly that his knuckles had turned white. His jaw was set in a way that added a sharp angle to his usually boyish features.

Nell didn't say anything, not even to ask where they were headed. He was driving in the direction of Rockhollow, so they'd be back to civilisation soon, at least.

The sun had come up by now, though the clouds were so dark and pregnant with their next rain that it still felt earlier than it was.

Finally, Oleg said, 'I know the sort of things Easter says about Autumn. I'm not stupid.'

Nell had never thought Oleg was stupid, but she knew better than to speak.

'I didn't mind Easter asking you to tell their story because you have ... intuition,' Oleg went on, hesitating as though he'd needed to find the right word. His grasp of English was impeccable, but it wasn't the language he used to form his thoughts. 'How could you ask me if Autumn is still alive? Did Easter fool you so easily?'

Nell stared at the road ahead. Suddenly she couldn't look at him.

'This is my third book,' she answered softly. 'But Easter isn't the third murderer I've interviewed. I've interviewed dozens, and I've researched dozens more. But do you know what all of those murderers had in common? Their stories were trapped in their cells with them. They could tell me whatever they wanted – that they were innocent, or that their victims had it coming – but at the end of the day, those words meant nothing because they were still behind bars.'

'I don't understand your point,' Oleg said.

Nell turned in her seat. She wanted to put her hand over his knuckles on the steering wheel. She wanted him to feel her, so that he would know that she was being sincere. But it probably would have made matters worse. In a moment, he was going to think she was as delusional as Easter. But she had to tell him the truth.

'Since the day I met Easter, things have started happening to my family,' she said. 'Someone has been leaving threats for me and my sister. And someone tried to kill me tonight.'

'Threats?' Oleg asked, hesitant. 'Letters? Calls?'

'No,' Nell said. And then she told him about Lindsay's car, and the mannequins. As they wove through the twisty desolate outskirts of Rockhollow, she told him about the text she'd received in the middle of the night. The address that didn't exist. The car that ran her straight into the swamp and left her there to drown.

He listened in silence, but his brows were drawn together by the time she'd finished. He couldn't accuse her of exaggerating when she was sitting right there in his car, damp and filthy with swamp water.

'You rang the police?' he asked.

'Yes,' Nell said. Her voice was high and hysterical now. In speaking her fears out loud, she had invited them into her mind, and now they ran rampant. 'Lindsay – that's my sister – she convinced me that the mannequins were a neighbourhood prank. She's – well she's good at pissing people off, let's just put it like that. Nothing like this has ever happened before, but it seemed like the only explanation. And things were starting to calm down until tonight.'

Oleg opened his mouth to speak, but stopped. He was so careful with words. He was like Easter in that sense. He knew how to wear a mask.

When he did speak, it was with measured patience, and Nell imagined this was how he had sounded when he first learned English. 'Are you trying to tell me that Autumn isn't really dead, and that she is somehow behind this?'

That was exactly what Nell was trying to tell

him. But as crazy as it had sounded in her head, it sounded even crazier when he said it out loud.

'Listen,' Nell said. 'When cases don't add up, I like to list all of the facts until they make sense and form a picture. Here are the facts: a skeleton was found by the river. The skin had been picked away by animals. Even the hair was gone. The only identifying remains were two teeth, which were used to match DNA, but they were found *near* the skull. The rest had been removed. It's all there in the police report.'

Oleg's arms were shaking now. His cheeks were flushed, his eyes glassy. Nell felt the vibration under her seat as he accelerated too much at once.

'It would be easy enough to remove two of your teeth,' Nell said. 'Isn't it at all possible that the victim by the river wasn't Autumn? Isn't it possible that the victim—'

'Don't call her that!' Oleg burst out. He spoke with so much force that spittle flew across the steering wheel. 'She wasn't "the victim". She was my sister. She was my little sister. She was the *good* one.'

Nell went silent. She waited for him to pull over and let her out, but he didn't. His foot eased up on the accelerator and he returned to the speed limit. Forty-five on the dot.

'You say that your sister pisses off a lot of people,' he said, in a calmer tone now. 'But what about you? You go nosing around these cases, looking for your next story. Maybe there's someone who doesn't like what you have to say.'

Nell nodded. 'I've considered that. And I shouldn't have said that about Autumn. I'm sorry.'

He didn't look at her. The flush was still on his cheeks, but he didn't look angry anymore. Tears were suspended in his eyelashes like raindrops in a web.

'Let me tell you what it was like to get a phone call that my sister was dead,' he said. 'My first thought was that there was some mistake. Easter had told me that Autumn had taken off for a while; she often did. And of course she was pretending to be Autumn to everyone else so no one raised the alarm. So when I got that call, it wasn't enough that the police told me her body had been found. I had to see it. They rolled her out of the drawer in the coroner's office. There was no muscle or tissue left. There was nothing to hold her together. All of her bones were laid out in their proper places, but not touching each other. I didn't think it was possible that this could be all that was left, and for a long time I didn't believe it. But in the end that's all any of us are – just bones.'

He shook his head. 'Autumn is not alive,' he said. 'Believe me before you believe Easter. I'm the one who wishes she were still out there somewhere.'

'I'm sorry,' Nell said. 'I'm so used to looking at things analytically, I forget that I'm talking about real people.'

'No you don't,' Oleg said. 'I've read your words. You know that they're real people.' He frowned, glanced at her for a second before looking back to the road. They were in Rockhollow's surrounding suburbs now. A school bus stopped beside them at the red light, its brakes squealing and its engine letting out a loud huff, as though indignant with its purpose in life.

'You've only just finished your last book, isn't that right?' Oleg went on. 'And without taking time to breathe, you've been thrust into Easter's world. She isn't easy to take. I know that. Maybe you should give yourself more time. Be patient with yourself.'

Nell felt sick with guilt. He was being so kind to her, after she'd woken him from his sleep and unearthed such ugly things for him.

'My motel is just on this block,' he said. 'Why don't we stop there so you can take a hot shower. Warm up. I'll buy you some breakfast. And then we're reporting everything you told me to the police.'

The motel was a small, single-storey building wedged between two high-rise apartments. There was a flickering neon sign advertising vacancies, and the air smelled like bacon from a diner across the street.

Nell had suspected Oleg had no desire to move to America permanently. He would leave when his travel visa expired. Still, she was taken aback by his dedication. He cared so much about his sisters and their story that he had uprooted his life to stay here.

His car must have been a rental too. The upholstery was so clean that Nell was self-conscious about soiling it with swamp water.

Once she was in the motel room, Nell tried Lindsay's cell again. It went straight to voicemail. If Lindsay had managed to find her own way home, why hadn't she rung Nell in the car to let her know, to tell her to turn around?

Nell was afforded a startling glimpse into what today would have been like if she'd drowned on that empty road. Lindsay was probably sleeping off her hangover somewhere and Sebastian was busy at work. She could be bloated and floating in her car and they would have no reason yet to worry.

She showered and then stood under the hot water until it began to turn cold. She'd left her clothes hanging on a towel rack above the heating vent. They were stiff and mostly dry, though they stank. Maybe that wasn't such a bad thing, she reasoned. It meant the police would be more likely to believe her story, unbelievable as it was.

Oleg knocked gently on the door. 'I'm leaving a jumper for you,' he said.

After he'd gone, Nell opened the door just enough to see the blue sweater he'd left folded on the floor.

It was soft when she put it on – cashmere. Her jeans were rough and uncomfortable by contrast, but Nell didn't mind. On some distant level, she recognised that she must be traumatised. She kept imagining the moment Lindsay and Sebastian would have realised she was missing.

When she emerged from the bathroom, Oleg was seated at the tiny desk in the corner. He was reading a well-worn paperback of Nell's first book. From where she stood, she could see Nathan Stuart's picture on the cover, the child victim of the Syracuse Strangler. He was staring wide-eyed, his finger pressed pensively to his lip, which was stained cherry red from the candy he'd been eating. It had been taken on the morning he'd lost his first tooth. His mother had requested that photo be used for the cover; it was her favourite.

Seeing Oleg hold a copy of her work made her feel self-conscious, though she wasn't sure why. Over a million copies had been sold over the years. But to see Oleg with a copy made her feel as though he could see clean through her words, to the girl she had been when she'd written them. It made her feel as naked as her body under his borrowed cashmere sweater.

She wrung her wet hair into a towel. 'You keep a copy of my book just lying around?'

'Of course.' He set it on the desk with care. 'It's the reason I'm here.'

He looked at her, and his eyes were the palest, clearest blue in the morning light. 'Are you feeling better now?'

'Yes, but I must look like a mess,' Nell said, laughing. She always laughed when she was frightened. It was strange how one could feel fear even after the thing to cause that fear was over.

'Hey.' Oleg moved towards her and circled his hand around her wrist. 'You're shaking.'

Nell shook her head. 'I'm fine. Everything is fine.'

'No it isn't,' he said. 'But it will be. I promise. Maybe we should skip breakfast and go straight to the police.'

'No,' Nell answered too quickly. 'No,' she said again, trying to sound calmer. 'Breakfast will help. I need time to sit and think.'

'All right.' His voice was as serene as his eyes. 'All right. It's just across the street. We can walk there.'

# 20
## THEN

On what would be her last Christmas, Reina was three years old. Eleven months later, she would disappear forever.

It was also the first year Nell went to visit Bonnie without Lindsay, who had practically surgically attached herself to Matthew Cranlin.

Nell brought Reina along instead. Ethan had offered to come too, but Nell knew he was hoping she'd refuse, which she did. 'I can't make you ride out all that way,' she said, standing in the driveway with her hand on the car door handle. 'You wouldn't like my mother anyway. You've heard the stories.'

'Yeah,' Ethan said. 'Drive safe. Call me when you get there so I know you're okay.' He hoisted Reina over to her. A second ago, Reina had been latched to his hip with her head tucked against his shoulder. She'd looked like a baby koala in her puffed mint-green coat, staring impassively at the lightly falling snow. But once in Nell's arms, she went slack and uncooperative. Nell had to tighten her grip so Reina wouldn't slip through her arms like a heavy bag of groceries.

She dreaded the drive without Lindsay there to balance things out. Lindsay's pettiness and contrarian nature didn't yield for toddlers. In Lindsay's mind there was no difference between a stubborn child and a burly mugger in the back alley behind a bar. If someone provoked her, she responded in kind and there would be no exceptions. If Reina threw one of her screaming fits in the grocery store, Lindsay would crouch down before her and scream too. If Reina pitched her cereal at the wall, Lindsay said, 'Is that all you've got?' and threw her drink. Whenever Lindsay brought Reina a present, the first thing Reina did was break it. So Lindsay bought more challenging and resilient things: a cast iron bank shaped like an alphabet block, a Rubik's cube whose little square buttons would not come apart no matter how Reina pulled at them.

It became its own sort of weird affection, and both participants got a kick out of it. Nell envied this. Lindsay had found a way to bond with her niece, even if she did consistently maintain that the child was a terror. It was something. Nell had observed the way Reina studied her aunt; doubtless Reina recognised someone who would challenge her – someone who didn't fear her tantrums or feel devastated when her gifts were smashed or peed on. They were playing a game.

Nell didn't even get that much out of her child. Reina had always known how to break Nell.

Sometimes when Reina sat catatonic in front of the TV or in her car seat, Nell suspected it was out of boredom. Nell was such an easy mark that there was no sport in it.

For the first hour of the drive, Reina slept, lulled by the thrum of the engine and the heat. Nell's gaze flitted to the rear-view mirror. She so rarely got to have a good, uninterrupted look at her daughter's face. She avoided looking when the baby was awake.

Everyone else looked at her, though. When Nell pushed her stroller through the grocery store or stood in line at the bank, there was always someone who remarked on what a beautiful child she had. Of course they only caught Reina in glimpses, and probably dismissed her permanent scowl as a moment of moodiness that would later be assuaged by a nap or a snack.

But it was true. Though everything about Reina's behaviour was grotesque, Nell had seen from the first day that her daughter was pretty. A perfect little machine with pink lips and cheeks, and lashes that were dark and heavy.

Watching her daughter sleep, Nell allowed herself to feel a bit of pride.

Her eyes turned back to the road just in time for her to see the rows of brake lights. Traffic had come to a stop.

She slammed the brakes; the car screeched and bucked and Nell jolted forward.

Her eyes closed in dread. She knew what was about to happen.

Reina awoke with a gurgling hiccup, and it turned into a shriek.

'Really?' Nell muttered. She wasn't talking to Reina, but to whatever grand force seemed to hate her so much. The gust of hatred she felt was strong enough to make her believe in God.

Reina screamed all through the traffic jam. She tugged at the seatbelt that wove through her car seat, trying to free herself. But Nell had safety-pinned it in place because she was on to her daughter's tricks by now.

As Nell eased the brakes and let the car roll forward in yard-long increments, she wondered why she went to such lengths to save her daughter from herself. Bolting the windows when Reina proved to be a little climber, installing a pressure lock on the fridge so she wouldn't drink the condiments until she threw up, pinning the seatbelt behind the car seat so she wouldn't rip out the buckle.

She imagined what would happen if she hadn't taken the extra measure of pinning the seatbelt down. She imagined Reina ripping herself free and pulling up the door lock and running out into traffic.

What would happen then? Maybe she would realise that cars and strangers aren't as easy to manipulate as her mother. Maybe she would realise that the world was vast and unforgiving, and that her mother was continuing to inch along the traffic jam without her, and she would return to the car before it was too late.

Or maybe she would run along the yellow dotted lines as far and as fast as her little red suede shoes would carry her.

Nell's fingers flexed and tightened around the steering wheel.

Reina's stamina was impressive. The screaming maintained its pitch. The pauses for breath were short and measured. Her face wasn't even red from the strain. There were no tears in her eyes.

By the time they reached the prison Nell had grown used to it, the way she always did if she was subjected to a long tantrum.

She was also used to the indignant stares she got in the visitors' queue, and the way the screaming echoed.

The worst part was carrying her. Reina knew how to make herself twisty and slippery like a snake, and she had mastered the art of throwing a tantrum while keeping her body miraculously limp.

Finally fed up with having to readjust her grip, Nell tried something new and draped Reina over her shoulder. She clamped down on Reina's ankles with one hand to keep her from sliding away. All this effort to hold on to something that hated her.

When at last it was her turn, she was led to a tiny room filled with tables and chairs.

This was a rare treat. Most visits with Bonnie were no-contact visits, because she was on probation for violating a rule or there simply wasn't room. Especially on holiday weekends.

Nell deposited Reina onto a chair, and the tantrum stopped. Reina had never been in this part of the prison before. She had only seen her grandmother through a sheet of shatterproof glass, which she would crawl up on the counter and lick so that she could spread her saliva around into nonsense shapes.

But this place was new. There wasn't much that should interest a toddler; no colours, nothing to grab or play with. But Nell knew that contemplative look in the child's eyes. She was going to find some way to sabotage this visit.

Bonnie was led to the table by a CO, and she sat slowly, grunting. She was not an old woman. Only forty-three but already arthritic with smoker's lung. Nell had watched her mother wither more with each visit. Her brown hair had turned grey, then silver and limp, and then it began to thin. Her skin had leathered. But she always took care of her teeth; they were bright and smooth and straight.

'Hi, baby,' she said to Nell, with a resigned weariness.

'Hi, Momma,' Nell said. 'This is a surprise, getting to see you without the glass.'

'Oh yeah.' Bonnie coughed. A wet, rattling sound. 'Delightful. I've been a good girl.' She looked to Reina, who was sitting upright in her chair and staring at her. 'Hey, kid.' When there was no response, Bonnie turned back to Nell. 'She still ain't talking, huh?'

'Yes,' Reina said, her cheeks fat with a scowl.

'Sometimes she speaks,' Nell said.

'She still smearing caca all over the house like a barn animal?' Bonnie asked.

This was a new word for Reina. *Caca*. It made her laugh. It wasn't a playful, little girl laugh. It was the same sort of laugh Matthew let out when Lindsay tripped or spilled something.

'Don't give her any ideas,' Nell said.

Bonnie's pitying look said that Nell looked as tired as she sounded. Seventeen years old and Nell felt haggard and sore.

Bonnie reached across the table and tucked a piece of hair behind Nell's ear. 'You're so pretty,' she said. 'This isn't what I wanted for you, baby girl, you know that.'

Nell held her tongue. Reina had taught her that level of restraint. What she wanted to say was: if you cared to raise me, why did you fuck it all up? Why was I born on the floor of your cell? What sort of future did you have in mind if that was my start?

'Caca,' Reina echoed, swinging her feet. She kicked at a table leg, and Nell ignored it, letting the table bounce against the floor. If she made a move to steady it, Reina would know she had found her new game.

Bonnie seemed to know it too. She knew a lot about babies, given how little attention she'd given her own. 'Where's your sister at?'

'She's not speaking to me,' Nell said.

'What crawled up her ass this time?'

Nell shrugged.

Bonnie leaned closer. 'That boy hits her, doesn't he?'

Nell preferred not to divulge Lindsay's private matters to her mother. The truth was that she wanted desperately to save her sister, not only from her husband but from herself. But Lindsay was a novelty finger trap – the more Nell tried to pull her away, the tighter she latched on to her convictions.

Her hesitation was her answer.

'Lindsay ain't mad at you,' Bonnie said. 'That's just an excuse so you don't come around and see what he did to her face.'

Nell hadn't considered this, but upon hearing the words she knew they were true.

Bonnie's jaw clenched. She shook her head. 'That girl's gonna end up in a body bag.'

'Mom,' Nell scolded. She glanced to Reina, using her child's presence to veer the conversation to something lighter. But Bonnie wasn't having it.

'I thought Lindsay'd be more the shotgun type,' Bonnie said. 'Thought she'd put a bullet in that son of a bitch and end up living here with me. But she's just gonna let him kill her.'

Nell could have lied and said this wasn't true, but Bonnie would see through it anyway.

'Don't you try nothing,' Bonnie said, pointing at Nell. 'Don't get yourself locked up trying to protect your dumbass sister. There's still hope for you.'

'This is why Lindsay doesn't want to visit you,' Nell said, trying to sound amicable. 'She thinks you play favourites with us.'

'I ain't playing,' Bonnie said. 'I love Lindsay, but you're the good one. You're gonna do the big things. I've always known that. You've had yourself a little setback, but you'll get back on your feet.'

Getting pregnant at fourteen had not been a setback. Having a child like Reina was the setback.

'Mom,' Nell said, and leaned closer. 'What was Lindsay like when she was little?'

'She was like a cat,' Bonnie said, not without affection. 'That girl got into everything. Wasn't much of a talker, but that's because she was always planning something.'

'But was it ever more than that?' Nell asked. 'Was she like –'

'Like this one?' Bonnie nodded at Reina. Reina had a finger up her nose, and she was digging so hard that blood was dripping from her nostril. Nell didn't try to clean it up; she didn't want to provoke another screaming match, and she would rather a messy child than a loud one. With Reina, she had to take what choices she was offered. And Reina was always scratching herself anyway. Her nails were long and sharp. Mrs Eddleton was the only one Reina permitted to cut them, and only when it suited her, like when she tore one apart trying to scale a tree or had gotten a splinter wedged in her nail bed.

'No, Lindsay was never like your kid,' Bonnie went on. 'If I had a kid like yours, I'd have left her with your father. Woulda been a better punishment than trying to shoot him.'

Nell could never be sure how much Reina understood. She plopped her bloody nail into her mouth and sucked it like a pacifier as she stared at her grandmother. Reina had only ever seen Bonnie behind a sheet of glass; maybe she had thought her to be a television show. But now she liked her – as much as she could like anyone.

'Do you like this place?' Bonnie asked Reina. She didn't bother to make her voice sweet or melodic the way that most adults did around children. Maybe that was part of Reina's fascination.

Reina nodded. It was a short, rapid little gesture that made her curls bounce over her eyes.

'That's good,' Bonnie said. 'I'll see you here when you grow up. Maybe if you're nice to me I'll show you how to make hooch.'

'Mom!'

Bonnie folded her arms and sat back. 'What's true is true,' she said.

# 21

# NOW

Nell cupped the warm mug in both hands and took a sip of her coffee. It was bitter, but it was hot, and that was all that mattered. 'Have you spent much time with Mr and Mrs Hamblin?'

'Is this for your book?' Oleg asked.

'No. I'm just curious.'

He covered his mouth to stifle a yawn. Nell wasn't the only one who hadn't gotten enough sleep. 'I spent a few weeks of my summers there after my sisters were adopted,' he said. 'I knew they did this for my sisters' sake. I could tell that sometimes I had worn out my welcome.'

'I find that hard to believe,' Nell said. She would never make such a leading statement in an interview, but this wasn't an interview. For the first time, she was having a simple conversation with one of the subjects.

'I think Mom Esther liked having me there,' Oleg said. 'She's the type of person who likes to take care of people. Mr Hamblin was the one who wanted me to leave.'

Mr Hamblin's title stood in contrast to Oleg's

affectionate nickname for Mrs Hamblin.

Oleg smiled at her. He canted his head. 'Shall I ask the waitress to bring a pen and paper so you can write some of this down?'

'This isn't an interview,' Nell reminded him. 'And anyway, I never forget anything.'

'How do you manage that?' Oleg asked.

'If it's the truth, you don't need to remember much,' Nell said. 'The pieces will all fit together no matter how you turn it over.'

'That's such an interesting sentiment,' Oleg said, and took a sip of his own coffee. 'And what about you, Nell? Do the pieces of your own life fall together as neatly as the events in your books?'

The question stirred up her anxiety again. Here was Oleg, giving so much of his time and his honesty to her, and she couldn't afford him the same.

He must have seen the change in her expression, because he added, 'I didn't mean to ask you anything personal. I'm sorry.'

'No, you're fine,' Nell said. 'It's just – my head's a mess after last night.'

Mercifully, the waitress brought their food at that moment. They ate in silence. The croissant was buttered to opaqueness and the scrambled eggs were dry, but Nell began to feel better as she ate.

The waitress came and took their empty dishes. She left the check, and Oleg grabbed it before Nell could reach for it.

She watched him for a moment as he read the piece of paper and began calculating the tip in his head.

Nell didn't know what made her say what came next. 'To answer your question, the pieces of my life *do* always come together eventually. The problem is getting others to believe me.'

✦

'Can you think of anyone who would be targeting you?' Officer Rayburn asked.

Once again, Nell found herself sitting in the hard plastic chair of an interrogation room.

Oleg was beside her. He didn't have to come along; he could have waited in the lobby, or just dropped her off outside the station and driven away. But without a word he had followed her when her name was called. Nell could smell the lingering cologne in the sleeve of his cashmere sweater when she brought her knuckle to her lips.

'I write about controversial things,' Nell said. 'The press release for my latest book just came out. It's sparked some outrage, but that's pretty normal. True crime writers get that all the time.'

Officer Rayburn raised an eyebrow. 'Is that so.' It wasn't a question. 'You live in the Ocean View apartments, right? The good news is that building has the best security in the city. My suggestion would be to stay home until there are new leads. We'll do what we can on our end.'

'That's it?' Oleg burst out. He sounded like someone else entirely when he was angry. It was jarring the way that he switched gears without warning – first this morning in the car, and now here. 'Someone tried to kill her. Do you understand that?'

Officer Rayburn held up both hands. 'I do understand. And Ms Way has given us a description of the vehicle. But without a licence plate or a description of the driver, there's very little that we can do.'

'It's all right,' Nell said to Oleg.

'How can you say that?' His eyes were wide, wild.

'Look,' Officer Rayburn said. 'My advice: go online. Search for your name. Look for anyone who may have issued any threats because of your books.'

Nell closed her eyes and let out a long breath. There was no way for Officer Rayburn to know that she did this all the time. But she only nodded. Her head ached and all she wanted to do was go to her own bed and sleep this off.

It was mid-afternoon when Oleg pulled up in front of her apartment building. 'I could come up with you,' he offered.

'No,' Nell said. 'Thank you. You've been more than generous.'

He hesitated. She could see that he really was concerned about her.

'I'm sorry for what I said about Autumn,' she said. 'I don't know how I could think that was a possibility.'

He shook his head. 'You've had a horrible night, and Easter has a way of getting in people's heads. I get it.'

'Still, it isn't like me to—'

'How about we make a deal?' Oleg interrupted. 'You get some rest, and the next time we speak, that conversation never happened.'

'I'd like that,' Nell said.

The apartment was quiet when she got upstairs. There was still the faint smell of body wash coming from the shower, and the bed was made with Sebastian's trademark neatness.

She napped fitfully on the couch for an hour, and awoke startled by a nightmare she couldn't remember a second later.

She stared at the ceiling. Afternoon light filtered through the clouds, making the room dreary. Then, she pushed herself upright. It was time to quit delaying the inevitable.

The Hamblins' chapter was waiting for her when Nell opened her laptop. She minimised the window and opened her web browser to a private tab.

The search field stared back at her, as though it were already accusing her of something. Nell typed: *Penelope Wendall*.

This was not the name on her manuscripts. It

wasn't the name Sebastian murmured, coiling his arms around her when he wanted five more minutes in bed. It wasn't on any of her contracts. It wasn't the way she was programmed into the contact list on Lindsay's phone. It wasn't on her driver's licence or her lease.

But it was her name, under everything. It was permanent, even though she'd had it legally changed nine years ago. Penelope Wendall: the baby who was born in Bonnie's prison cell. The name the Eddletons were still cursing to this day.

Her heart sped when she read the search results, the way it always did. As usual, there weren't many hits, and none of them were tied to her legal name now. Penelope Wendall and Nell Way had never met, but they were each a ghost haunting the other's castle.

Nell had memorised the first page of search results. They hadn't changed at all this month. There were old news articles that had never archived their comment section, and every so often there was a new comment asking for an update. Usually nobody replied, because nobody knew or cared. But occasionally there was an adamant theory that she was a pop star, or a voice actress for car commercials, or that she had died of an overdose in prison.

Nell steeled herself and read through every comment looking for anything she could connect to what had happened last night. There was nothing.

On the second page of search results, at the very

top was EarlyAngels.com. Again, Nell braced herself. She had been to this website many times when researching the Widow Thompson case. It was a collection of fan-maintained online memorials for children who had been murdered or gone missing. The fans were thorough; there had even been information about Daisy Thompson, the thirteen-month-old. Nell recalled a prominent photo of her grin, wrapped up warm and safe in a towel with a hood meant to make her look like a baby chick. The online obituary said that she had loved staring at the lights cast by the prisms hanging over the kitchen sink. She would only nap if her car seat was left to rattle on the running dryer. Her favourite food was bananas.

Reina was on there too. Nell knew this, of course. She had searched many times, only to stare at the blue underlined link of her child's name and never clicking it.

She clicked on the search result now, and immediately 'Angel' by Sarah McLachlan blared from the speakers. Nell hit the mute button in a panic. Her lungs felt tight. The room got darker. Her stomach flipped, and a sick taste filled her mouth.

There was a slide show of Reina's photos. Only three had ever been leaked to the press, but whoever put this memorial together had gotten creative, using colour filters and a glittery shooting star effect as one image blended into the next.

In the clearest picture, Reina stood in tall blades of grass wearing a blue and white striped shirt and denim overalls with metal hearts for buttons. Her thick, silky curls spilled over her eyes, and she held them away from her forehead with one hand, clutching the grass with the other. Her mouth was open, a row of pearly little teeth, perfectly gapped. It looked as though she was smiling.

Below it, the text in swirling purple calligraphy: *Baby Reina, 2006–2010*.

Nell was faced with that picture every day for weeks. She had been there when it was taken, and she knew the truth, which was that Reina had not been smiling but squinting at the sun. The camera had clicked at just the perfect moment to create the illusion that she was a happy child, a normal one.

But once Reina was gone, Nell had stared at that picture and made herself believe that the little girl in the picture was smiling. That she was sweet and bright as the voices on the evening news declared. It made her feel less alone in her grief. And she did grieve, desperately. So much it surprised her.

Ten years later, Nell still thought of Reina every day; she couldn't help it, and she accepted it as her penance, not only for losing her daughter, but for bringing her into the world at all. But the photos were still a shock, because she had come to remember Reina abstractly, like details from a dream. But there she was: dark eyes and curly hair. Sweet, people would call her. Pretty. Reina had been pretty, and that was what made her disappearance less suspect. Nobody is surprised when pretty things get taken. They're horrified, outraged, but not surprised. Pretty things are always at risk. The earth splits open just long enough to swallow them whole.

Unconsciously, with one hand on the track pad, Nell's other hand pressed against her stomach, as though to make sure there would never be room for another creature to pass through her womb; as though to make sure no one could see that she had ever carried a child there, and certainly so they could not ask her where that child was now.

Because the answer was its own terror: her child was nowhere, and she was everywhere.

The slideshow was still playing on a loop when Nell scrolled to the bottom of the page. There was a link that read: <u>condolences (5689)</u>

Nell clicked. The comments were sorted with the oldest first.

November 28, 2010: rest in peace, sweet angel

November 28, 2010: I'm sorry your mother didn't treat you like the gift you are. Rest in peace.

November 28, 2010: I have a son your age and I promise to protect him from monsters like the one who hurt you. Rest in peace.

Nell sorted the comments so that the newest came up first.

January 9, 2020: Is there any update on the mother? Is she in jail?

March 27, 2020: She was acquitted of all charges. But I know karma will get her.

## 22
## NOW

Before Nell could register the sound of keys in the door, Lindsay had already burst into the apartment. A phone was pressed to her ear. 'Yeah,' she said, to whoever was on the other line. 'Yeah, she's here. See you soon.' She slammed the phone on the counter. 'What the fuck, Nell?'

Nell clicked out of the memorial site, but Lindsay had already seen it. Lindsay's eyes moved from the screen to her sister, her face a mix of outrage and horror. 'Do you know we have been out looking for you all goddamned morning?' she said.

Nell stood and moved to close the apartment door, which was still wide open. Though she was trying her best to appear calm, her legs felt rubbery and weak. Her throat felt dry, and she had the sense that no sound would come out if she tried to speak.

'Don't scream at me,' Nell said, her shoulders pressed to the door, the doorknob clutched in both hands behind her back. 'I was out looking for *you*, to clean up your latest mess. But the address you gave me didn't exist, and you haven't been answering your phone. I left you about a dozen messages.'

Lindsay reeled back, blinking. 'Looking for me? What are you talking about, Nell?' She waved her phone in a frantic gesture. It was not her usual phone with the pink and gold leopard print casing and the smudged screen. This phone looked factory new, rose gold without any personal embellishments. 'I lost my phone yesterday.'

'Lost?' Nell echoed back, hollowly.

The tension in Lindsay's shoulders eased. She was calming down now. 'I lost it at the salon. I'm positive that's where I had it last. I've been trying to reach you all morning, but you weren't picking up. I figured you didn't recognise my new number, so I left a bunch of voicemails. Finally I called Sebastian at work. He said he thought I was with you.'

Nell shook her head. 'You texted me last night.'

'I didn't have my phone.' Lindsay said the words slowly, punctuating the space between them, the way she used to when she was dealing with a particularly dense foster sibling. She reached forward, picking at the cashmere of Oleg's sweater. She wouldn't know it was Oleg's, of course, but it was clearly a man's sweater and it wasn't Sebastian's style.

'I don't have *my* phone!' Nell burst out. 'It's at the bottom of a fucking swamp, along with my car, because *you* texted me that you needed me to come get you.'

Lindsay stared at her for a long moment. Her

eyes were blue, but not pale and warm like Oleg's. They were bright and deep and commanding. She grabbed Nell's forearms. 'I was home last night, Nell.'

'What about the police car?' Nell asked. 'You said a police cruiser has been parked outside of your house, right? Maybe we should make sure nobody followed you home, took your phone—'

Now it was Lindsay's turn to be on the defensive. Her thumbs traced circles against the cashmere. 'About that,' she said. 'I lied.' As Nell wrestled from her grasp, she added in a louder voice, 'I knew you were going to worry needlessly, so I said what I thought would calm you down.'

'Worry needlessly?' Nell cried. 'Lindsay, someone has been threatening us. Someone burned your car—'

'I got a new one through the insurance,' Lindsay said, as though that were the point. 'And I told you, it's probably just that old bat on my street.'

'Really?' Nell's voice had gone hysterical. She was shaking now. 'Did that old bat try to kill me by running me off the road?'

'Hey,' Lindsay said. 'Hey. What are you talking about?'

She guided Nell to the kitchen counter, and before Nell could argue, Lindsay was uncorking a bottle of white wine and grabbing a pair of glasses. It was early, but Nell downed her glass as soon as it was

223

handed to her. Lindsay climbed onto the barstool at her side.

In a voice that was eerily calm, Nell told her sister everything about the night before, leading into the early morning argument with Oleg about Autumn, up to the report she'd filed at the police station.

Somewhere in this retelling, Lindsay had wormed her fingers between Nell's and was now squeezing her hand.

'It's okay,' Nell said, staring into her empty glass. 'It's okay.'

Lindsay didn't speak for a long time. She was thinking, calculating. Any time their lives fell into chaos, Lindsay had always been the one to fix it. But she couldn't fix this. Nell knew that somehow. The police couldn't fix it. No one could fix it.

'Is that what you were doing on those let's-lynch-Penelope-Wendall message boards when I walked in?' Lindsay asked. It was jarring for Nell to hear her sister say her full name. It had been years since they'd left that ghost behind in Missouri.

Nell nodded, still staring at her glass.

'All right.' Lindsay took a breath. 'Do you remember ten years ago, when – let's just be honest – I abandoned you and left you with the fucking Eddletons?'

Nell already knew where this was going. 'This isn't like that.'

'You were traumatised. Reina' – even Lindsay

couldn't say the name without a tangible modicum of strain – 'was gone, you were under a microscope, the Eddletons threw you to the wolves, and I was too busy with my marriage to see what was happening to you.'

'This isn't like that,' Nell said again. 'I didn't hang mannequins in your yard, Linds. I didn't set your car on fire.'

'Of course not,' Lindsay said. 'But can you at least entertain the idea that the mannequins were a prank by my psycho neighbour, and the stress of all that, plus this new book, are bringing up a bit too much of the past?'

'What are you suggesting?' Nell said. 'That I hallucinated your text messages?'

Lindsay didn't answer. She knew that saying it would only bring up a fight. But it was too late.

'Get out,' Nell said.

Lindsay squeezed Nell's hand, but Nell jerked back so hard that her barstool tipped and she had to clutch the counter to keep from falling.

'No,' Lindsay said. 'I'm not leaving you alone right now.'

'Why not?' Nell bit back. 'You've left me alone to deal with worse.'

'You're right,' Lindsay said. 'You're right, and I'm sorry.' She was being uncharacteristically contrite, and it made Nell feel like a bratty child, once again rebuffing her sister for trying to look out for her. 'I'm just trying to see this logically. There's an explanation for the mannequins. There really is, Nell. And as for what happened last night, I don't know. But here's what we do know: someone took my phone. I never texted you. And Autumn Hamblin is as dead as my love life.'

'My car's gone,' Nell said. 'I didn't make that up. Someone is trying to hurt us, Linds. Both of us. Someone clearly stole your phone and used it to lure me to the middle of nowhere.'

'Or a drunk driver ran you off the road,' Lindsay said, and Nell could see that Lindsay was steeling herself against the imagery. Lindsay didn't dwell on things; Nell was alive and that was all that mattered for now. 'There's not even a police department out there, only a sheriff. People go speeding down those back roads all the time, you know that.'

Nell stared into her glass again. A moment ago, she'd been furious that Lindsay didn't believe her. She'd been certain of exactly what had happened to her. But now it was all falling to pieces in her mind.

'Am I being crazy?' she asked, her voice hoarse.

'No,' Lindsay said. 'I know that it feels like the universe is trying to punish you, but hey.' She grabbed Nell's chin, tilting it so that Nell's eyes met hers. 'It's been ten years, and you have to let this go now. You've gone through hell and you made it out the other side.' She was so adamant that Nell found herself believing it. 'The universe is not punishing you. Nobody is.'

It didn't matter how big they were now; it didn't matter that Lindsay had grown wealthy off her failed marriages, or that Nell had grown wealthy off her books. It didn't matter that they had found stability, or love, or any other desirable thing that sparkled to anyone on the outside looking in. They were still abandoned children at the end of the day. The world had given them to each other to make up for everything else they'd lacked.

Lindsay scooted her barstool closer, and Nell rested her head on her shoulder.

'I'll never let you get pulled back into that place again,' Lindsay said, tucking her chin on top of Nell's head.

'Sebastian can't know,' Nell said. 'He can't know about who I was. He'll leave me. I'll lose everything.'

# 23
# THEN

When Nell heard about missing children on the news, she'd always watched and wondered how the sequence of events happened. Did the parent march to the help desk, ask to speak to a manager, and explain the situation? Or was a missing child such a catastrophe that the police somehow sensed it and showed up with their squad cars and sirens?

When it happened to Nell, she had her answer. She just started screaming.

She walked to the frozen and refrigerated food aisle of the grocery store. Raw slabs of beef and chicken hung on bits of twine, swirling in cold mists. Eggs watched from their cartons like eyes. A bulb in the fluorescent ceiling light flickered like an interrogation lamp.

Someone ran to her. He wasn't a manager or the police. He wasn't anyone in authority at all. He was a teenage boy with a nametag and a button-up shirt who had been restocking the yoghurts; Nell remembered seeing him as she came in.

Through her hysterics, she heard him asking what had happened.

'It's all my fault,' she said. 'It's all my fault that she's gone.'

Nell was eighteen years old, but having a child like Reina had aged her a hundred years. A thousand. She was beyond any measure of sanity most days. Reina's absence flooded in through the sliding glass doors of the supermarket like an ocean wave.

The store was on lockdown immediately. Customers were kept lined up by the doors with carts of shopping bags, unable to leave. Reina's description was blasted over the speakers, cutting through Mariah Carey's rendition of 'All I Want for Christmas'.

All of this as Nell sat, useless, on the rickety bench beside the deli counter, sobbing into a wet tissue. Sobbing because she knew that Reina was not going to turn up hiding behind the lobster tank or under the rolling cart of ground meat. A cashier in a black apron wasn't going to come walking up one of the aisles, holding her by the hand.

Nobody knew this except for Nell, who was used to not being believed when it came to her daughter, and so she didn't bother to explain. Reina was not here. She was already gone.

It wasn't Reina who emerged from the crowd an hour into the search. It was Ethan. Nell was still sitting on the bench, but she stood when she saw him and they ran to each other. His arms locked tight around her, and in her dazed confusion, Nell could almost mistake his affection for love.

'Hey, Penny,' he whispered against her ear. It was a nickname he'd given her before Reina was born, and he was the only one who used it.

'She's gone,' Nell croaked. 'She's gone. I lost her.'

'She's not gone,' he said. 'We're going to find her. I promise you we will.'

It was the only promise he would ever break. Nell responded the way she always did when she had already given up. 'All right,' she said. 'Okay.'

When they drew apart, he took her hand. He wasn't crying, but Nell's face was slick with tears. *Strange*, she'd thought. He'd always loved Reina, and she'd been certain he would be the one to cry if anything ever happened to her. But there was grief in his stoicism, and Nell would only realise this years later, looking back. He had mourned for their daughter in a way that was profound because of how selfless it had been. How selfless it still was.

'Come on,' he said. 'The police are here to escort us to the station.'

Nell found that idea comforting. Here in the grocery store, she was just floating in space without anything to anchor her to the earth. But at a police station there would be a story to tell and action to take, and all of this would make time move forward again.

In the interrogation room, she was handed a

bottle of Coke. Officer Brady, a woman whose hair was so blond it was almost white, asked questions in the gentlest tone she could manage.

'How old is your daughter?'

'She's four.'

'And what was she wearing?'

'Light blue jeans. A brown suede coat with pink fur trim.' Nell tugged at the sleeves of her sweater. 'She kept opening the door to the freezers and trying to climb inside. She wanted to test how warm she would be in her coat.'

'Is that where she was when you lost sight of her?'

'No. We moved on. It was the next aisle over, with the loaves of bread. At first I thought she was hiding – she does that.' Nell almost said more, but she stopped herself. If she went on, she would have said that Reina loved to test them. It was a mean little game she played, and she was willing to freeze to death or risk falling into a lake and drowning just for the satisfaction of making Nell come undone. Wherever Reina was now, she would enjoy this. If she had heard the police sirens and known they were for her, she would feel like she'd won her greatest victory yet. Maybe she had.

The police sent them home after that. Nell couldn't believe that this was what they did, without any sort of fanfare. Just 'your job is to go home and wait'.

Mrs Eddleton was in hysterics. All five thousand square feet of the house was electric with

232

her nervous energy. She was on the phone with the police, demanding a thorough rundown of the search, when Nell and Ethan entered the kitchen.

'The police are incompetent. We're forming our own search party,' Mrs Eddleton said, slamming the phone on its cradle. Mr Eddleton was seated at the kitchen table, staring sullenly into his cup of black coffee.

Nell felt sick with the taste of her own tears and the smell of fear that permeated everything. She had done this to them. To all of them. She had brought Reina into this world, and her reasons for doing so had been selfish. She had wanted something of her own that she could love, and at the time it had not seemed so outrageous to assume a child would love her back.

Reina had come out screaming. In a pained delirium Nell heard it. She opened her eyes and saw the bloody, squirming silhouette against the searing overhead light. No one prepared her for how powerful babies were.

The Eddletons loved Reina. Even Ethan, who had never used the word 'love' in his life. Even Mr Eddleton, who seldom spoke, preferring to grunt in acknowledgement of his wife's rants. And Nell loved her, though it drained everything from her. Though it aged her. Though it made her sick and certain that her life was no longer her own.

But Reina did not love any of them. She could have

been born into this suburban mansion or any other house on earth, to rich grandparents who adored her or parents who neglected her, and it all would have been the same to her. Reina was all about utilising her environment, manipulating whoever was naïve enough to cow to what she wanted.

Reina did not love them. That was the truth. Nell repeated it over and over in her head, hoping it would make her absence easier.

By the top of the hour, Mrs Eddleton had summoned no fewer than two hundred people to search for Reina. Mrs Eddleton was nothing if not socially conscious, and now the cul-de-sac was filled with families from church, middle-aged alcoholics from the country club and rubberneckers from the three-block radius. It was dark, so everyone brought their own flashlights and spread out.

Nell and Ethan walked slowly, stiff with fear like small animals frightened by car headlights. Ethan kept murmuring words to comfort Nell, while Nell mumbled her assent. She only walked. She didn't look. Reina was not going to be in a ravine or behind a fallen tree. She was gone. Gone. The word was too small to describe such a big and unchangeable thing.

It was late when she and Ethan returned to the house. Usually the light in the kitchen and the study would still be on – Mr Eddleton pouring his ninth cup of coffee, Mrs Eddleton organising fundraisers and sending busybody emails to the congregation. But the entire house was dark, and neither Nell nor Ethan bothered with the light. They passed by Reina's nursery and Nell didn't look inside, but she felt Ethan leaning back as they passed, as though to make sure their daughter hadn't been asleep in her bed this whole time.

Nell awoke to the sound of Sebastian's voice, muffled by the bedroom door and the comforter over her head. She couldn't make out the words, but he sounded furious.

Rain was coming down sideways, slamming into the bedroom window. The clouds made everything so dark that for a second Nell thought it was night. Thunder boomed, drowning out the city traffic far below.

It wasn't night-time, Nell realised. She was waking up to the same awful day. She remembered crawling back into bed at Lindsay's insistence, after her second glass of wine. Somehow she'd fallen asleep.

Now, she pushed open the bedroom door. Sebastian had just set his phone angrily on the counter, and now he ran to her, wrapping her in his arms.

Startled, she circled her arms around him too.

Lindsay was lying on the couch, staring at the screen of Nell's laptop, which rested on her stomach.

'I've been on the phone with the police trying to find out what they're doing to catch this guy,' Bas said. He drew back, gripping Nell's shoulders and studying her face like he was inspecting her for damage. 'They're useless. Completely useless.'

'Lots of drunks out driving in the bunks,' Lindsay said, not looking up from the screen.

Sebastian was stroking his thumb over Nell's temple, and she realised now that her skin ached there. In the shower at Oleg's motel room, she'd noticed the scrapes and cuts from the glass on her arms, but hours later bruises were beginning to form too.

Nell was grateful that Lindsay had apparently filled Bas in on the details, because she was too exhausted to relive it again. And all her theories, which had seemed so certain and so clear hours earlier, had turned to mush in her mind. She wondered if she had a concussion.

Lindsay slammed the laptop shut and got to her feet, tucking it under her arm. 'I've been researching your insurance policy online,' she said. 'The accident wasn't your fault, but that'll be tough to prove.' She gently steered Nell back towards the bedroom. 'Come on, I'll help you sort everything out.' She whispered something over her shoulder at Bas, but Nell couldn't make it out.

As soon as Lindsay had closed the bedroom door, Nell said, 'I don't care about the insurance.'

'What?' Lindsay said. 'No. We're not doing that. I just said that so Sebastian would leave us alone.'

She waved her hand dismissively and tossed the laptop onto the bed. Then she sat on the edge of the mattress and patted the space beside her in a gesture for Nell to sit. 'I've spent the past couple of hours going through every possible search result for your old name. And yes, the shit I found was dark, but it was also old.' She squeezed Nell's shoulder. 'Nobody is coming for you. Nobody knows where you live now.'

Nell doubled forward. 'I don't know what to think anymore,' she said. 'This morning I was so rattled that I actually thought it was Autumn Hamblin.'

'The conjoined twin?' Lindsay said. 'Isn't she the dead one?'

'Yes,' Nell said. 'But Easter keeps insisting that Autumn is alive and that she's evil, and – yes, I know how this all sounds.'

'Well, I don't know who ran you off the road,' Lindsay admitted. 'But I can confirm that it's not the ghost of an evil conjoined twin, and it isn't anyone from an internet message board looking to exact revenge on you ten years after you left Missouri.' She patted Nell's knee. 'Sebastian has talked the insurance into sending someone out there to fish your car out of the swamp with a crane. The police will be able to take paint samples from the bumper and hopefully match it to a make and model. That's something.'

'He did all of that?' Nell asked.

'Of course,' Lindsay said. 'He's a good one, Nell. Don't fuck it up.'

'Trying really hard not to,' Nell said.

※

# THEN

After Reina disappeared, entire hours slipped down the drains of the Eddletons' bathroom sinks. Morning was gone, and then the afternoon.

The Eddletons' house was never empty. Mrs Eddleton was especially relentless, inviting every news station and journalist in the country to her house. The living room had become a studio. The couches were pushed back against the walls, leaving only a set of dining chairs in front of the fireplace, which was a shrine of baby photos. A camera was always pointed at those chairs. Someone was always pressing for answers.

Nell did almost none of the talking but she bore the worst of the backlash. The Eddletons were the loving, warm grandparents. Nell was the reckless teenager who had been given the most precious gift in the world and fucked it up.

Ethan was never in the papers. Fathers didn't sell stories. It was always the mothers. There were the Eddletons, printed in black and white, each clutching a corner of a framed photograph. And there was Nell in a tabloid photo that had been taken through the bushes, sneaking out the back door for a moment to breathe, a beer bottle in hand.

Lindsay was nowhere that day, and later Nell would find out that Lindsay had in fact been there, only to be turned away by the extra security hired by Mrs Eddleton to keep the photographers back.

No one looked after Nell. No one brought her food or asked how she was faring or told her to get some rest. Not even Ethan seemed to notice her. He had always been a lazy, passive sort, but the child's absence awoke something in him. Every daylight hour he was with the neighbourhood searches, wading through tall grass and dumpsters. He tore open bulging trash bags, hoping they wouldn't birth Reina's corpse like a putrid womb. He came home only to stand over the kitchen sink, forcing down a thirty-second meal and then disappearing again. His muddy footprints and the crumbs on the counter were the only traces of him.

Nell felt herself slipping out of her body. She had become like the charcoal drawings she saw in art classes before the students painted them. Lines on top of lines, new positions on top of old, until everything blurred and it was impossible to know which version was really there.

She slept only in fitful naps, and never for long. She dreamed sometimes of maggots crawling from eye sockets or a tiny body sinking in the ink-black water of a well out in an empty field. She dreamed of shadowed figures and car doors closing, and she always woke up wondering if Reina had cried out, wherever she was. If she even cared whether she lived, much less whether she made it home.

Nell was wondering this when Mrs Eddleton opened her bedroom door and said, 'We're going to church in an hour.' And then she was gone.

The ride to church was filled with Mrs Eddleton's nervous prattling and Mr Eddleton's solemn grunts of affirmation. Ethan and Nell were in the back with the empty baby seat between them. They were staring off in different directions, but then Nell felt his hand eclipse hers. His long, slender fingers wove into her grasp and he squeezed.

She stared down at their hands, startled. All day she had been invisible. She had been nothing. But Ethan was telling her that not only did he see her, he needed her.

Maybe he was even trying to comfort her at the same time, but it didn't work. She felt even worse, if that were possible.

She slid her hand from his grasp and went on staring out the window. She could see his face reflected in the glass. There was a hurt expression there, boyish and vulnerable; the kind of look he could only give if he believed no one was looking.

Nell tried to concentrate on what Mrs Eddleton

was saying. She wanted to prepare herself for whatever was about to come next.

'We'll each light a candle for Reina—' Mrs Eddleton's voice hitched as she said the name, but she went on. 'And a prayer for her will be said after the sermon. After that, I've arranged for caterers to set up a luncheon back at the house. I've invited the *Tribune*, the *Missouri Post*...' Nell began to lose focus again. What did any of these things matter? Candles? A candle was not a magnet, and Reina was not an earring that had gotten lost somewhere in the couch cushions. And a luncheon. Nell pictured platters of cheese cubes and crackers shaped like butterflies. More strangers to flash photos of her and type stories of what a wretched mother she was.

None of those reporters knew the truth, which was much worse than anything they were going to write. They didn't know what sort of child Reina Eddleton was. They hadn't seen the things Nell had seen, or thought the things Nell had thought.

They made it halfway up the church steps before Nell started to shake. It began as a low tremble, like musical vibrations, until it spread out to her fingers and her feet. Her mind went hazy, and with the next step she collapsed to her hands and knees.

Someone was screaming. A crowd began to form. Cameras flashed, and Nell realised the screams were coming from her.

Arms wrapped around her. Ethan had taken off

his jacket and he draped it over her head, shielding her from the reporters.

It was a small gesture of such profound kindness on his part. But Nell didn't want him. She wanted Lindsay. Her sister, who was nowhere. *Maybe the police ought to be looking for her too*, Nell thought through sobs. Maybe she had slipped under the water in her new massive marble bathtub and gotten sucked into the Bermuda Triangle.

'It's all right,' Ethan said in her ear. He had never been one for platitudes. Surely he didn't mean that this was all right. Maybe he only meant it was all right that she couldn't make it to the church. 'Come on. Can you stand?' He didn't wait for her to answer before he wrapped his arm around her waist and pulled her up. She gripped his coat and kept it tented over her face as he guided her to the car. She heard him tell a reporter to fuck off.

He pushed her into the car and followed after, locking the doors. The windows were tinted, mercifully, but that didn't stop the photographers from trying to get their perfect shot. Cameras flashed through the glass.

'I really need her,' Nell sobbed. 'Where the fuck is she?'

'I know,' Ethan said, gathering her into his arms. 'I know, Penny. I need her too.'

Looking back on that day, Nell would never be certain whether she had been talking about Reina or Lindsay.

# 25

# NOW

Three days after Nell drove her car into the swamp, a crane came to fish it out. Nell, Lindsay and Sebastian stood on the shoulder of the road, watching the massive metal arm dip below the surface of the water.

It was a murky swamp, surrounded by fronds and tall grass, and the late morning sun revealed shades of green and yellow.

The crane began to lift, groaning mechanically. Up came Nell's 2010 Buick LaCrosse in metallic midnight blue. A waterfall was pouring through the broken driver's side window.

'Holy shit,' Lindsay whispered.

Sebastian wrapped his arm around Nell's shoulders, reeling her close.

Nell numbed herself to what she was seeing, forcing away the knowledge that it could have been her grave. Since that night, her sleep patterns had become more erratic than usual. She'd been shaky one minute, hyperactively cleaning the entire apartment the next. And she'd been thinking about Reina, not as the four-year-old Nell remembered, but as the little girl being memorialised by strangers and well-wishers on the internet, who called her a precious angel and said things like 'rest peacefully, sweet girl'.

In her constant thinking about Reina, Nell wondered who her daughter had really been. Had she been the monster Nell remembered, or was Nell the monster? She thought about how backwards it seemed that she could find the humanity in a woman who had drowned all of her children, but no matter how many memories she replayed, she couldn't find the humanity in her own child.

After the ruined car was deposited onto the tow truck, Sebastian sprinted over to the driver to give directions to their preferred mechanic, then got in his car to follow, raising a hand in farewell to the sisters.

'Well, that happened,' Lindsay said.

Nell didn't let herself look at the car for a second longer. She was afraid that if she did, her mind would go back to that night, and she would only drive herself crazy with all of her unanswered questions. Instead, she turned to her sister. 'I need a ride.'

It was more than a thirty-minute drive to the Hamblin family's brownstone, and to Lindsay's credit, she didn't utter one word of protest even though she hated that Nell was still researching their story.

'It's this one on the left,' Nell said, as Lindsay

cruised between rows of slender trees in boxes on the sidewalks.

'Brownstone,' Lindsay echoed. 'Nice. The Hamblins make bank.'

'They're both retired now,' Nell said. 'But Mrs Hamblin was a tenured professor at Juilliard and Mr Hamblin was a private attorney, specialising in medical malpractice.'

'You've done your research,' Lindsay said.

'I've been trying to establish what the twins' childhood was like.'

'Fancier than ours,' Lindsay said, gesturing to the brownstone after she'd thrown the car in park. 'How long are you going to be?'

'I can text you when I'm done,' Nell said. 'I have some questions for Mrs Hamblin. I was afraid that if I called to set up a time, she would blow me off. It took a dozen attempts just to get her to meet with me the first time.'

'It's cool, I'll wait here,' Lindsay said.

Nell paused, her hand on the door. 'You're afraid to leave me alone.'

Lindsay stared at her. 'Okay, fine, yes,' she admitted. 'I don't want to find you wandering down Main Street in your underwear.'

Nell rolled her eyes. 'I'm feeling much better.' It wasn't entirely true, but she hoped it would put her sister more at ease.

Lindsay waved her off with a theatrical flick of

her hand. Sunlight gleamed off her red manicured nails. 'Go do your thing. There's a flask in my glove compartment if I get bored.' Her plaintive stare said that she was kidding.

Nell made her way up the sidewalk. There was a page in her manuscript that had been blank all week, and only the mother of Easter and Autumn could possibly fill in the gaps.

The doorknob turned even before Nell could knock.

She had seen Mr Hamblin in newspaper articles and on television. In her research, she'd even found old law firm commercials from the early 2000s on YouTube. But now as he stood before her in his doorway, he looked taller. His skin was ashen, almost as grey as his neatly combed hair. Even in retirement, he was sharply dressed in a white button-up shirt and twill pants, and he smelled of cologne. It was a smell Nell recognised lingering in the living room when she'd interviewed his wife.

Nell put out her hand. 'Mr Hamblin? I'm Nell Way—'

He had thick, dark eyebrows, and in that moment they accented the fury on his face.

'You have some gall showing up at my home,' he said.

Nell steeled herself. Grief often turned to anger, and she had seen this reaction many times before.

'Mr Hamblin, I'm here because I—'

'I don't care why you're here.' His voice was a growl. 'You've undone months – *months* – of progress my wife had been making. Do you know what it was like, being under the constant scrutiny of every reporter in the state of New York? The horrible things they said about us?'

Nell didn't respond.

'Things had finally settled down. The letters had stopped. Everything had stopped.'

'I'm sorry,' Nell said, realising a second later that it was probably going to make matters worse.

'Last night,' Mr Hamblin began, shaking for all his fury, 'we were woken up by the floodlight in the back yard. When I went down to investigate, I found what looked like a body floating in our pool. It was two shop mannequins someone had melted together to look like my daughters before their surgery.'

He looked as though he might reach out and strangle her, or burst into tears. Nell couldn't tell which. She took a step back.

'Mr Hamblin, I—'

She didn't know how to finish that sentence. But it didn't matter. He slammed the door before she could make another sound.

## 26
# THEN

Nell woke from a fitful half-sleep. Ethan was crawling into the bed beside her. It was dark, and she could just make out the outline of his messy black hair, damp from a recent shower. He smelled like body wash and clean laundry. And suddenly, Nell wanted to lose herself in that smell, because it reminded her of newness, as though it had the power to erase everything they'd gone through together.

The truth was that Reina was the only thing keeping them together. They'd conceived her on the night they met, and by morning, their fates were sealed. Nell went back to her group foster home. Ethan went back to his six-figure-a-year private school, both of them expecting to only see each other at parties, or maybe never again.

But instead, they were here, living in separate bedrooms on opposite sides of the hallway that also housed Reina's nursery. And even though Reina was gone, here they both were. Tethered together like astronauts floating in space.

'Hey,' Nell whispered. She rolled over to face

him, and found herself slipping perfectly into his arms. She wanted to ask what he was doing in her room, but the words didn't come.

He swept the hair back from her face, and she eased onto her back. He bowed his head and pressed his lips to hers in a gesture too light to be considered a kiss. It had been nearly a year since they'd done even this much, but it unlocked something in each of them. His next kiss was forceful and desperate, and Nell gasped, coaxing him on.

The door was slightly ajar, letting in a sliver of light from the hallway, but neither of them moved to close it. The house was silent. They were silent.

When he moved inside of her, it woke her from the haze that had ensnared her since that day at the grocery store. No – that had ensnared her since the day Reina was born and everything changed. *This is the way being a teenager was supposed to feel*, she thought. Forget yesterday, forget tomorrow. Forget the reporters and the grief and the aching in her bones. Forget everything but this moment, which Nell believed could last forever if she held on tightly enough.

The only sound was the mattress hitting against the headboard and the rustle of sheets. When he was through, Ethan collapsed onto her chest, all of his weight crashing back down to earth. He buried his face in the hollow of her neck, still inside of her, and sobbed.

It was the first time he'd broken down since it happened. His skin was clammy and warm, and he let out the most piteous wail against her skin.

'It's my fault,' he gasped between sobs. 'I wasn't there to protect her.'

She ran her fingers through his hair, rubbed circles on his back and shushed him. Their little moment was over. Gone. Just like everything else that had ever been good in their lives.

They fell asleep clinging to each other, and in the morning they were both awoken by Mrs Eddleton's loud knock on the door. It was as though she knew what they had done the night before and wanted to punish them for it.

Nell winced at the light burning in through the windows.

'Penelope, the police are here to speak with you,' Mrs Eddleton said. 'Get dressed.'

'Just Penny? Not me too?' Ethan asked groggily, but his mother was already gone. They could hear her heels slapping on the marble stairs.

Two officers were waiting in the foyer when Nell descended the staircase in a long-sleeved t-shirt and jeans, accompanied by Ethan.

'Good morning, Penelope,' one of the officers said. 'We have a few things we'd like to go over with you, if you wouldn't mind coming down to the station with us.'

'She'll be happy to,' Mrs Eddleton said. Grief had

made Mrs Eddleton more focused and ferocious than ever. Every waking second, she was contacting the press and heading search parties. Her current project was a candlelight vigil, scheduled for that evening, which the mayor would attend. The mayor meant press, and press meant more news coverage, and news coverage meant Reina's photograph in more living rooms for the evening news.

In the shadow of Mrs Eddleton's efforts, Nell felt more useless and incompetent as a mother than Reina had ever made her feel. She felt the full weight of how small and helpless she was.

Nell tugged at her sleeves. 'All right.'

'Can I go with her?' Ethan asked.

'We need you here,' Mrs Eddleton said, gathering him under her arm like a mother hen shielding her chick. 'She'll be back in a little while.'

Nell rode in the back of the police cruiser. The ride was mostly silent, except for when one of the officers glanced back at her from the other side of the metal mesh and asked her, 'Have you ever ridden in a police car before?'

'Yes,' she said.

In the interrogation room, Nell was offered a cup of coffee or something from the vending machine, but she refused.

'Are you sure?' the officer asked. 'You look uncomfortable.'

Nell was the most uncomfortable she could ever

remember being. More uncomfortable than being squished against Lindsay in the bottom bunk like sardines. More uncomfortable than the prison pat-downs when they visited their mother.

The room was cold and she tugged her sleeves over her knuckles. She hadn't cleaned herself up the night before, and she'd been in such a rush to get downstairs this morning that she hadn't even gone to the bathroom. Now she had to pee. And she could still feel the remnants of last night inside of her, dampening the inseam of her jeans.

She crossed her legs. She was going to get a urinary tract infection, she was sure of it. But worse, what if she was pregnant? Her sex life had been so nonexistent that she often forgot to take her pill.

If she and Ethan made another child, would it be like Reina? Would it hate her too?

'Penelope?'

'I'm fine.' Her voice was soft. 'Thank you.'

'Fair enough.' The officer slid his laptop across the table, turning the screen so that it faced her. 'We've obtained security camera footage of the grocery store from the afternoon your daughter went missing. We should have accessed it sooner, but there were technical issues. But we have it now. I'd like you to take a look.'

He tapped the space bar and the footage began to play. There were four squares, presenting the store from multiple angles. One of the screens showed

Nell getting out of her car in the parking lot. She already knew what she was going to see, but she watched anyway.

Nell exited the car and entered the store alone. Reina wasn't there. The car seat, visible through the back window, was empty.

Nell sat in the interrogation room and watched the small, sharply detailed image of herself enter the store and stand beside the shopping carts, staring at her shoes. Her shoulders rose in sharp, rapid breaths. In the video, she was hyperventilating and trembling, already in tears.

Finally she made her way down one of the aisles and screamed. She had lied about everything else that day, but the scream had been real.

The officer slid the laptop aside, so that he and Nell were once again facing each other. 'I want to help you, Penelope, and I *can* help you if you're honest with me,' he said. 'Where is your daughter?'

For the first time all morning, Nell met his eyes.

'I'd like to call my attorney,' she said.

# 27

# NOW

Oleg seemed relieved when he entered the diner and locked eyes with Nell. She'd called an hour earlier and asked him to meet her for a working lunch. She'd chosen a small, crowded diner downtown because it was walking distance from her apartment.

'Hey,' he said, sliding into the seat across from her. 'I'm so glad to hear from you. I was worried, but I didn't want to call. I thought you might be avoiding me.'

'It was nothing like that,' Nell assured him. 'If anything, I owe you an apology for what I said about your sisters in the car that morning.'

He flashed her his easy smile. 'You've already apologised.'

'A hundred more times should do it,' Nell said. 'It was completely unprofessional of me. So was calling you to come get me. I think I was in shock, but that's no excuse.'

'I'm glad you called me,' he said. 'It's nice to be needed.' He raised an eyebrow. 'Is that strange of me to say? Since my parents died, I get this feeling like I'm not useful. I have nobody to take care of. Even when I came to visit my sisters, they only seemed to need each other.'

'I'm sure they were glad to have you,' Nell said.

'Autumn was very active,' he said. 'Even though she knew I was only visiting for a week or two, she'd spend half of that time off doing her own thing. She let her phone die constantly. It made Easter furious, not being able to reach her.'

'Really?' Nell rested her chin on her fist. 'Where would Autumn go?'

'Off with friends, I assume,' Oleg said. 'She didn't bring them by the apartment. I think she was embarrassed by Easter.'

His gaze got distant, and Nell suspected there was something he wouldn't tell her. He remained loyal to his sisters even after Autumn's death and even with all Easter had done.

'I'm grateful for the time I did spend with them,' Oleg finally said. 'I'll always torture myself wondering if I could have done more for them, but they were so impenetrable. They wouldn't allow themselves to accept help. They barely accepted love.'

Nell offered him a smile, though from where she sat, that smile felt haggard and weak. 'You have the burden of being the eldest sibling,' she said. 'My older sister always likes to feel needed too.'

'I didn't know you have a sister,' Oleg said.

Nell shrugged, taking a sip of her coffee. She

nodded to the waitress to bring a cup for Oleg. 'I don't usually tell my interviewees about my life,' she said. 'It's not relevant, and they never ask.'

'It's relevant to me,' Oleg said. He rested his chin on his fist and stared contemplatively at her. 'I know where you attended college, and that you dropped out when you sold your first book. I know that you get your inspiration from mid-century poetry, and it shows in your writing.'

Nell laughed, a warm flush spreading across her cheeks and behind her ears. 'Someone's been reading my book jacket.'

His smile had adopted a wistful, almost sleepy quality. 'And I know that you entertain every possible theory,' he went on, inching out of the way as the waitress poured his coffee. 'Even if that theory is absolutely impossible.'

He was referring to her theory about Autumn, Nell knew. She cleared her throat, forcing herself out of the trance his observations evoked.

'I wanted to talk to you about the Hamblins.'

Oleg's sober expression made her feel guilty. 'The mannequins in the pool,' he said.

'Yes.'

'That was a new one,' Oleg said. 'When the story was first on the news, someone threw a rock through their window. There was red paint on the car. Phone calls, letters. Russia halted adoptions to American families after there were allegations that

Iskra and Klavdiya had been abused by their adoptive parents.'

'Were there any direct threats?' Nell asked.

'Some,' Oleg said. 'Things have been mostly quiet since the trial. People find something new to be angry about.'

'But the fact that I'm writing a book might have brought it all back,' Nell said. It wasn't a question. Even though there had been no formal press release or even a sale yet, rumours spread like wildfire in book club message boards. Someone had apparently spotted Nell at the penitentiary. The same penitentiary that was housing one of the country's most famous murderers.

'Mom Esther told me that Mr Hamblin chased you away when you came around for an interview,' Oleg said. 'But she's glad you're writing the book. I am too. The world needs to hear their story. Now that Autumn is gone and Easter will never be free again, their story is that much more important.'

'I'm glad to hear you say that,' Nell said. 'I feel the same way.'

Oleg was smiling again. 'If we're going to talk about my sisters, we'll be here a while,' he said, and raised a finger to get the waitress's attention. 'May as well order some food.'

His kind, honest quality made Nell want to be honest with him. She wanted to tell him about her childhood in foster care, and how unwanted she had felt, and that was part of what had drawn her to the twins' story. She wanted to tell him about her past, which Easter had uncovered in the newspaper archives of the prison library. She wanted to tell him all the things she had done, and see if he still liked her then. But perhaps Easter had already told him? No, surely he would have brought it up. It was too awful a thing to remain unspoken.

Three hours into their interview, Oleg told a story that made Nell laugh so hard, the group of teenagers two booths over all turned to look at her. Nell cupped a hand over her mouth. 'She really threw your clothes out into the street? My God, that's so theatrical.'

They were no longer talking about the twins, and Oleg had transitioned into a story about his own failures in love. 'Galina was … spirited,' he said, laughing before taking a swig of coffee.

'She must have been mad as hell,' Nell said.

'I guess I have that effect on women,' he said. 'I make them mad as hell.'

'I don't get that impression,' Nell said.

He winked. 'Trust me.'

'Galina.' Nell tried to say the name in the proper Russian accent and failed.

'Gah-LEE-nah,' Oleg said. 'Say it through your bottom teeth.'

Nell made another attempt, sticking her jaw out in an exaggerated fashion. Oleg laughed, which made her laugh harder.

'You got it that time,' he said.

Nell noticed the darkening sky through the window. Alarmed, she grabbed her phone and checked the time.

'Have somewhere to be?' Oleg asked.

'I need to get home before—' she cut herself short. She had almost said 'before Sebastian gets home' but she stopped herself. She was usually so good at keeping her guard up when interviewing subjects, but something about Oleg put her at ease. 'Before it gets dark,' she said. 'I have to walk home. I haven't replaced my car.'

'I'll give you a ride,' Oleg said, sliding out of his booth.

'That's all right,' Nell said, and came to stand beside him. He was so tall, and she found herself imagining what it would be like to lean forward and rest her head against his chest. Would it be soft? Solid? Either way, she knew it would be warm. 'I'm only a block away.'

'I'll walk you then.'

'You don't have to,' Nell said.

'I know.' He was already heading for the door, and she hurried to keep up with his broad strides.

It was a frigid night. Nell tugged up the lapels of her wool coat to cover her ears.

Oleg was still talking as they began to walk. His breath made dissolving clouds. He recounted another of his failed romances, a young woman named Akilina, who'd left him for another man, leaving him to care for the pet raccoon she'd domesticated. 'Pooped in the dish where I kept my keys,' Oleg said. 'One morning I reached for my keys and picked up a pile of raccoon poop.'

'Stop,' Nell laughed. 'What did you do with the racoon?'

'I set him free,' Oleg said, with wistful mock-pride. 'I like to think he's still out there, majestically foraging for garbage behind apartment buildings.'

Nell snorted with her next laugh, and promptly covered her nose with her palm.

Oleg smirked, looking straight ahead. 'It's good to see you feeling better.'

Nell stepped onto the front step of her building's entrance. Even then, she was nearly a head shorter than Oleg. 'This is me,' she said. She took the keys from her pocket, volleying them between her fingers. 'Thanks for walking me.'

When she raised her eyes, she saw that Oleg was watching her. His eyes were bright, like burning blue galaxies against the winter sky. *They're so beautiful*, Nell thought. He was beautiful, his cheeks bright pink from the cold. His eyebrows were the same white-blond as his hair. His lips were full and smooth; her eyes settled on them. She saw his Adam's apple move under his skin when he took a breath.

He started to say her name, or maybe to say

goodbye, but he changed his mind and kissed her instead.

She sucked in a breath and tasted the coffee on his tongue. She heard him breathing in her ears. His fingers were feather light under her chin.

Nell forced herself to break away, and as she did so, she realised how much effort it took.

'I'm sorry,' Oleg said, when Nell averted her eyes. 'I thought you wanted me to.'

Nell shook her head. 'It's all right,' she said. 'I should have told you that I'm seeing someone.'

Seeing someone. Bas would be heartbroken to hear their relationship put so simply, but what was she supposed to say? 'I'm living with a man who wants us to buy a house and a dog together'?

Or she could tell him the truth. That she was so damaged that it was a wonder she'd found someone who was passionate, and good, and drop-down-dead in love with her. That she spent every day terrified of ruining it, and she loved him too much to let that happen.

'I'll call you when I need another interview,' she said, and the words felt clumsy on her tongue. Before he could respond, she was up the stairs and through the glass double doors.

## 28
## THEN

Within an hour of asking for an attorney, Matthew Cranlin showed up at the police station. Nell didn't know his home number, but she had found his law firm listed in the phonebook beside the station payphone.

The first thing he'd asked her was, 'Are you under arrest?'

'I don't know.' She'd been trying not to cry.

'Did you ask if you're free to go?'

'No,' Nell said. 'I—'

'Don't say anything, do you hear me?' Matthew told her. 'Keep your mouth shut until I get there. Don't even answer if they offer you a glass of water.'

Nell had done as he said, sitting with her hands knotted in her lap. She flinched when Matthew entered the room. Nell had only met him in person a handful of times – at his wedding to her sister, and standing in the doorway waiting impatiently whenever Nell drove Lindsay back home.

He was tall, with lean muscles and golden blond hair. He had sparkly green eyes, and he was pretty in the way that Lindsay was pretty. Side by side, they looked like the photo that came with the picture frame. But Nell had never liked him. She didn't like who Lindsay was since meeting him, either.

But Nell was desperate. The Eddletons had an attorney, but if they saw what was on that security footage, Mrs Eddleton would drive Nell to the county jail herself.

'You're Ms Wendall's attorney, I take it,' the officer said.

'That's right,' Matthew replied, taking his seat beside Nell. 'Is my client under arrest?' There was a menacing gruffness to his voice.

'Mr…' the officer began, giving a pause for Matthew to introduce himself.

'Cranlin,' Matthew said, reaching across the table to shake the officer's hand. There was nothing civil about it; even Nell could see that.

'Mr Cranlin, your client reported her four-year-old daughter missing two days ago, and it's the job of this unit to find that child. Your client is withholding information that allows us to do that.'

'Withholding information?' Matthew pushed back his chair and looked under the table. He grabbed Nell's shoulder and pushed her forward, so he could inspect the space between her back and the chair. 'My client doesn't appear to be hiding a child under her clothes, officer. I'd like to see what evidence you have that's so compelling you'd subject a frightened teenage girl to a police interrogation.'

The officer played the security footage for Matthew, who remained reactionless from start to finish.

'What did I watch?' Matthew said. 'That was just a woman entering a grocery store. The last I checked, that's not illegal in the state of Missouri.'

'Your client,' the officer said, pausing for dramatic emphasis, 'had the entire grocery store on lockdown looking for a child she knew full well wasn't there.'

Matthew was still unmoved. 'Is my client under arrest or isn't she?'

'Not yet,' the officer said, slamming the laptop shut. 'But I hope for her sake you're a damn good attorney.'

# 29
# NOW

Nell opened a new Word document and made a list of everything that was possible:

- The mannequins were a prank by someone in Lindsay's neighbourhood
- The mannequins were a prank by someone angry about the book
- Autumn has faked her own death and is responsible for all of this

The last item on that list should have made the least sense, and yet it was the most plausible. Nobody would suspect Autumn. Nobody would be looking for Autumn. Nell stared at the list for a long time, trying to come up with a fourth item that would put her mind at ease. Something that would be easy to explain.

Without stopping to think, she added:

- Someone knows about Reina

When the apartment door opened, Nell quickly

hit CTRL + A, highlighting the text. One press of the delete key, and the Word document was blank again.

'You're home early,' she said, spinning in her chair to face Bas.

'You weren't answering any texts,' he said, and Nell could see the effort he was making to sound light. 'I was a little worried.'

'Sorry.' Nell blinked. 'I guess I was just really into what I was doing and spaced out.'

Sebastian dropped onto the couch. He patted the space beside him, and Nell fell into place. He wrapped an arm around her and kissed the crown of her head. 'I've been thinking we should go away somewhere,' he said. 'What about Hawaii? We can stay away all winter and spend it on the beach.'

'You know I can't do that,' Nell said. She had been leaning against him, but now she sat up. 'I have interviews to conduct for this book.'

'The book can wait a little, can't it?' Bas said. 'It's not like you have a deadline. You could still back out if you wanted to.'

'Back out?' Nell blurted. 'Sebastian, I made a commitment. Oleg left his home in Russia to stay in a crappy motel, just to be here for this project.'

'Well who asked him to do that?' Sebastian shot back, raising his tone to match hers. 'I don't get why he needs to be here anyway. They have phones in Russia.'

'It's because he cares about his sisters,' Nell said.

'He cares about something,' Bas muttered.

Nell stood. 'What's that supposed to mean?'

'It means I think you two are spending a little too much time together, Nell. You called him in the middle of the night when you were stranded.'

'Because you never pick up your phone when it's important!' Nell cried. Her entire body felt hot, electric with anxiety and anger.

Sebastian stood and brushed past her. 'Forget it,' he muttered. He made it halfway to the kitchen before he spun around to face her. 'You know, sometimes I wonder if there's any point to this, Nell. You'll never love me as much as your work.'

'Any point?' she echoed. 'You're asking if there's any point to what? To us?'

He shook his head. 'Forget it.'

'No,' Nell said. 'No, I can't forget something like that. If you have something to say, come out and say it.'

He stared at her, breathing hard, the way he did when he was extremely upset. Nell had only seen it a handful of times. The first had been the night she told him about her C-section scar after he'd grown fed up with how closed off she was. The other times had all been because of something outside of their relationship – his sister's asshole boyfriend, or trouble at work.

She hated this side of him. It was a stranger who

broke into their apartment and vandalised their lives.

'All right, I will,' Sebastian said. 'I don't like all the time you're spending with that man.'

'Oleg?' Nell blurted out. 'Sebastian, it's for my book!'

'Maybe to you it is, but I think he has another idea.'

'You've never even met him,' Nell said.

'I don't have to meet him to know he's the one you called when you were stranded. I don't have to meet him to know you came home wearing his clothes.'

At that, Nell took a step back. When she spoke again, her voice was quiet. 'What are you accusing me of?'

He ran his hand roughly through his hair. He didn't want to say what he was thinking, but he didn't have to.

Nell spluttered an incredulous breath.

Just a moment ago, nestled against Sebastian, she had felt calm and warm and tranquil. He had that effect on her. Right from the moment they met, when she spurned his advances and ignored his increasingly obvious affections, he had put her at ease. He cut a tall figure, but he was gracious. He didn't hold open doors or pull out chairs, but he knew how to move in tandem with her erratic pace. Whatever bizarre dance she put him through in their courtship, he found a way to make it work. It was a hypnotising calm. But when it turned ugly, it was overwhelming.

She headed for the bedroom and he followed after her at a distance. She wasn't angry with him for the accusation; she was angry with herself because he was right. She had kissed Oleg, not because she'd wanted to but because it was in her nature to sabotage everything. Everything. Even Bas.

'Nell, wait—'

She kept her back to him as she pulled clothes from her dresser drawers and began stuffing them into her laptop bag.

'Where do you think you're going?' Sebastian tried to stop her by putting his arm on the doorframe, but she squeezed past him. When she pulled open the apartment door, Sebastian reached over her shoulder and slammed it shut. 'Nell!'

The outburst startled her. This was not the Sebastian she knew.

She turned, her back against the door, pinned under his arm.

'Say something,' Sebastian burst out. 'Christ, Nell, you drive me insane the way you do that – you just look at me like I'm a blank page in your book and you haven't decided what story you're going to tell me.' His eyes were wild with anger. Frustration.

He was right. Nell couldn't see her own expression, but she knew that must be exactly how she was looking at him. He felt just like a blank page in that moment. This man she had slept beside for two years. How could she tell him what she was thinking when she couldn't admit it to herself?

'Bas,' she said. Her voice was quiet, but it was a warning. 'Let me go.'

His eyes were still locked on hers as he lowered his arm. He took a step back.

'I can't do this anymore, Nell,' he said. 'I never know which version of you I'm going to come home to.'

Poor Sebastian. That's what she wanted to say. He hadn't known he was taking on such a lost cause when he first smiled at her. What had it been? Her dress? Her eyes? Or maybe he had sensed that she was broken and wanted to fix her. Children who aren't loved grow up to have a certain palpable quality. Nell possessed enough self-awareness to know that about herself.

Lindsay, at least, embraced it. She capsized the heart of any man who made the mistake of loving her. She wasn't afraid to scream and slam doors and shatter vases. She wasn't afraid to get a good divorce attorney and take everything the law could extract from her captive.

Nell liked to believe she was better than her sister in this regard, but she wasn't. The only difference was that she had no interest in Sebastian's money, or his car, or his friends. She only wanted to be what he believed her to be. She wanted to look like a woman who had not been broken, whose mother was not in a prison cell and whose father wasn't burning through his liver. She wanted to be childless. Truly childless. She wanted the faint, shining scar that ran from her hip to her breastbone to be gone.

Nell was not childless, though. Reina would always be somewhere on this earth, long since rotted away, but still hers. And Nell would always be the broken thing that had lost her.

'I can't do this anymore either,' she said, and opened the door.

*

It wasn't often that Nell let herself cry, but that night she did. It was the sort of ugly, screaming, guttural cry that left her stomach feeling clenched and sore.

Lindsay sat on the couch, holding Nell's head in her lap and rubbing circles against her back. She hadn't asked for an explanation when a cab pulled up outside and deposited her sister on her doorstep. That was the beautiful thing about Lindsay; while Nell obsessed over every detail, Lindsay only cared about the result, not the cause.

When Nell finally did offer an explanation, it was without any prompting or expectation. 'It's never going to happen, Linds.'

She sat up, her hair flying in static-charged wisps around her face.

With a pitying expression, Lindsay yanked a tissue from the box and dabbed at Nell's leaking nose.

Nell sniffed. 'We're never going to have that life. A marriage, a house, a dog maybe. It doesn't matter how close we come to it. It's never going to change that our lives are trash.'

'Hey now,' Lindsay said. 'I like my trash life. It comes with a housekeeper and a view of the river.'

Nell laughed at that, and Lindsay gave a triumphant smile.

The amusement was short-lived though.

'Sebastian and I had a fight,' Nell confessed.

'I figured as much,' Lindsay said.

'It was about work,' Nell said. 'He thinks I'm too intense about it. And he's jealous about all the time I spend with Oleg. He insinuated that I'm cheating on him.'

Lindsay tucked a piece of hair behind Nell's ear. 'Men are all in a pissing contest with each other,' she said. 'Once Sebastian calms down, he'll realise he was being an idiot. It isn't really about Oleg, Nell. Oleg is just the manifestation.'

Nell blew her nose. 'Manifestation of what?'

'He thinks he's competing with your job,' Lindsay said. 'Deep down, all men want to marry June Cleaver and be the provider.'

Nell smirked into her soggy tissue. 'I don't know about all that.'

'So your boyfriend wants to be a bigger part of your life,' Lindsay said. 'Apparently that's something normal people do.'

'Was Robert like that?' Nell asked. Lindsay had never offered much about her second marriage and Nell had never asked. Robert had seemed decent enough, if a little too good-natured. More than once Nell wanted to warn him off. When she and Lindsay were children, sometimes they would have a foster sibling who latched on to them. Lindsay was pretty and she was charismatic, and she lured the weaker, nicer souls into her light like moths. Those were the kids whose few precious trinkets went missing; the first thing Lindsay did in any new neighbourhood was locate the pawn shops. And Robert – debonair, handsome, attentive Robert – had been just another foster child with something shiny that Lindsay could turn into a profit. It wasn't that Lindsay didn't love him. She did, and it had frightened her.

'Oh, Robert was always interested in me,' Lindsay said. She got up and walked to the kitchen, calling over her shoulder as she went. 'Sometimes I think he was asking about my childhood just to gauge how fucked up our kids would be if they were like me.' She came back to the couch with a glass of water and handed it to Nell, who realised that she was dehydrated from crying.

'How did you handle it?' Nell asked.

'You know how I handled it.' Lindsay shrugged. 'I've never pretended not to be a mess. It isn't my fault he thought he could turn me into one of those mothers you see on TV talking about which brand of peanut butter they feed their little angels.'

'I guess we have a type,' Nell said. 'Men who want to fix us.'

Lindsay's expression turned soft, and it worried Nell. Lindsay was not one for warm sentiments, and she had to be very concerned if she was resorting to them. 'You were more than just a smart kid, Nell. Even with the paltry crumbs we were thrown from the education system, I always knew you'd do something big with that brain of yours. You weren't going to be like me, or any of those other kids that shuffled in and out of our lives wherever we went.' She put her hand over Nell's. 'But that kid of yours, Nell. You really tried. You tried harder than Bonnie ever did with me, and harder than anyone ever did for you, but you met your match with her. Right from the day she came out of you, she started chipping away at your life.'

'She was only a baby,' Nell said, staring into her glass. Those were the words she was supposed to say out loud, even if she didn't believe them.

'No,' Lindsay said. 'She was never just a baby. She's been gone for more years than she was alive, and she's still ruining your chance at happiness.'

278

She took the now-empty glass from Nell's hands and placed it on the table. With nothing else to focus on, Nell met her sister's eyes.

'Sebastian is giving you the love you have always deserved,' Lindsay said, and her earnestness made Nell's vision blur with new tears. 'He's giving you what you never got from Bonnie, or from Chuck, or those *idiot* teachers who didn't see what a genius you were. This is the life you deserve, Nell. You're trying to ruin it because you've been taught that life always turns bad when your guard is down. I'm not going to let you ruin it.' She grabbed another tissue, this time dabbing at Nell's eyes. 'You can sleep here tonight, but tomorrow you're going back home.'

# 30
# THEN

After the interrogation, Matthew escorted her out of the police station. 'Get in the car,' he told her, as she struggled to keep up with his pace.

Once inside the vehicle, he slammed the gas, and her heart leapt.

'You're lucky they didn't arrest you, you know that?' His fingers clenched around the steering wheel. 'They want you for murder, Penelope.'

'I didn't kill my daughter,' Nell said, and it took all her bravado not to jump from the moving car, she was so terrified.

'I don't care what you did,' Matthew said. 'What happened doesn't matter. What matters is what we can convince a jury of. And this *will* go to trial. Where's your cell phone?'

'I don't have it,' Nell said.

'Don't have it?' he parroted back, annoyed. 'What do you mean you don't have it? You're a teenager; you should be glued to that thing.'

'I left it at the Eddletons'. I was in a hurry.'

'Christ.' He ran his hand down his face, tugging aggressively on his lower lip. 'Is there anything incriminating on that phone? Pictures? Texts?'

'No,' Nell said. Her voice was quiet. She was staring at her lap.

'No?' Matthew asked. 'You're sure? Because it's only a matter of time before that phone ends up admitted as evidence.'

'If you take me back home, I can get it,' Nell said.

Matthew laughed, loud and without humour. 'You're not going back to the Eddletons,' he said. 'Before the day is over, the police will show them that footage. Your boyfriend will be in an inter-rogation room, getting grilled on what type of mother you are. He'll panic and throw you under the bus.'

*He wouldn't do that.* That's what Nell wanted to say. They may not have had a Hallmark Channel romance, but he loved her, in his way.

Suddenly she thought back to their fights about Reina. All the times he'd called her crazy. The way he never believed anything she said.

'Listen to me,' Matthew said. 'Was your phone on you the day Reina went missing?'

That morning, Reina had been screaming when Nell scooped her up from the kitchen floor and wriggled her arms into her coat. Mrs Eddleton was shouting to be heard. She was prattling off a list of things she wanted Nell to buy at the grocery store because the housekeeper was out with the flu. Ethan was already waiting in the car and he'd honked the horn for the third time in as many seconds. Nell was supposed to drop him off at the entrance to his university for an 8:30 class.

Reina had gone dead weight and she refused to walk, so Nell had to haul her out to the car like a sack of grain. As she shouldered her purse, she saw her phone resting on the table in the foyer. It had been a conscious decision to leave it there, so that Mrs Eddleton would have no way to reach her. One more conversation about the groceries needed for the perfect hors d'oeuvres and Nell was going to have a mental breakdown.

'I left it at home,' Nell said.

'You're sure?' Matthew asked.

'Yes.'

He smiled at the road ahead. 'I hope you're as smart as Lindsay keeps bragging you are,' he said. 'You're going to need it to get through this.'

They pulled up to the massive suburban mansion Matthew and Lindsay shared. Before the car had even come to a full stop, Lindsay was running down the front steps, the folds of her asymmetrical sweater flying around her like wings. She gathered Nell into her arms and clung to her. 'I'm so sorry,' she whispered. 'I've been trying every day to see you and they wouldn't let me in. I'm so sorry, but you're home now.'

There would never be such a thing as home.

❋

After a week spent at Lindsay and Matthew's house, Nell understood that Lindsay's invitation for Nell to stay there was not just to protect Nell from the press, police and the Eddletons. It was also so that Nell could protect Lindsay from Matthew.

When they weren't rehearsing what Nell should say the next time the police summoned her, Matthew was amiable to Nell at best. And in Nell's presence, he didn't just kiss Lindsay – he groped her, with the greedy possessiveness of a man trying to compete with a formidable lover. He knew almost nothing about Nell except that she and Lindsay had a bond he couldn't compete with. Not truly.

Nell wondered if Lindsay had lost her mind. She seemed to like that she drove her husband wild. She exaggerated the handsomeness of men on the television and sighed that she wished she could find a lover like the hero in whatever romance novel she was reading.

It wasn't a marriage. It was a game. Being caught in the middle like an animal trapped between two lanes of traffic was preferable to the press and the Eddletons, but that wasn't saying much. A kick to the spleen would have been just as preferable.

But the human mind was adaptable. Nell adapted to waking each morning under the crushing weight of being a childless mother. She adapted to the slammed doors, the fights, the stench of vodka and espresso, and the nauseating knot in her stomach.

Nell had become so used to all of these things that the silence was the thing that woke her. It had rained the night before – thunder tearing the sky to shreds while the rain applauded its efforts. But the morning was so still that even birds weren't singing.

'Lindsay?' Nell whispered. The quiet felt too fragile. Her footsteps were light as she slid out of bed. She opened the door and stepped out into the hallway. The upstairs was a mezzanine that looked down over the living room, and from here Nell could see the crackling fire in the hearth. A blanket was wadded on the floor beside the gaudy tiger-skin rug.

Nell didn't call for Lindsay again as she made her way downstairs. Something warned her not to.

Something crashed in the kitchen. The ceramic sound of it breaking tore through the entire house. Nell ran even without understanding what had compelled her to move so fast.

Matthew was kneeling on the tile floor. Lindsay was pinned under him, clawing at his hands that were clutched around her throat. Her face was red, her eyes shining and wide. Her tongue bulged between lips that had already begun to turn blue. Her bare feet slid helplessly against the tiles.

Nell grabbed the skillet from the stove. Eggs were sizzling on its surface and the cooking steam trailed after the motion as Nell swung it, screaming, at

Matthew's head. She felt the force of the impact, and even though she saw him fall back, she was certain she hadn't hit him hard enough. He was going to get up. He was going to kill them both. She hit him again. She tried to hit him a third time, but he staggered to his feet. He was dazed and clumsy, and he clutched the door frame. 'Fucking crazy,' he blurted out. 'Both of you are fucking crazy.'

Nell could smell the alcohol on him and she knew that he was drunk. She didn't stop him as he made his way through the living room and out the front door. Nell heard the sound of his car starting, and she craned her neck to look out the window. The car never left the driveway. Matthew passed out cold against the steering wheel.

Lindsay was the one to take the skillet from Nell's hands. 'You shouldn't have done that,' she said. Her voice was hoarse. Her breath reeked, and in a moment of clarity Nell saw that the force of drawing air back into her lungs had made Lindsay vomit on the floor. 'You shouldn't have,' Lindsay said again, and sagged wearily against her. 'It wasn't his fault. It was mine.'

Nobody called the police.

Lindsay and Nell crouched together on the kitchen floor and cleaned up the shards of the plate with little daisies painted on it. They mopped up the eggs, vomit and blood with hand towels and they left Matthew to sleep it off in his car.

He didn't wake up for a long time, and Nell thought about what she would do if he died there. She tucked Lindsay under the cashmere blanket on the couch and brought her a glass of lemonade, and she thought about burying Matthew Cranlin in his own back yard.

It wouldn't be difficult. When she read about crimes in the paper, in hindsight they always sounded messy and doomed to fail. But here in the quiet of this house with all the neighbours cordoned off by shrubs and trees, it seemed easy. She wouldn't even need Lindsay's help.

First, she would prepare the burial site. This often got overlooked by murderers. They were too panicked by the enormity of what they had done, and their flaws weren't in the execution of the plan itself, but in the cover-up.

She would go outside. She would take a spade and the cloth gloves from the shed. She would gingerly dig up the tulips and begonias that framed the walkway, taking care to preserve their roots. Then she would dig a hole in the malleable earth. She would drag him to the grave and then she would place the tulips and the begonias on top of him, neatly patted down as though nothing had ever happened. There were a dozen flowerbeds along the walkways and around the well and the property line. The softened earth wouldn't be suspicious at all.

She sat on the couch. Lindsay yawned and put her head in her lap.

*It would have been possible*, Nell thought. *I could have done it.*

# 31

# NOW

After a long and embarrassing cry, Nell retreated to the guest room upstairs. There were technically three guest rooms, but all of them were being used as storage and only this one had a bed.

In addition to the twin bed there was also a crib, still furnished with a cornflower-blue mattress, occupied only by an unopened box of baby monitors. The curtains were drawn, and the door to this room was always closed. In lieu of a nightstand, a resin train lamp sat upon a stack of cardboard boxes of blankets and clothes.

Lindsay might have donated the contents of this room to charity, if only she could bring herself to open the door. Her marriage had died in this room. It was a shrine to her panic. After going through all the trouble of humouring her husband, she ultimately confessed that she wasn't going to give him the babies she'd promised him. Not because she couldn't, but because she didn't trust herself enough to try.

Robert had been kind and far more patient with Lindsay than most of her suitors, but his wife had promised him children, and without that there was nothing left to talk about.

Nell knew that she was to blame for this as well. If she'd never had her own child, Lindsay wouldn't be so afraid of what tragedies might be waiting to happen.

Though it resembled a nursery, the room smelled more like an old woman's closet: mothballs and lavender scent packs. Nell closed her eyes and tried to sleep.

A short while later, she awoke to the sound of a car door slamming. Keys jingling. Footsteps.

She opened her eyes. It was still night, and she knew she hadn't been asleep for very long. She moved to the window and looked out onto the driveway. There was a white Mercedes she didn't recognise, but she knew the man who had stepped out of it. Matthew Cranlin was making his way to the front door.

Nell was about to move, to run and shout a warning out to Lindsay. But then, from where Nell stood at the window, she saw the front door swing open before Matthew could reach for the bell.

'Didn't you get my text? I told you not to come here tonight.' Lindsay spoke in a hushed voice, but it still echoed through the house. She hugged her silk robe around her, shivering at a breeze.

'I haven't had a chance to check my phone,' Matthew said. 'I sped over here as soon as my flight touched down. All I could think about was you.'

He slapped his hands on either of her hips, reeling her against him.

Lindsay relented when he kissed her. Even from up here, Nell saw her sister falling under Matthew's spell. Her shoulders slackened and she wrapped her arms around his shoulders.

When the kiss ended, Lindsay slapped his cheek playfully. 'Get out of here. My sister's upstairs.'

'She's a big girl,' Matthew said, grinning as she leaned in for their next kiss. 'Come on. We'll go somewhere. I've been flying all day to see you.'

Of all the things Nell would have expected to come rolling up Lindsay's driveway in a shiny white Mercedes, Matthew Cranlin had not been one of them. But it disheartened her to realise that she wasn't surprised. Her sister's bad decisions always bubbled back up to the surface, like a bloated corpse in a swamp.

Nell stood in the darkness and watched as Lindsay, giggling and tripping over herself, grabbed her purse and let Matthew open the passenger side door for her. A minute later, they were gone.

Nell could have taken Lindsay's car and followed them. She could have called Lindsay to ask what the hell she thought she was doing. But she didn't. She stormed back to the bed and fell onto the mattress, furious. Furious with her sister, and furious with herself.

*No*, she told herself, as she closed her eyes and

tried to fall back asleep. She was furious with Matthew. And in the morning, when Lindsay snuck back into her own house and tried to pretend nothing had happened, Nell was going to remind her of everything that man had put her through. She was going to shatter the bubble that protected her sister from reality.

❈

In the morning, Nell woke to the unfamiliar ringing of her new phone. It had a cleaner and more musical sound than her old one. She lay still for a moment as she tried to place the song.

'Hello?'

'Hey.' Sebastian's voice.

Nell sat up. 'Hey.'

'Slept like shit,' he said with a nervous laugh. 'What about you?'

Nell had slept in the graveyard of Lindsay's non-existent child. She dreamt of the mobile spinning and the music box on the dresser creaking open. There had been a tiny figure spinning slowly. Too slowly. It never turned all the way for Nell to see its face, but she'd somehow known it would frighten her.

'Lousy,' she said.

'Come home tonight,' he said. 'Let's talk about this, Nell. Please.'

She doubled forward, still pressing the phone to her ear. Sebastian. Her love for him was the only stable romantic love she'd ever experienced. Desperate at times, but always a load-bearing pillar in her life. She could see herself having a life with him, being happy. Not with children, but with a dog maybe, even one of those modular houses he coveted and she so openly despised. All that mattered was that he was the one to climb into bed beside her at night.

But there would always be a wedge between them. Reina's ghost on the mattress, reminding Nell that she could play the part but she would never be what Sebastian thought she was.

'Nell?'

For one maddened, vulnerable moment, she wanted to tell him about Reina, and the day she disappeared. She wanted to tell him all of it. After years of sleeping beside this man, she could anticipate his reaction to almost anything, but not this. There was no promise that he would understand, much less love her. He might even insist on telling the police. One guess was as good as another. This was uncharted territory.

The police couldn't punish her, but the court of public opinion could. She feared that the most: hundreds, thousands, millions of people gathered outside the doors of her publisher, screaming for her head or her career – whichever they could have the quickest. She would have nothing. No more stories entrusted to her care, no more words and no more pages. No more Sebastian. No more apartment overlooking the dragonfly city. No more Nell Way, who was no relation to Penelope Wendall. And as always, no Reina.

It was the hundredth time she considered telling Bas the truth, and the hundredth time she kept quiet.

'Yeah,' she said. 'I'm here.'

He let out a relieved breath. 'Okay,' he said. 'Love you.'

'Love you,' she said. 'So much.'

She could tell by his pause that she'd startled him. She told him she loved him all the time, but always withholding her earnestness. She was either afraid to give him too much, or it felt too unbearable to acknowledge.

She hung up before either of them could say anything more, and she closed her eyes. She could smell the presence of a new baby in this room. Little bottles of lotion and diaper cream in a basket under the crib, and the liquid-resistant rubber liner over the mattress.

The Eddletons had given Reina a beautiful nursery like something out of a fairy tale, with a mobile of little crocheted bears and stars spinning in their own galaxy.

Mothers often talked about the scent of their new baby, how they dreaded the day that it would fade.

Nell never had a baby that smelled of sweetness and powder. There was no softness. Not a single time had she walked to her daughter's crib eager to fill her arms with the weight of her. During her pregnancy, she'd romanticised motherhood. She had dreamed of a little piece of herself to love, but she gave birth to a sobering reality instead.

Nell tried to remember now what it had been like to hold her own child. Had there ever been a peaceful moment? Surely there must have been. Four years was a long time to go without a second of happiness. All of that time blurred together now, like one long dream. Nell had the sense that if she thought too long on it, her past would reach up like skeletal fingers from the grave and pull her beneath the earth.

She heard Lindsay clattering about in the kitchen, and then the loud whirr of her Keurig heating the water for coffee. Nell descended the stairs and found Lindsay standing in front of the open refrigerator in an oversized t-shirt.

The refrigerator was an abysmal display: a bottle of raspberry zinfandel, a carton of blueberries with fuzz on them and half of a fast-food burger loosely wrapped in its paper.

'Good morning, sunshine,' Lindsay sang. She turned on her heel to face Nell. 'Coffee?'

'You're in a good mood,' Nell said, falling into a chair. She knew exactly what this was. Matthew was so much of a drug that he might as well have been in a syringe. He built Lindsay up only to drain her spirit away, and the only one incapable of seeing it was Lindsay.

'Why wouldn't I be?' Lindsay sat at the table. She cradled her mug in both hands; there was a cartoon cat pouring whiskey from a bottle on it.

Nell stared at her. 'Are you going to make me say it?'

The glow drained from Lindsay's face. 'You saw me leave last night.'

'Yes, I saw you leave last night,' Nell said. She was trying not to raise her voice. As a result, her tone sounded eerily calm. 'What happened, Lindsay? I thought you left him behind in Missouri. Doesn't he live there?'

Lindsay took a measured sip of her coffee, swallowed audibly and set the mug on the table. 'Nell, you seem to be operating under the belief that I haven't given these things any thought. I have. I just don't think you'll like what I have to say.'

Nell waited for her to go on. She had the sense that any response she gave would be the wrong one anyway, and if Lindsay blew up into a defensive rage, there would be no bringing her to reason.

'My marriage to Matthew had nothing to do with you,' Lindsay said. 'I know you think that the mannequins in my car and in my back yard were meant to send you some message, and if you want to know the truth, I think that's shitty of you.'

'Shitty?' Nell balked.

'Yes,' Lindsay said. 'Shitty. You think everything is fodder for one of your goddamned books and you're the omniscient narrator who gets to tell us about it.' She pointed her mug at Nell, spilling a few drops of coffee onto the table. 'That's right. I know big words too. It hasn't even occurred to you how *I* might be feeling about this. I'm Matthew's ex-wife, Nell. Me. Not you. Someone was trying to scare me, and it worked.'

Lindsay broke eye contact to stare out the window, at a world buried in autumn leaves.

'Wait,' Nell said. Her chair scraped against the tiles as she pushed it back. 'Wait a minute. Are you telling me that Matthew has been visiting you in Rockhollow this entire time, and he might have something to do with all of this?'

'There's a lot you don't know about the time I was married to Matthew,' Lindsay went on, her voice quieter but still with an edge. 'Not because I was deliberately keeping it from you, but because it didn't seem important, especially with all you were dealing with that year. It was right before your trial.'

Nell reached across the table and took Lindsay's hand. Her way of apologising. Lindsay was right. Nell couldn't argue. She *had* made this all about herself. 'Like what?' she asked.

'It doesn't matter.' Lindsay's effort to sound non-chalant contradicted her words. 'He had a couple of affairs. One of them was his secretary – how clichéd is that?' She laughed coldly. 'Anyway, I guess she was under the impression that he'd leave me and go be with her. She couldn't let it go. She scooped a dead squirrel out of the street and put it in our mailbox. She smashed in my car windows while I was getting a hot stone massage. Might have gotten away with that one if someone hadn't seen her running out of the parking lot.'

'Lindsay, oh my God,' Nell said.

Lindsay rolled her eyes. 'It was nothing. You were dealing with the press and the … fucking Eddletons. This kind of shit wasn't worth worrying you over.'

'What happened to this woman?' Nell said. 'Where the hell is she?'

'Matthew handled it,' Lindsay said. 'I thought.' She shrugged. 'It isn't the first time she's done something crazy. That's all I'm trying to say.'

'What does that mean?' Nell pressed. 'What else has happened?'

Lindsay heaved a theatrical sigh. She threw back the rest of her coffee and then moved to the sink with the empty mug. 'She moved in with Matthew after I left him. Good riddance, right? She can have him. But a dog's a dog, and eventually he cheated on her and left her too. She had it in her head that it was because of me.' She sat in her chair again, never managing to meet Nell's eyes. She made a production of how unconcerned she was with what she was saying. She straightened the stack of napkins in the apple-shaped holder.

'It's been a few years since she sent me any surprises. The last one was a hate letter smeared with what I'm going to assume was period blood.'

'Lindsay, what the fuck?' Nell said. 'Why didn't you tell me?'

'Because you were finally picking yourself back up,' Lindsay said. 'You took those night classes to get your diploma and then you went to college.'

'Don't act like you did this for me,' Nell said. 'You shouldn't have kept this to yourself.'

'Whatever,' Lindsay said. 'I think the mannequin nonsense is coming from her.' Her voice went soft, all her edge and steel giving way to something softer, more human. 'That's what I told the police. They've been investigating it. I didn't tell you because I didn't want you to freak out. And, Nell, she isn't the one who ran you off the road. That had to have been a drunk driver. This woman's crazy, but the police checked and she has an alibi that night.'

'What's her name?' Nell asked.

'Candace something, I don't know.' She surely did know, but Lindsay never liked admitting how much thought she gave to things that troubled her.

Nell reached across the table to take both of Lindsay's hands in hers. Lindsay stared down at them. Her expression was guarded and she was trying too hard to look unfazed, but Nell could see how upset she was. What else had she overlooked?

'Linds.' Her voice was gentle. 'Tell me her last name.'

'Nielson.' Lindsay spat the word like a piece of gum that had lost its flavour.

Nell tried to picture it, like words being drummed into a sheet of typewriter paper: Matthew's jilted lover destroying Lindsay's life. If Candace Nielson truly hated her, she would want Lindsay to feel the same injustice she felt. So she resorted to her old trick of leaving a bloody animal for Lindsay to find, only this time it was the mannequins. It wouldn't be the gore that scared Lindsay. It would be the fact that Candace had been able to break into her back yard, leaving no trace. It was a show of power.

'Lindsay,' she murmured, finally understanding. 'I'm so sorry. You're right. I've made this all about me because Reina's anniversary messed with my head. I wasn't even thinking about you.'

Lindsay sniffed. Her eyes were wet with tears she was too stubborn to let out. 'You've been kind of selfish, yeah.'

'But there's something I don't understand.' Nell squeezed her hands. 'Why would Candace do this to you now? You've been divorced for years. Matthew's surely had a thousand other little liaisons since then.'

Lindsay lost her nerve again, lowered her gaze, turned red. 'It doesn't matter.'

'Don't do that,' Nell said. 'What more do you know? Tell me.'

'Because I'm pregnant,' Lindsay burst out. It was almost a scream. 'It's because I'm fucking pregnant, okay?'

## 32
# THEN

It didn't take the press long to find Nell at Matthew and Lindsay's address.

Nell awoke, panicked, to the sound of fists pounding at the door. She looked out of her window and was greeted by flashing cameras and what seemed like a thousand people crowding the front lawn.

'Penelope!'

'Ms Wendall!'

Nell's heart was pounding when she burst into Lindsay and Matthew's bedroom. It was empty, the bed already neatly made. Nell looked at the clock on the bedside table. It was nearly 2 PM. After a fitful night, Lindsay had given Nell one of her Ambien, and it had apparently rendered her comatose for the entire morning.

At this hour, Matthew would be at work. And Lindsay – God only knew where she was. Lindsay had abandoned Nell the second she'd married Matthew; apparently this was true even when they were living under the same roof.

Nell paced through every room of the house, calling Lindsay's name, screaming it. Her brain was still hazy from the Ambien. Reporters were still pounding on the door, and it felt like the entire house was shaking.

Her reflection in the ornate hall mirror was skeletal. She sat at the marble table under the mirror and picked up her phone. The world moved in slow motion as she scrolled through her contacts list looking for Lindsay's number.

It rang for an eternity, and then there was only the sound of a beep, followed by silence. Lindsay used to have a playful outgoing message that began with the song 'Spiderwebs' by No Doubt, singing, 'I'm walking into spiderwebs, so leave a message and I'll call you back' followed by a giggle and Lindsay saying, 'Leave a message, bitches!' But Matthew had disapproved, and now it was just a beep.

Nell left a message for her sister, and she didn't remember all of what she said. It was a torrent of obscenities, she knew that much. And 'How could you leave me?' topped off with a shrill 'I hate you!'

The rest was a blur. Nell was swimming in a world that had gone underwater with her tears. It was only in that state, lacking clarity, that she was able to face the reporters outside. She stormed through the cloud of them. Two or three of them followed her down the street, shouting, 'Penelope!' 'Did you murder your daughter? Penelope Wendall!'

She broke into a run. She cut between two manicured lawns and into the woods behind them. She ran until there were no longer footsteps coming after her, and she didn't stop until she reached the road on the other side. There was a divided highway, blurred by speeding headlights.

Later, Nell would learn that she had been walking through the woods for hours before reaching that overpass. But in the moment it only felt like a handful of seconds. How could she be expected to feel the passage of time? She didn't even feel the cold as it raked her lungs.

She only knew that she was tired. 'I'm sorry,' she murmured. 'I'm sorry, Reina.'

It was the last time she ever intended to say the child's name. In her four years as Reina's mother, she had often dreamed of her being gone. She had dreamed about leaving the party at Ethan's house, rather than staying behind and giving him her virginity. She had dreamed of taking Lindsay's money and having an abortion. She had been stupid to think there was anything redemptive about motherhood.

She could have forgiven herself if she'd had the abortion. She would have cried a little, been angry with herself and spent the rest of her life wondering what might have been. Years would make the memory of it smaller and smaller, though, until it was just a ghost. But once Reina was here, that was another matter entirely. Reina Eddleton would never be erased from this world like some bloody pieces in a medical waste container. She would forever have existed. She would forever be in Nell's nightmares.

*I don't want Reina to disappear*, she realised. *I want to be the one to disappear.*

She stopped and gripped the railing of the overpass. Below her, cars sped towards the city on one side and away from it on the other. Between the cars there was the road, shining with moonlight and rain. That was where she would jump – for that gleam of brightness in the black. It would hurt for a second, but then she would be gone.

She hoisted one leg over the railing and pushed herself forward.

Something reeled her back. In her daze, Nell thought it was God.

It was Lindsay. She slapped Nell hard across the face, creating a blossom of starbursts, and then she grabbed her shoulders. She was shouting, but Nell couldn't hear the words. Her breath came in loud rasps. Her only chance at escape was gone.

*Pregnant.* Nell's mind went black for a moment. Her brain was trying to disregard the word. It was too impossible.

Getting answers out of Lindsay was a delicate balance. Nell knew that she couldn't press too hard. That sort of thing would get her thrown outside like a stray cat. But she also knew that if she didn't push at all, Lindsay would manoeuvre her way out of discussing it.

'Linds.' Nell's voice was gentle but not placating.

Lindsay raised her eyes in a stare that could be mistaken for mean but that Nell knew to be resignation. 'All right,' Lindsay said. 'Okay. I'll talk about this, but your mouth stays shut unless you're pouring coffee into it.'

Nell's silence was her agreement.

'I ran into him at the country club,' Lindsay began. 'He was in town for the week, rubbing elbows with his lawyer friends for some legal convention. It was a year ago. I know you don't think it's possible for people like him to change. Maybe you're right, but we started talking and I figured it couldn't hurt to let him take me out to dinner. It wasn't anything much. Robert has also been "taking me out to dinner".' She emphasised her meaning with air quotes.

'I made sure it was a shitty diner with no ambiance. I wanted to see Matthew's face in the harsh lighting. I thought it would show me all the sun spots and the wrinkles and pores and remind me that he's a piece of shit. But he just' – she tugged at a piece of her hair and twined it around her fingers – 'looked like the man I used to be in love with. And he started seeing me whenever he was in town.'

Nell's ability to remain silent was a testament to how much she wanted to hear the rest of the story. She regarded Lindsay the same way she had regarded the Widow Thompson when she described killing all eight of her children and then laying their corpses on her bedroom floor so she could sprinkle them with holy water.

She had many questions, and if she was patient, she would have her answers. But not now. Some would take days to coax out of Lindsay.

'I wasn't going to tell him I'm pregnant,' Lindsay said. 'I was just going to get rid of it. I got in the car and I drove to the doctor, and then I don't know what happened. It's like I had a stroke. My hands wouldn't let go of the steering wheel and my heart started racing.' She was staring past Nell, trapped in her memory. 'I had this thought that if I went through with it the ugliness would never go away.

I'd never feel good again.' Her eyes moved to Nell and she let out a bitter laugh. 'So much for that, right?'

Nell thought of the nursery upstairs. Had the basket of baby lotion always been under the crib, or was it a recent addition? No, it hadn't been there six months ago, when she'd last spent a night at her sister's house. It wasn't like Nell to miss a detail, but then Lindsay was so good at making them blend in. She was a chameleon of deceit.

'You've decided to keep it,' Nell said. It wasn't a question.

'I told Matthew earlier this month. I wanted it to be right before he left for his trip, so he wouldn't smother me. He's started getting clingy.' She squirmed as though there were spiders crawling up her back. 'That was a mistake. I should have told him it was someone else's.'

Lindsay was right. Telling Matthew was a mistake, but the true mistake was conceiving a child with him in the first place. Now she was forever tethered to this horrible man. This sinister tarp of skin and violence and poison. Years ago, Bonnie had said that Matthew would be the death of Lindsay, and she was right. As long as he was in Lindsay's life, it was only a matter of time before he killed her.

'Lindsay—'

'You don't get to say anything,' Lindsay snapped. 'That was the agreement.'

Lindsay was pregnant. The idea wouldn't register. Nell thought back to the wine Lindsay had uncorked the other day at her apartment – had Lindsay even taken a sip of it? Nell could only remember her swishing it in the glass and taking the occasional sniff.

Lindsay was looking at her. A chunk of blonde hair fell across her face and clung to the corner of her mouth.

In that moment Nell realised it wasn't just teenage girls who were intimidated by positive pregnancy tests. There was something about the entire fiasco that could make anyone feel small. Even a woman who kept knives and hammers under her couch cushions.

Lindsay had never seemed small before. Even when Matthew nearly killed her, she picked herself up like a boxer rising from a blow with seconds left to spare.

'Is there any way that it isn't Matthew's baby?' Nell asked. She felt nauseous at the thought of that man being back in their lives, this time with a permanent tie to her sister. 'What about Robert? How can you be sure?'

After a long pause, Lindsay nodded, staring down at the table. 'The timings line up. You could be right, but I just … have a feeling, you know?'

Nell reached across the table and took her hand. 'That doesn't mean you have to let him back into your life, Lindsay. You don't owe him anything.'

'Please don't turn this into a fight, Nell,' she said. 'I don't want to fight.'

'You already know I'm on your side,' Nell sighed, resigning herself to holding her tongue. 'And until that psycho woman is in jail, you're not staying here.'

'Here is the safest place for me,' Lindsay said. She moved to the drawer where the silverware was kept and extracted a .48-caliber pistol. Then, she lovingly laid it back amid the spoons. 'They're all over the house. I'll be fine.'

Nell laughed. She didn't know why; there was nothing about any of this that she found funny. But it was all so absurd that she couldn't help herself.

Lindsay scooted her chair closer and wrapped her arms around Nell's shoulders. 'I won't blame you for being weird about this.' She was talking about her pregnancy, something that hadn't existed in Nell's world five minutes ago. Something she never would have deemed possible.

What surprised her most was that Lindsay hadn't been able to go through with the abortion. They had that much in common. Nell understood the exact feeling her sister had described: the idea that there was no certain path to true happiness, but there was, at least, a path of despair to avoid.

'We shouldn't tell Bonnie,' Nell said. 'Next year we should just show up with a kid on your hip and watch her hit the floor.'

Lindsay snorted a laugh.

'Linds,' Nell said, and her tone sobered them both. 'Please come and stay with me and Bas. At least for tonight while we sort this out. There's round-the-clock security and I'm in the penthouse. No way anyone is going to breeze into the lobby to leave dead shit in the mailbox.'

'Your couch sucks for sleeping on,' Lindsay said.

'Yeah,' Nell said. 'But that's Sebastian's problem.'

Lindsay smiled. It was her first genuine smile since her revelation about Matthew, and it warmed Nell to see it. 'So you've decided to stop being an idiot and go back to him.'

'Yeah,' Nell said. 'I guess I love him enough for that.'

'There is no "love him enough",' Lindsay said. 'You love someone or you don't. Love is an emotion, not a unit of measurement.' She dispensed her casual brilliance, and Nell's heart went back to hurting. Nell had been the one to go to college and have the career; she had a boyfriend who loved her, an agent who emphatically waved pompoms around her efforts, and thousands of emails from adoring readers.

But Lindsay was a genius; from the moment Nell was first placed in her arms, Lindsay allowed herself to go without if it meant Nell could have the best their circumstances allowed. The softest side of the bed, the one chicken nugget in the carton that was shaped like a heart, the chance to rise above their station. It was Lindsay who sat on the floor with her after school, teaching her fractions and punctuation. It was Lindsay who tested Nell's intelligence by feeding her the lessons from her own homework sheets, three grades ahead, and ruffling her hair and saying 'that's my girl' when she got them right.

Lindsay was brash and calculated, and in anyone else's story she would be the villain. But to Nell she had always been everything.

❋

# THEN

The morning after the incident on the overpass, two policemen knocked on the door. Lindsay was the one to answer, and when one of the officers asked if Nell was home, Lindsay planted her hand on the doorframe, using her arm to bar entry. 'Do you have a warrant?'

Matthew put his hand on her shoulder. 'It's all right, sweetheart,' he told her. Then he nodded to the officers. 'What is this about?' He guided Lindsay out of the way so that the policemen could step inside.

Nell was standing on the threshold of the kitchen, a half-eaten carton of yoghurt in one hand and the spoon still suspended between her lips. At the sight of the officers it began to churn in her stomach.

'Penelope Wendall.' One of the officers stepped towards her and the other followed suit. 'You're under arrest for the murder of Reina Eddleton.' He drew a pair of handcuffs from his belt, and Nell could only stare at them. Somehow, the spoon and the yoghurt container were gone, and she had the vague sense that she had just destroyed the carpet by dropping them.

The officer grabbed her shoulder and spun her around, so that her hands were behind her back. 'You have the right to remain silent,' he said. 'Anything you say can and will be used against you in a court of law. You have a right to an attorney—'

'Lindsay,' Nell whimpered. But Matthew was gripping Lindsay's arm so tightly that her skin was turning red.

'If you cannot afford an attorney, one will be provided for you. Do you understand the rights I have just read to you?'

'Don't say anything,' Matthew called out as Nell was shoved through the door, out into the breezy winter air. 'Don't say anything at all! I'll be right behind you.'

Yesterday, the Ambien had left a fog in Nell's brain, even after the overpass incident. And now she felt like she was trapped in another delirium. The cold black upholstery in the police cruiser. The smell like cigarettes and coffee and crisp linen uniforms and leather belts. The jingle of keys, the gleam of their badges. The way her shoulder immediately cramped when she fell against the seat with her arms behind her. Lindsay standing in the doorway, her messy gold hair burning around her like a wild sun. Matthew mouthing 'say nothing' as Nell stared helplessly back at them through the glass, as the car pulled out of the driveway.

# 34
# NOW

Nell drove her new rental car to Royal King's State Penitentiary, and eased up on the gas when she realised she was going ninety miles per hour.

Lindsay was beside her, staring intently at her phone. Each time she flicked her thumb there was a small victory trill from whatever game she was playing. A cartoonish voice said things like, 'Great shot!' and 'Triple bonus!'

Nell didn't mind. She didn't feel much like talking. Lindsay had insisted on coming along and had already decided she would wait in the car.

It was a bright day. The sun was candied in its blue winter sky, and it made the interior of the car feel warm, despite the wind chill outside.

Lindsay didn't bother looking up until Nell had navigated the prison parking lot and found a space.

'Sure you don't want to come in?' Nell asked. 'You could visit your best friend Bonnie.'

Lindsay snorted and turned back to her phone. 'No thanks. Have fun interviewing the murder twin.'

'You're amazing!' came the voice from Lindsay's

phone, accompanied by the sound of victorious trumpet music.

'I'm leaving my keys in the ignition. Don't drive off and leave me here,' Nell said.

'Uh-huh.' Lindsay didn't look up, and Nell rolled her eyes.

It only took half an hour for Nell to reach Easter today. As she stood to have the contents of her purse inspected, she saw a group of teenagers exiting the hallway that led to the visitation areas. They were quiet, despite their gleeful smiles. Their carefree stride and bright-eyed expressions told Nell that they were not visiting a loved one. Rather, they had the flustered excitement of someone who'd just met their idol backstage at a concert.

Prison groupies were a phenomenon few would understand, but Nell had seen it dozens of times. Even Bonnie had fielded letters, calls and visits from hundreds of them over the years. In Bonnie's case, it was mostly men. The groupies got the thrill of racy phone calls from a real-life cult celebrity, and Bonnie got a few extra dollars in her commissary; it was a win-win.

Prison groupies weren't always about romance. Sometimes it was an intense fascination that caused them to project their own ideals onto the inmate. And for commissary dollars and something to break up the monotony, inmates were good at catering to such delusions.

Nell couldn't fault anyone who found crime and punishment fascinating. It wasn't every day that you met someone capable of shooting her husband or murdering his neighbour after their extramarital affair. She supposed her own fascination with high-profile crimes wasn't much different; she just took the time to see more of the details, and then she wrote them down.

When Nell sat before the glass and picked up the phone, Easter greeted her with a smug smile. 'You're my third visitor this week,' she said, favouring her Russian accent.

'Oh yeah?' Nell said. Being in a prison might have set most people on edge, but Nell found it oddly calming. From the time she was a child, she learned that any emotion she betrayed in a prison could be exploited. Inmates used to call out from behind their bars when she came to visit her mother. They only ever honed in on Nell, never Lindsay.

Finally Lindsay told her, 'It's because they want to see what you'll do. They can tell how scared you are. Just pretend it doesn't bother you.'

On their next visit, Nell walked down the corridors with her gaze fixed ahead of her. She thought about movies and song lyrics and the stray cat she'd been feeding behind the school. She learned that Lindsay was right; if she betrayed no emotion then no one could touch her.

She did this now as she faced Easter, thinking

319

about how to best approach today's line of questioning. There were things she needed to know, but she couldn't let on how important they were. Easter relished whatever power she could get.

'Have you had visits from adoring fans?' Nell asked.

Easter sat back in her chair and let out a small laugh. It had the croaking quality of an old desk chair. 'My parents,' she said, 'and my brother.' Easter nodded to Nell's empty pad. 'Are you asking for your book?'

'I could be,' Nell said. 'Would you like to tell me what they had to say?'

Easter shrugged. 'I haven't seen my parents since the trial. Oleg visits, but they never do. My mother only stared at me, but my father – he was in tears.' Easter said this without any emotion. Perhaps she didn't feel anything for the people who had raised her, or perhaps she was playing the same game as Nell.

'My father has always been an emotional man,' Easter said. 'Here in America, I guess you'd call that sweet. In Russia, nobody respects a man who weeps like a little girl. But my mother' – Easter sat back in her chair – 'my mother is a stoic woman when she needs to be.'

Nell thought back to her one and only visit with Mrs Hamblin. Stoic had not been the word. Nell found her to be warm, loving and deeply hurt. But she utilised that hurt in a productive way. It was true that she didn't break down into tears, like so many others Nell had interviewed. Her home was tidy, she was well-dressed, and she spoke about her girls in a way that was honest and beautiful and practical, not sentimental. If Easter admired her mother, Nell could see why.

'My father begged me not to let you go ahead with the book,' Easter went on. 'Apparently the parasites are back to give them more trouble.'

'Parasites?' Nell asked.

'Yes,' Easter said. 'And I don't mean the press. My parents think it's those little shits with their laptops in their parents' basements, making prank calls and playing games.'

Nell sat very still, but her heart was pounding. Easter was talking about the mannequins left in the pool. This was the very thing Nell had wanted to ask her about, and now she had an opening to let Easter think this subject matter was her own idea.

'People have been giving you trouble?' Nell asked.

'It's all Autumn,' Easter said simply. 'I told you. It's always been her.'

'Does Autumn ever try to contact you?' Nell asked.

'Of course,' Easter said. She tapped her fingertip against her temple. She had small, dainty hands, which were in contrast to the rest of her haggard

321

frame. She looked as though she had been assembled using pieces from both the elderly and the young.

Nell afforded Easter a quizzical expression. She knew that Easter wanted this reaction.

'I bet you think we're like psychic twins you'd read about in a horror novel,' Easter said. 'But the truth is we were more like an old married couple than anything. You spend every day literally joined to someone at the hip, you get to memorise each other, and then it doesn't matter that you've been cut apart like a string of paper dolls.' Easter cradled the bottom of the phone in her palm and leaned closer to the glass. 'I get letters in here,' she said. 'Most of them are garbage, but some of them are from Autumn. She doesn't sign them, but I know they are from her, even if no one believes me, not even Oleg. They say things only she would know.'

'What does she say in her letters?' Nell asked, trying her best not to sound sarcastic.

'Maybe one day I'll show you.' Easter stared at Nell, considering. 'I don't know for sure whether or not you're guilty. But that's fitting, isn't it? I don't know whether to believe you, just like you don't know whether to believe me.'

# 35
# THEN

On the morning of her arraignment, Nell stood, shivering, in a corner of the courtroom, partitioned by metal mesh. She was in a cage, her hands cuffed before her.

Not five yards away, Nell spotted Lindsay seated in the wooden pews. She met Nell's eyes, and her expression was stony and guarded; she was trying to coach Nell to do the same. Nell did her best.

Several rows behind Lindsay, she saw Ethan, and she thought she felt her heart go still. To his right sat Mrs and Mr Eddleton. None of them looked at her.

The judge banged her gavel, and Nell flinched. She hadn't opened her mouth and yet she'd already let Lindsay down.

Nell tried to focus on the judge. She was a middle-aged woman with jowls and a disinterested gaze.

'Penelope Wendall,' the bailiff said, his voice echoing in the tiny courtroom. 'Case number S9 dash 839218.'

'Is council present?' the judge asked.

Matthew raised two fingers of his left hand. 'Yes, your honour.'

'Read the charges,' the judge said.

A woman in a grey pantsuit read from a stapled stack of papers in her hand. 'Reckless endangerment resulting in the death of a child under the age of eighteen, which is a felony under Missouri state law, obstruction of justice and first-degree murder.'

'How does the defendant plead?' the judge asked.

It took Nell a moment to realise everyone was looking at her. 'Not guilty,' she managed, her voice hoarse.

Matthew took a step forward. 'Your honour, defence requests the accused be released on bail to her family. The defendant has no passport or contacts outside of the state of Missouri. There's nothing to indicate that she's a flight risk.'

The woman in the pantsuit was quick to argue. 'The defendant is accused of murdering her child and hindering the investigation.'

'I'm aware of the charges,' the judge said. Her flat expression indicated that she heard terrible things all day and she was unmoved by one more. 'Bail is set at one million dollars, with the defendant to be released to a blood relative and monitored by an ankle bracelet.'

'Thank you, your honour,' Matthew said. The judge slammed the gavel again. 'Next case on the docket, bailiff.'

Nell was transported back to the county jail and shoved into her cell. She had spent her first night in solitary confinement because her face was all over the news on the TV in the lounge.

She had just sat down on her bunk when a CO came to get her. 'Let's go, Wendall. You made bail.'

Nell was rushed through processing and changed back into the clothes she'd been wearing when she'd been arrested: pink cotton pyjama pants with sheep on them and a grey men's hoodie that said GAP across the chest in large white embroidery, which belonged to Ethan and still smelled like him even now.

'There you go, tagged and tracked,' a female CO said, after fitting a black monitor around Nell's ankle. 'It's waterproof, shatterproof, idiot-proof,' she said, clearly giving a memorised spiel. 'If you try to break it, it beeps. If you step outside to get the newspaper, it beeps. If you go anywhere without court approval, it beeps.'

Nell was escorted out into the lobby, and when she saw Lindsay standing there with teary blood-shot eyes, Nell ran faster than she ever had in her life. They clung to each other, and Lindsay kissed the top of her head. 'I'm so sorry,' Lindsay whispered. 'I posted bail as fast as I could.'

'You had a million dollars?' Nell sniffed.

'No, kiddo.' Lindsay drew back and wiped Nell's tears, and then her own, with her sleeve. 'You only have to put down ten per cent. We'll get it all back when you make your court appearance.'

She hadn't called Nell 'kiddo' since they were children. Nell realised now that she hadn't felt like a child in years and years. Before Reina was born, she had been someone entirely different. Motherhood had only been a small fraction of her life, and yet what motherhood lacked in quantity it made up for in volume. Even now without a child to reach for, she was drowning in it, like a mosquito in slow-drying resin.

Outside it was raining, and it was so dark that Nell wondered if the sun would ever come out again. As she ran for the car, with rain making her sweatshirt cling to her shoulders, she thought of Reina. Was she out there? Was she cold? Did she still think that her mother was coming to find her?

Matthew was in the driver's seat, and Lindsay climbed into the passenger seat next to him. The second the door was closed, he started driving. They had an hour to get home before Nell's ankle monitor would sound the alarm. She was being tracked in case they tried to take any detours.

'You did good in there,' Matthew said, though there was no kindness in his voice. 'The press will be all over our house by morning when they realise you made bail, so the blinds stay closed from now on. No looking outside for any reason, got it?'

Nell nodded, suddenly too exhausted to speak.

'Good,' he said. 'We'll start going over your

defence tonight. Once the jury has been selected, I'll get a better read on which angles to play.'

Lindsay reached into the back seat and grabbed Nell's hand, giving it a hard, reassuring squeeze. But Lindsay didn't offer any words of comfort. Of the two of them, Nell had always been the story-teller, and Lindsay had never learned how to spin an ugly truth into a pretty lie.

# 36

# NOW

It was raining by the time Nell turned out of the prison parking lot.

Lindsay had fallen asleep waiting in the car, but she stirred when the car hit a pothole. Nell glanced over and saw her eyes start to open.

'You have a better shot at this,' Nell said.

Lindsay pushed herself upright, blinking groggily. 'At what?'

'Motherhood,' Nell said. 'You raised me, and look how well I turned out.'

Lindsay smirked at the windshield wipers. 'Like a soufflé,' she said with a dazzling French accent.

She meant that sincerely, Nell knew. Growing up, it had never been Chuck or Bonnie's approval she sought. Her parents were distant relatives she visited sometimes, bearing drawings and wilted dandelions she'd plucked from the sidewalk. Lindsay was the one who was proud of her.

Thinking about it now, Nell was furious with Lindsay for enduring this pregnancy alone, but angrier still with herself for not thinking to check in with her sister. What was wrong with her? She was ordinarily so logical; ten anniversaries had passed since her daughter's disappearance, and with practice she had numbed herself to them. But not this year. The meteoric rise of her career may have had something to do with that, and Sebastian's increasing hints at an impending proposal. She feared marriage for the same reason Lindsay had ended hers: the expectations of a domestic life were too daunting.

'Hey.' Lindsay's eyes brightened. 'You took forever and I'm starving. Wanna get waffles?'

'Sure,' Nell said. 'Just so you know, Sebastian and I are due to have one of those long boring talks about our relationship.'

'You two are so disgusting when you're sweet,' Lindsay said.

'Linds?' Nell ventured. 'I think maybe I'm going to tell him the truth.'

'Truth?' Lindsay echoed, letting the word fill her mouth like a giant gumball. Then her eyes went wide. 'About—'

'About Reina. It's either tell him or end things now,' Nell said. 'I'll never be able to have an honest connection with him if I keep a secret like this.'

'First of all, you sound like an article I'd read in the gynaecologist's office,' Lindsay said. 'Second, there's no such thing as an honest relationship. Everyone lies to the person they're sleeping with.'

'Sebastian doesn't lie to me,' Nell said. 'Nine out of ten times, I know when the people I'm interviewing are lying to me. There's a quality.'

'A quality?'

'If they look at me the way you look at the entire world, I know they're lying.'

'Okay, now you're just being an asshole,' Lindsay said.

'I thought you'd be happy,' Nell said. 'It was *your* suggestion for me to tell him not that long ago.'

'That was to get ahead of Easter. I didn't know what that psycho was going to do, but now I think she was just playing with you. She won't tell him anything because it'll mean losing you as her little chew toy.' Lindsay sounded angry all of a sudden. This was how she used to get when she caught Nell smoking in middle school, and when she couldn't talk her into having an abortion. 'And what about your career? What if he not only leaves you but he goes to all your good friends at the press? They'll pick your life apart. You want to go through that again?'

'He wouldn't do that to me,' Nell said.

'Anyone is capable of anything,' Lindsay countered. 'You know that. Nell, this will ruin your goddamned life.'

'My life was already ruined that day,' Nell said. 'Do you honestly think that things can ever be normal for me? For either of us? Don't kid yourself, Lindsay. You love to say that we're unbreakable, but we're already broken. We started out broken.'

'You're just feeling sorry for yourself,' Lindsay

said. 'You do that. You make everything out to be catastrophic just so you have an excuse not to fight when things get hard.'

'You're one to talk.' Nell snorted. 'What about Robert? You gave up on someone who was good for you because you didn't want to start a family with someone who loved you and treated you like the fucking centre of the universe. And for what? To have a baby with the man who tried to murder you.'

'Matthew did not try to murder me!' They were both shouting now. The tendons in Lindsay's neck bulged and her face had turned pink. 'You weren't there for all of it. You don't know anything about it!'

'I know what it looks like when someone is trying to kill someone,' Nell cried.

'I provoked him, Nell. I provoked the hell out of him that day. You didn't see that part.'

Nell shook her head. 'Oh my god,' she muttered. 'You haven't learned anything at all. You're really going to take him back. You're going to make me bury you.'

'Don't be dramatic,' Lindsay said.

'You think I've never written this one?' Nell said. 'I have. Right now Matthew has you vulnerable and he's playing to that. You think he's changed and he'll worship this baby and treat you like a queen. He won't, Linds. He'll panic. He won't want to be shackled to a baby – all the screaming and the smell of shit and how tired you'll be. Your stomach is going to get bigger and Matthew will have his epiphany that he'll always be second to this baby. He won't be able to control you.'

'Nell,' Lindsay growled; a warning.

'He'll kill you both. You'll be on one of those missing posters, everyone praying for a miracle. Meanwhile you and your giant stomach will be anchored to the bottom of the Hudson. Did you know that the body expels the foetus post-mortem? It's called a coffin birth. All the gases in your stomach will build as you decompose until it just pushes everything out. That's where you'll be while church groups are combing fields with flashlights and calling your name.'

'Shut up!' Lindsay roared. Nell looked over and saw tears streaming down Lindsay's face; her lips were wet and quivering. Lindsay sobbed and wiped her nose with her wrist. 'Just shut up.'

Nell wasn't sorry. Lindsay needed to hear it. She needed to be scared. She needed to be reminded of what Matthew Cranlin was. He wielded his masks with finesse, but Nell had not forgotten the putrid monster he was underneath all of them.

They weren't even on the interstate yet, and already she and Lindsay wanted to kill each other. This was so typical, to get into an argument in the middle of nowhere. She said nothing, though the anxiety of it made her stomach hurt. She stared

333

ahead at the road that revealed itself through the November fog.

Too late, she saw something lying across the asphalt. A plank, Nell thought, or a dead coyote. She felt strangely calm as she slammed the brakes and swerved. She heard the thuds as the tires were blown out by a spike strip. She felt the force of the car spinning. Her head hit something, hard. The world filled with stars bleeding stars.

# 37
## THEN

Matthew never asked what happened on the morning Reina disappeared. Instead, when they returned to the house, he sat across from Nell at the kitchen table and he asked her only what he thought was relevant. He paused after each of Nell's responses to take notes.

'Were you alone with Reina when you left the house that morning?'

'No.'

'Who was with you?'

'Ethan.' Nell tugged at a piece of her hair.

Matthew raised his eyes. 'Stop that. Don't fidget. When you get into the courtroom, jurors are going to analyse your every move. You need to learn to sit still. Have no reaction no matter how upsetting some of these things will be to hear.'

Nell straightened her posture. She folded her hands neatly on the table.

'Was Ethan with you when you went to the grocery store?'

'No.'

'Good job. Where was he?'

'At school,' Nell said. 'I dropped him off.'

'I didn't ask you if you dropped him off.' Matthew pointed his pen at her. 'Never volunteer extra information. The prosecutor will be a shark. Anything you say will be turned into something incriminating.'

Nell wanted to cry but she didn't let herself.

Matthew stared at his notepad, considering something. Though the interrogation frightened her, Nell preferred this side of Matthew. It was more predictable, at least. He was focused and driven and calm. It didn't matter that he hated her. She had landed herself at the heart of a high-profile case and he was determined to win it. This was going to bolster his already thriving career. For now, Matthew loved her, because Matthew Cranlin loved anyone he could use.

'How did you meet Ethan?' Matthew asked.

'At a party,' Nell said, mindful not to volunteer extra information.

'You had sex that night?'

'Yes.'

'Were you drunk?'

'A-a little.' Nell's voice faltered. She'd had a couple of beers in red Solo cups, but she hadn't exactly been too drunk to know what she was doing. She remembered the entire night. She'd been dragged out by Shayne, the only girl in her latest group home who was nice to her.

'How old were you, do you remember?' Matthew pressed.

'I was fourteen.'

'And how old was Ethan?'

'Seventeen.' It was easy for Nell to recall little details like this. She was always storing them in her brain like pieces of trivia. She collected things that weren't important to anyone else, the way children collected seashells and pebbles and called them treasure.

Lindsay was sitting on the counter, sipping a glass of merlot. She found Nell's eyes and gave her the same look of encouragement she'd given Nell when she answered a question right on her homework. *Great job, kiddo.*

Matthew was grinning at his notepad.

'What is it?' Lindsay asked. 'Did you figure something out?'

'The age of consent in the state of Missouri is seventeen,' Matthew said, ignoring Lindsay's question and looking at Nell. 'It doesn't matter how drunk or sober you were. He was old enough to give consent and you weren't. That's statutory rape.'

'Rape?' Nell parroted back, her voice too loud. 'He didn't rape me.'

'Actually, he did.' Matthew tapped the back of his pen against the pad. 'And we've just found our defence.'

Lindsay slid off of the counter and took the chair beside Nell. 'What do you mean?' she asked.

Matthew's eyes were bright. He was excited, inspired. 'How could anyone think you'd kill your daughter?' he said to Nell. 'You didn't have the agency to do something like that. You've never had any agency in this relationship at all. You were an underage girl who met a young man at a party. He took advantage of you and got you pregnant. Then, because he had all the money and the influence and you had nothing, he kept you in his parents' home. He used you for sex whenever he wanted it, and then he went back to his expensive school, and later to college, leaving you at home to take care of his child.'

Nell felt sick hearing the spin he put on her relationship with Ethan. On the surface, much of what he said was true. Nell had been forced to drop out of high school when the toll of caring for Reina was too taxing, but Ethan had never so much as been late for a class. He didn't even appreciate it; he hated school, he didn't know what he wanted to do with his life. Nell was the one with dreams, and nobody ever asked about those.

But Ethan wasn't the one who held her back. Ethan wasn't the one who chipped away at her confidence and her social life and her ability to write. That was all Reina.

Wasn't it? Suddenly it all felt murky. Nell had been too many days without her daughter, and she couldn't get a clear picture of her face.

'Did Ethan have other girlfriends?' Matthew asked.

'Sometimes.' Nell shifted uncomfortably in her chair, then remembered to sit still. Because Matthew had told her to never volunteer extra information, she didn't tell him that she'd never cared who Ethan slept with, as awkward as it was when Nell got up late at night to pee and heard his latest conquest flushing the toilet. They loved each other the way that old friends did, but there was no expectation that they would ever marry or be exclusive. Even when they did have sex, there was no romance. There never had been.

'Did you have other boyfriends?' Matthew asked.

'No,' Nell said. Again, she didn't volunteer the rest. She didn't date anyone else because nobody would want a girl with a child, much less a girl who lived with the father of that child. But this was irrelevant anyway, because she was too tired for sex, and her ineptitude as a mother made her feel too ugly and unwanted to try.

'Ethan Eddleton stole your life, Penelope,' Matthew said, slamming his hand on the table and making Lindsay flinch. 'You were a young girl. A young, *intelligent* girl with her whole life ahead of her, and he took control over everything you did. And the prosecution wants to accuse you of murdering your child? Please. You didn't have the power to do that.'

'No,' Nell burst out, finally reaching her limit. She jumped to her feet. 'I'm not going to say that. I'm not going to say that Ethan raped me, or that he killed Reina.'

'Maybe he didn't kill her on purpose,' Matthew shot back without missing a beat. 'Maybe it was an accident, and he panicked, and he forced you to cover it up the way he forced you to do everything since the night you met. And now he's home with his parents while you're the one going to trial.'

'Stop it,' Nell cried.

'Sit down,' Matthew said.

'No!'

'You've already spent most of your teen years in a cage,' Matthew burst out. 'Do you want to spend the rest of your life in one?'

Nell stood there in silence, letting the words sink in.

Then she sat back down.

# 38
# NOW

The turn signal was ticking. It was a tiny heartbeat in a world that had gone still.

Nell opened her eyes. Her skirt was wet and clinging to her thighs. At first she thought it was blood, but clarity returned and she realised that it had begun to snow, and it was coming in fast through the broken windshield.

Lindsay was beside her, slumped over the dashboard in a shower spray of glass.

Nell tried to call for her, but no sound would come out. She wrestled with her seatbelt, tugging weakly until she found the cognisance to press the release.

She leaned over to her sister. 'Linds.' Her voice was hoarse. She wanted to scream. Why couldn't she scream? 'Lindsay.'

Lindsay moaned. She tried to lift her head off of the dashboard but fell unconscious again.

'Lindsay.' It was all Nell could think to say. It was the only word that meant anything. 'Lindsay!'

Nell could taste blood in her mouth and she knew that she was going to lose consciousness too.

Screaming at her sister would do nothing. If she fell asleep now, they would both die here.

She struggled with the door. Her arms felt so weak. Her vision blurred and doubled. Tugging on the handle did nothing. She threw her weight against the door, toppled out into the wet grass and mud.

The road looked as though it were a thousand miles away. Nothing made sense. And still, something told her to go forward. She crawled, sliding in the mud, grasping at grass that broke apart in her fingers. She fell against the earth, and it was so soft, cold at first and then warmed by her skin. Her eyes closed.

*No*. She forced herself back awake. Making it to the road would have to be enough. It was all that she could do.

Headlights burned against the fog. There was the sound of tires skidding. Brakes. A door opening.

'Nell?' She knew that voice.

She saw his shoes, and that was the thing that made her remember. Oleg was always particular about his loafers. They were polished shiny leather, but now they were caked with mud.

It was strange that he was here. Nell knew this, on some distant level.

Arms hooked under her armpits, hoisting her up. She tried to take a step and staggered forward. He was here, and he was trying to help her. She collapsed against the side of his car. It smelled familiar, bringing up the faraway memory of the morning he'd picked her up. And it smelled like him. How had she never noticed that? It smelled the way he'd tasted when he kissed her out in the cold.

He was saying something, but he sounded like he was underwater and Nell couldn't make out the words.

'Wait,' she heard herself saying. 'My sister is still in the car.'

She collapsed against something hard. There was the sound of a door slamming, and then silence.

✳

# THEN

Reina disappeared in November, and by January of the following year, the case had gone to trial. Nell sat at the defence table beside Matthew, her muscles tense and her gaze set forward. Despite the chill in the air, she could feel the sweat gathering in her armpits and above her upper lip. She could taste the tears in her throat, but she didn't cry. They had been rehearsing this at home. Matthew called her every awful thing the press was going to dole out. He called her a slut, a baby killer, a manipulative psychopath. He said it over and over, until Nell learned that they were only words and that they had no power over her.

But despite everything, the prosecutor's opening statement pierced through her defences. She was a tall, slim woman whose high heels slapped the tile floor with every step. Her dark hair was pulled into a severe ponytail.

'Ladies and gentlemen of the jury, good morning. My name is Belinda Ambrose and I represent the state of Missouri. There will be several witnesses called in this case. The first will be a clerk from the Saveway grocery store where the defendant reported her daughter missing. The next will be a professor from the university where the defendant's boyfriend attended class at the time of this incident. The third will be a paediatrician who treated the defendant's child after a near-fatal allergic reaction to a bee sting.' She strode to the trial exhibits and hefted a 2x4 piece of cardboard and brought it to the easel beside the witness box. She flipped the card-board to face the jurors and the courtroom as she set it onto the easel.

It was the photo of Reina in her denim overalls with hearts for buttons. Her hand was up over her forehead, sweeping the curls from her dark eyes and heavy lashes, and her mouth was open and upturned as though about to smile.

The prosecutor went on. 'One witness who will not be called to the stand is Reina Eddleton, because the defendant is accused of killing her. The defence will try to portray the defendant, Penelope Wendall, as a defenceless little girl because she was a teenage mother. This is an act the defendant has used for her entire life.'

Nell's mind went dark. Her vision clouded until nothing made sense. The photo of her daughter was just a blur of colours and shapes. She heard, but didn't understand, the rest of the words the prosecutor was saying.

Ethan was in the room, seated somewhere behind her. She could feel his eyes boring through her. She could feel what he was thinking, and it frightened her.

When the prosecution was done, it was Matthew's turn. He stood, adjusting his cufflinks, and flawlessly dispensed the story he'd been rehearsing for months. Not to appear rattled by the prosecution's tactics, he left the photo of Reina on the easel.

Nell wanted the photo taken down. She wanted it gone. She felt sick, but she couldn't look away.

Matthew told the courtroom that Nell had been a young mother, that she'd been manipulated, mentally abused and shut up in the cage that was the Eddletons' home.

Through the corner of her eye, Nell saw a woman holding a giant pad and pastel pencils. She was sketching the courtroom, and Nell wondered how she must have looked, sitting there in the itchy white blouse and grey pencil skirt Matthew had chosen for her. She wondered if she looked like a teenage girl or a cold-blooded murderer.

The court adjourned for lunch at noon, and Matthew held Nell's forearm under the table, keeping her in place until the courtroom was empty. Then, he led her out into the hallway.

Her legs were shaking and she leaned against the wall, beneath a placard that read COURTROOM B.

'You did great in there,' Matthew said. 'But focus on keeping your mouth in a straight line. It looked too much like you were trying not to cry.'

Nell *had* been trying not to cry, but all she said was, 'Where's Lindsay?'

'I asked her not to speak to you here,' Matthew said. 'We're not in the courtroom, but the people are still looking for any opportunity to scrutinise you. Right now, we focus on getting you something to eat and maintaining your stamina.'

In all the commotion of the crowded courthouse, Nell didn't hear the telltale clatter of high-heeled shoes.

'Penelope?'

Nell spun around to see Mrs Eddleton standing in the hallway. Her hair was pulled back into a beehive, teased and sprayed to hide the fact that it was thinning. She towered over Nell in height, as always, but she looked smaller somehow, as though she'd shrunk in the months since Nell had seen her last. Her eyes were steely and bright and shining with tears. She raised a hand and slapped Nell across the face.

The sound echoed against the tiles.

'Fuck you,' Mrs Eddleton hissed between her clenched teeth. It was the first time Nell had ever heard her curse. Security ran to detain her and she didn't fight the guard who took her by the arm. Her eyes were still on Nell as she was pulled back. 'I hope you burn in hell.'

# 39
# NOW

The cold woke her. It bit into her skin like thousands of tiny teeth.

Nell opened her eyes and found that she was staring up at the darkening sky. It was just after sunset, and there were still ribbons of light fading away on the horizon.

Her vision blurred. She tasted blood, and then she remembered losing control of the car. She remembered Lindsay slumped over, barely breathing. This was the thought that gave her just enough adrenaline to move.

Her wrist was sprained. Hot red pain shot up her arm when she tried to move it.

She tried to move again, and a loud groan escaped her. She was in the woods, she knew that much. But the woods had been set back far from the road, hadn't they? Nell tried to think. Had she been thrown from the car?

Oleg. Had she dreamed him? No. She was sure that she'd leaned against his car. She'd felt the cold metal of the door handle, pressed her forehead against the open doorframe.

'Lindsay?' she managed to croak. She pushed herself up using her good arm. Her legs were numb with cold, and most of her body felt like dead weight, but she didn't think anything was broken.

'Lindsay!'

She heard the sound of something scraping. Heavy breathing. Grunting. Her vision filled with stars. She tried to breathe, and slowly the stars settled.

But even though her vision was clear, she didn't understand what she was seeing. Oleg was standing three yards away, holding a shovel and stepping on the blade so that it cut through the frozen dirt. What was he doing here? Why had he left her on the ground?

He didn't seem to notice her at first, but then without looking up, he said, 'Did you have a nice nap?'

Snow was still falling in wisps, and the grass was covered with it.

'Oleg?' her voice was scratchy. Her mind was full of questions, but her brain wouldn't latch on to any of them. They were so far into the woods that she couldn't even see the road. But she saw Oleg's car parked in a clearing twenty, maybe twenty-five yards away.

Her eyes went back to the shovel in his hand. The ground was so frozen that he must have been here digging for hours.

Her blood ran cold. No, he hadn't been digging for hours. He'd dug the hole for Nell already, and now he was just widening it so that it could fit Lindsay's body too. It was clear that Lindsay was an unexpected complication.

'Lindsay!' Nell screamed with everything that was left in her. Somehow, she managed to get to her feet. She took one step before Oleg swung the shovel at the back of her knees, and she fell. But she didn't stop screaming. Not until he knelt over her and put a hand over her mouth.

'Listen to me,' he said. 'Your sister isn't going to answer. Nobody can save you.'

Nell stared up into his eyes. They were the same familiar blue. His hair was still neatly parted, only a little dishevelled at the front. He was the same and not the same all at once.

She could taste the fibres of his gloves, and she inhaled deeply. If he was going to murder her, she wanted those fibres in her mouth, in her lungs. It might be the only evidence the police had to go by when they found her. If they found her.

❋

# THEN

'Your honour, I'd like to present Exhibit G,' the prosecutor announced.

A hush fell over the courtroom as Belinda Ambrose hauled Reina's car seat, encased in a large evidence bag, across the courtroom. She slammed it down on the table that had been brought to the centre of the court.

'You'll notice safety pins and duct tape on the seat-belt,' Ambrose said, gesturing to the evidence like a grim Vanna White. 'Ladies and gentlemen, people of the state of Missouri, you'll hear testimony from Reina's grandparents that these accessories were *routine.* You'll hear them testify that the defend-ant' – she pointed to Nell – 'duct taped and pinned her child into this car seat, claiming it was because she knew how to escape. Please refer back to my earlier Exhibit A.' She tapped her finger against the enlarged photo of Reina, still resting in the easel.

'This picture was taken just weeks before Reina Eddleton was reported missing. Now direct your atten-tion back to this car seat. It's a new model. It appears to be in proper working order. Ladies and gentlemen, the entire purpose of a car seat is to keep children safe and secure. Reina was not Harry Houdini. She didn't possess superhuman strength. She was only a little girl, powerless to her mother's whims.'

Nell was sitting beside Matthew at the defendant's table. She held her breath until her chest ached. Over the course of the morning and afternoon, she'd lost count of how many times her daughter's name had been used. It was like a weapon being drawn against her, this name she'd given her daughter when she first held her in that hospital bed. She never could have imagined that it would come to this.

'See this, here?' Ambrose went on. Extending her manicured finger, she traced a line in the air around the car seat. There was a stain in the upholstery. 'This stain is urine. That urine belongs to Reina Eddleton, who was so terrified of her mother's abuse that she wet herself.'

'Your honour, objection!' Matthew stood, sounding more irritated than angry. 'That's pure speculation.'

'I'll withdraw,' Ambrose said quickly. But her smile said that she had already made her point. The jurors had already formed the image in their minds. Nell didn't let herself look at the jurors. She didn't dare. But she could feel their eyes on her. She could feel their disgust.

✳

# NOW

Nell didn't scream again. She had to appear compliant, or Oleg might kill her before she had a chance to escape.

He let go of her and allowed her to sit up, her back pressed against a tree.

*Where's Lindsay?* Was she in Oleg's car? In the trunk perhaps? He wouldn't have left her in Nell's vehicle by the side of the road; someone might have spotted her and called for help.

Nell tried to think. She couldn't hear traffic, but that didn't mean they were far from the road; they had been on a back road when they crashed, and not a lot of cars came by.

'Why are you doing this?' Nell asked, though she didn't expect a straight answer. A conversation would prolong the inevitable, giving her time to regain her strength. She felt for the pepper spray she kept zippered in her coat pocket, but the pocket was empty. Oleg must have taken it when she was unconscious. 'Is this about money? Because—'

'This isn't about money,' Oleg said, and for a moment he sounded like the congenial Oleg she had known. He changed as easily as Easter switched between her Russian and American accents.

Night had fallen, and it was getting harder for Nell to see him. He was kneeling a few feet before her, setting up a tripod and mounting his phone so that the screen faced Nell.

He was going to record her, Nell thought.

'This is about the truth,' he said. 'Yours. Mine.'

Nell tried not to let her shock show on her face, but she could see her expression on the screen, a mix of horror and surprise.

'Easter told you about my daughter,' she said.

Oleg smirked. 'Of course she did. Who else does she have to talk to? I'm the only one who visits. And she was so excited that you might write about her. Prove her innocence.'

Nell heard something rustle in the leaves. She cast a fleeting glance toward the sound, and then her attention fixed back on Oleg. She hoped it was Lindsay. Her situation would only be made worse if Oleg had an accomplice.

'You hide who you really are,' Oleg went on. 'But I can see it. Do you know why?' He leaned closer, though he stayed behind his phone so that his image wouldn't be recorded. But what about his voice? Surely someone would recognise it. *No.* He could edit it however he wanted, distort his voice.

'It's because you're just like Autumn,' Oleg answered his own question.

Nell's breathing hitched.

'As long as Autumn was attached to Easter, she was trapped. But even as a child, she found ways to do it without getting caught. Dogs, rodents.'

Nell wondered if she was delirious, if she was hallucinating. But the more Oleg spoke, the more awake she felt. She was trapped by her own horrified curiosity.

'Easter tried to stop her,' he went on. 'She would scream. But one day, Autumn jumped in the small pond near our house, pulling Easter with her. Easter tried to fight her, but Autumn held them both underwater. She stayed underwater until she'd made her point. If Easter didn't let her have her way, Autumn would kill them both.'

Easter, screaming for help. Easter, covered in bruises and burns, which Autumn told Mrs Hamblin were self-inflicted. Easter, recoiling into the shadows and taking all the blame.

'It was Autumn?' Nell managed to ask. 'Who killed the rabbit? Who hurt those children?'

'Of course it was Autumn!' Oleg snapped. 'You should have figured that out by now. The killers are the ones who look just like us. Who look just like you.' He paused. 'We did it together.'

Nell shook her head. 'I didn't kill my daughter, Oleg.'

'Reina's body was never found. We both know your defence was bullshit, but the jurors voted not guilty. They couldn't justify putting a teenage girl to death without any physical evidence of a murder.'

'There's no evidence because I *didn't do it*. I didn't—' She gasped, sobbed. 'I didn't kill her.'

356

He shook his head, his white-blond hair practically glowing. 'You want to do this the hard way.'

'Why are you doing this?' Nell let her words come out as a whimper. 'What do you want?'

'It's only fair,' Oleg said. 'You deserve some justice.'

'I was found not guilty!' Tears sprung to her eyes.

'Don't take it so personally,' Oleg said. 'Really, this is about me. Do you know what it was like, watching my little sister get away with killing anything she pleased? She could finesse her way out of anything. Anything. All she had to do was smile.'

Nell's mind spun furiously. A new picture emerged, not of one homicidal child but of two. A brother who dreamt of murder and a sister who pulled it off. Over and over.

Understanding this meant understanding that he was going to kill her. She refused to accept it, even as her body sat frozen. If she couldn't run, she would bargain. She would buy herself some time.

'If Easter didn't kill Autumn then who did?' she asked, as though this was just another interview at the diner.

In answer, Oleg reached for the phone mounted on the tripod. Not to record, Nell realised, but to show her something.

The video began someplace grainy and dark. In woods just like these, late in the evening as the sun was beginning to set. The camera moved erratically and there was heavy breathing.

The camera eventually settled on a child lying face up in the dirt. The dark lighting covered most of the features, and all Nell could clearly see was a red coat and a smattering of bright red hair.

No. Not hair. It was blood.

'What did you do?' Oleg's voice was breathy and raw from the camera. It was his voice, to be certain, but Nell had never heard him speak in this tone.

'He was a spoiled brat.' Easter's voice, in her full American accent. She sounded giddy, effervescent. The camera moved to her shoes – red ballet flats with white bows at the tops. 'Always egging our door on Halloween, pissing in the window boxes.'

'We agreed,' Oleg said. He sounded frustrated, but not at all horrified or surprised.

'*You* agreed,' Easter said. 'You and your stupid rules. What is that? Are you recording?'

The camera was raised, showing her face for the first time. And in that moment Nell realised that she could tell the twins apart, after all. Through her interactions with Easter, she'd learned her gestures. She had the presence of a child who had grown up unwanted, who had learned to shrink into the shadows, and who could only feign confidence in short bursts. Nell was like her in that way.

But Autumn had the stony gaze of someone who feared nothing because she felt nothing. There was something missing from her pretty face. Something that Easter, for all her own hardships, had managed to keep.

The woman staring back at Nell on the screen was Autumn Hamblin. She was sure of it.

Oleg turned off the screen. 'I could show you the rest, but it's a family affair,' he said. 'Autumn and I had an understanding – or so I thought – that we would keep our games to smaller creatures. There's no story on the news if a couple of neighbourhood dogs go missing. But she couldn't control herself. I had to put a stop to it.'

*He killed Autumn*, Nell thought furiously. *Easter is innocent.*

Oleg rose to his feet. Nell lost sight of him in the darkness, then he was illuminated by the dim light in the trunk of his car. He reached for something inside. And then there was another figure being pulled to its feet.

A flash of blonde hair.

No. Nell's breathing came in rapid bursts. She saw her own reflection in the phone screen, gasping. Oleg strode briskly towards her again, dragging Lindsay, who stumbled. Her hands were bound together, Nell realised, and there was a strip of duct tape wrapped around her head, covering her mouth.

Oleg shoved Lindsay and she fell hard on her side at Nell's feet. Nell wanted to reach for her, to pull her upright, to comfort her. It was instinct, what they always did. But she knew that showing any affection towards her sister would only provoke Oleg.

Oleg stood over them. He reached for something at his hip, and then there was the unmistakable click of a handgun. Beside Nell, Lindsay was stone still, and Nell knew that her sister was plotting her charge.

'Don't,' she whispered. *For once in your life, Linds, listen to me.*

'Have you figured it out yet, Nell?' Oleg asked.

How had she missed so many signs? Oleg had presented himself as the long-suffering brother, who struggled to forgive his sister for doing the unthinkable. But Nell could see the new image that emerged. He and Autumn were the same. And Easter was the perfect scapegoat. Was that all she had ever been to them? The weaker twin. The alibi.

'You killed Autumn,' Nell said. As she heard the words, she realised they made sense. 'Easter is innocent.'

Oleg laughed. 'Easter will believe whatever I tell her. It's a game Autumn and I used to play with her. I suppose we're still playing it even now. I told her that Autumn had gotten herself into some trouble and run away. I convinced her to dress as Autumn to cover for her – it was easy enough; nobody ever saw them both out in public together. I send her letters as if from Autumn, make her think she is still out there. Make everyone else think she's crazy for saying so. Contrary to what everyone thinks about twins, Easter hated our sister.'

'Whaa?' Lindsay mumbled through the tape over her lips. Nell kicked her so she'd be silent. She couldn't trust Lindsay not to infuriate their captor.

'It was you, wasn't it,' Nell said. 'The mannequins, and chasing me off the road that night.'

'You're the one who drove yourself into that swamp,' Oleg said, sounding irritated. 'I was only going to scare you.' He smiled. 'Autumn and I always enjoyed playing with our kills. It is better for them to be scared before the end.'

Nell remembered Lindsay's stolen phone. How Oleg had arrived a mere twenty minutes after she had called him. Hadn't she thought at the time that it was too quick? But of course, he hadn't been coming from the motel. He'd just had to turn around. She forced herself not to be combative, even as the anger and the fear ran laps inside her brain. All she said was, 'Why?'

'Autumn upped the ante, not me,' Oleg said. 'She put up quite a fight. Stabbed me in the side. Thankfully she didn't hit anything vital – don't know how I would have explained it if I'd gone to the emergency room.' He gave a congenial laugh that chilled Nell to her core. 'But I gained the upper hand. And as I was strangling her there in the dirt, beside her final victim, I was already mourning her.

What would I do without my favourite sister? Who else could possibly understand me? I even cried as I cleaned up her mess.

'But after that? After that it felt satisfying. I want to clean more messes like that. When Easter told me about what you'd done to your little girl, it was like Autumn sent me a gift from the great beyond. Poor Easter. She thought she'd found another innocent, falsely accused, someone who would believe her.'

Oleg fiddled with the phone again, and Nell could hear the chime it gave as he pressed record.

'And of course, there is the matter of your book. I could not allow you to write it, to perhaps discover the truth. You see, I truly believe you are good at your job. Easter must stay where she is. For my sake.' He leaned over her, so close she could feel the heat of his breath on her lips. 'And I will enjoy this necessity. I'm going to rid the world of another killer.'

❋

# THEN

Ethan sat tall on the witness stand. If his mother appeared to have shrunk since Reina's disappearance, Ethan appeared to have grown. He was taller than Nell remembered. His hair, normally messy, was gelled into neat curls that resembled Reina's.

Belinda Ambrose asked him to state his name for the record, and when he did, his voice was deeper than Nell remembered. She had known him since he was seventeen years old, and living across the hall from him had familiarised her with all of his moods. But now, at twenty-two years old, for the first time he looked like a man.

'Please tell the jurors your relationship to Reina Eddleton,' Ambrose said. She turned theatrically to face the court.

Ethan bowed his head closer to the microphone. 'I'm her father.'

Nell made herself look at him, but he didn't look at her.

'Mr Eddleton, would you say that you were Reina's primary caregiver?'

'No.'

'And who was her primary caregiver?'

'Penelope.' It was strange for Nell to hear him say her name like that. For years, he had only called her Penny.

Ethan pointed at Nell and their eyes met. Nell looked for any sign of the boy who'd sobbed into her shoulder on their last night together. But she barely recognised him at all.

'Mr Eddleton, would you say the defendant was a good mother?'

'She was okay.'

'Just okay?'

Ethan shrugged, and for a moment Nell recognised him. Even dressed in a custom-tailored suit, he had never been comfortable with formalities.

'Mr Eddleton, please elaborate.'

'She lost patience with Reina a lot,' he said. 'It caused fights between us.'

'Objection, your honour,' Matthew said, standing. 'My client isn't on trial because she argued with her boyfriend about diaper rash.'

Ambrose rolled her eyes. 'I'm establishing intent, your honour.'

'I'll allow it,' the judge said.

Nell's jaw tensed. Matthew picked up on it immediately and nudged her foot under the table.

'Mr Eddleton, did the defendant ever strike your child?' Ambrose asked.

'No,' Ethan answered.

'Did she ever yell at your child?'

'No. She always took it out on me.' Ethan squirmed uncomfortably. 'But I worried about leaving her alone with Reina when she was angry.'

'Please elaborate.'

Ethan lowered his head, and Nell's stomach clenched. If she'd been able to eat anything today, she would have vomited right there on the table. She knew this look. He was averting his gaze, and his voice had lowered to a mumble. He only did this when he was lying.

'Because one time she told me, "I can't look at her. I'll kill her if I do."'

The lie bore straight through her, and for the first time during the entire trial, Nell had to restrain herself from standing up and screaming her protest.

She stared at Ethan, willing him to look at her. But he didn't.

\*

# NOW

Oleg was dragging Lindsay away from Nell towards the hole. She twisted in his grasp, kicking the tripod over in her fury. The phone fell into the snow with a soft thud, and Nell flinched. Oleg threw Lindsay to the ground, and Nell was certain that Oleg was going to shoot her. She rose, scrabbling frantically to find her feet, and sprinted towards them, hearing the phone's screen shatter under her heel as she ran.

Oleg shouted something in Russian and pointed the gun at her. Nell knew she couldn't stop now. She charged forward with what strength she had left and launched herself on top of him, jamming her knees into his torso. Pain shot up from her wounded wrist and she screamed, primal. She screamed in pain, and she screamed for Lindsay to get the gun.

Lindsay was upright now. She raised her taped

hands over her head, and in one deft, fast motion, swung her arms down. The force of the movement ripped the duct tape, and she was free. Something she'd doubtless learned in those self-defence classes she took after divorcing Matthew.

Nell reeled back and punched Oleg, hard. Then she heard a loud bang, saw the muzzle flash.

*Lindsay's shot him. She'll be put on trial for murder.*

Then she felt the burning pain in her side, and the world shook on its axis. Oleg was still holding the gun, and he let out a roar and threw himself forward, Nell pinned beneath him. She drew up her legs, trying to kick him off, but the pain made her body lock up. All she could do was thrash under the weight of him.

The cold barrel of the gun touched her temple.

'Tell me what you did to her!' he grunted. 'Tell me what you did to Reina!'

There was the click of the barrel turning. Nell knew that he was going to kill her.

Then there was a loud thump of the shovel. Oleg moaned and turned to dead weight on top of her.

'Come on,' Lindsay was saying, the duct tape now hanging from her chin. She grabbed the gun from Oleg's slack hand and kicked his sodden form, until he rolled off Nell. 'Come on, come on,' Lindsay said again, and Nell didn't know who she was talking to. Stars exploded across her vision, but she managed to get to her feet. She climbed into the passenger side of Oleg's car, and Lindsay fired up the ignition. She spun the car into a U-turn and sped down the narrow path between the trees.

'Shit, shit, shit,' Lindsay said. 'Nell? Goddamn it, Nell, open your eyes. Stay with me.'

'Is he following us?' Nell's voice came as little more than a breath. Her eyelids were heavy, but she lifted them just enough to see trees blurring by, lit up by the high beams.

'No,' Lindsay said.

Nell shook her head. It rolled lazily against the headrest of her seat. 'Linds, we have to tell the police where he is.'

'Fuck Oleg. I'm more worried about you.'

'Listen to me.' Nell's words were starting to slur. 'We can't just leave him there.'

'He's probably dead,' Lindsay said. 'I hit him pretty hard with that shovel.'

'Tell the police,' Nell panted, 'about his phone. They can still get his video from the cloud. Proof you acted in self-defence.'

'Tell them yourself,' Lindsay said.

'This is important,' Nell said. 'I'm trying to save your fucking life.'

'Fuck that – I'm trying to save yours!' Lindsay cried. Nell could feel the engine vibrations under her feet. She didn't know how fast they were going, but the world was a blur.

'I'm sorry,' Nell murmured.

'Nell.' Lindsay's voice was loud and stern, but it wasn't enough to keep Nell awake.

'I'm really sorry.'

'Nell!'

First, everything went quiet. And then it went black.

# 40

# THEN

After Nell was acquitted, she would see Ethan one last time. It was a year later. Though northern Missouri was still peppered with missing posters of Reina's face, the trial was old news. The nation was now obsessed with a wealthy Massachusetts couple accused of running a sex traffic ring out of their Zumba studio.

Lindsay was in the final stages of her divorce, and in one week's time, both sisters would leave Missouri. Penelope Wendall would become Nell Way; she would make it official once she became a resident of New York State.

Nell had been sitting in the courtyard behind the hotel where she and Lindsay were staying. Ethan's shadow eclipsed the pages of Nell's notebook, and she looked up.

'You're writing again,' Ethan said, with a contrite smile. 'I'm glad to see it.'

She looked back at her page. 'What do you want?'

Ethan sat on the bench beside her. The smell of his cologne and shampoo took Nell right back to the Eddletons' house. Back to the life that felt like it had ended a million years ago.

'The prosecutor coached me,' he said. 'She made me say those things.'

'Funny, I didn't see any marionette strings,' Nell replied.

'She said that the defence would blame me. And she was right. But you were the one on trial, so as long as you were acquitted in the end, I knew we'd both be able to move on after the verdict.'

Nell shrugged. 'What does it matter now? Everyone decided I was a monster whether you confirmed it or not.'

Ethan shouldn't have even been here. After the acquittal, Matthew had filed a lawsuit against the Eddletons on Nell's behalf for emotional distress and harassment as a result of Mrs Eddleton's slap in the courthouse. The suit was settled privately, and one of the terms was that the Eddletons were no longer allowed to speak to or about Nell in a public setting; they weren't allowed to implicate her in Reina's disappearance. In return, Nell wasn't allowed to give any interviews regarding the Eddletons.

'My attorney said you were going to get off,' Ethan said. 'She knew that the prosecution had a weak case and the death penalty was too ambitious without proof.'

Nell shrugged. She drew a spiral on the page. She imagined that it was the portal to another dimension, and that she could reach a place in the universe where none of this had ever happened.

'I knew you could handle yourself and that you'd be okay, Penny. You always are.'

She sighed. 'You should go. Lindsay will kill me if she knows I'm talking to you.'

'I know, I just—' His voice caught, giving way to a moment of vulnerability.

Nell looked at him. 'Why did you come here?'

'I just miss her, Penny.' His eyes filled with tears. He knitted his hands together and stared down at them. 'You're the only one who would understand.'

Nell did understand. She had grieved for Reina over the past months. While the nation grieved for a sweet little girl with curly hair who disappeared into a late autumn sky, Nell had grieved for the real Reina. The child who never wanted to be held, who was only clever when she'd thought up some way to be cruel. The child who frightened her. The child who fascinated her. The person she had been, and the person she would never grow up to become.

But she couldn't bring herself to feel anything for Ethan. Not anymore.

'You shouldn't have said those things about me in court.'

'I'm sorry,' Ethan said. He sounded desperate and sad. 'I wish I hadn't. Everyone thought you were a monster and I confirmed it.'

'I don't care what the world thinks of me anymore,' Nell said. 'I just care about what's true.

And I never said that I wanted to hurt my daughter. I only said that I was tired of her hurting me.'

Ever since hearing Ethan's testimony against her, Nell had hated him. And even now, as she sat so close to him that she could smell his tears, she wasn't sure how much of that hatred was her own and how much of it had been put into her head by Matthew.

Had Ethan really controlled her for all those years? Manipulated her? Maybe. She didn't know.

But now that the trial was over and her duffel bag up in the hotel room was packed, she wasn't angry anymore. Ethan Eddleton was never meant to be a permanent place for her. He was just a prolonged foster home, and now that Nell was an adult, her days of sleeping in other people's houses were over. It was time for her to grow up and find a place of her own.

'Do you think we'll ever get her back?' Ethan asked.

'No,' Nell answered truthfully. She turned up the volume on the evening news whenever a body was found. She read the crime reports in every online newspaper in the country. All she ever saw were photos of children who didn't belong to her, and the start of someone else's horrible journey.

Ethan nodded. 'I guess I wanted to know if there was ever a time when things were … you know, good. Even if it was just for a minute.'

If Nell appeared to be considering this, it was

only because she had to muster the strength to say what she was thinking. Ethan had never asked her such a thing. No one had, not even the predatory reporters who'd asked her everything else. But Nell had asked herself a hundred times, and she knew the answer.

'Her last Christmas,' Nell said. 'I'd taken her to visit my mother in prison, and she was terrible the whole way there. But then on the ride back, I guess she'd exhausted herself. When we were getting close to the house, we passed that field near the elementary school. I stopped, because there were a bunch of wild turkeys crossing the street out in front of us. I thought Reina was asleep, but she sat up in her car seat and she asked me where the turkeys sleep at night so nothing eats them. I told her that they're wild birds. They fly up into the trees and they hide there until it's morning and the threat is gone. I looked at her in the mirror, and she was watching me. She had never been interested in any of the books I'd read to her or any of the stories I made up, but for once she was interested in what I was saying. She said, "I never saw a turkey in a tree," and I said, "That's because you never looked up." She smiled. But she caught me watching her in the mirror and she stopped.'

Nell was still staring at the courtyard, watching leaves skitter as they were pushed across the walkway by a gentle breeze.

'I've pictured every horrible thing that could have happened to her,' Nell said. She had seen what happened to missing children. She knew. 'But I think the reason we never found her in a ditch or stream or shallow grave is because she isn't in any of those places. She's hiding out of sight where the wild birds sleep, and she doesn't want to be found.'

✳

# NOW

'Fuck,' Lindsay said. Her voice was breathy, desperate, and the first thing Nell heard when she opened her eyes. 'Fuck,' Lindsay said again, and she leaned forward to kiss Nell's forehead so hard that it hurt. 'You scared the living piss out of me.'

*Are we still in Oleg's car?* That was Nell's thought. The room felt overly bright and unreal.

'Linds—' Her throat was so dry that she choked. Her body bucked and shuddered with pain.

'Don't move,' Lindsay said. 'You had surgery. There was a bullet right next to your fucking kidney.'

Nell focused on her sister's face. There were bruises on her forehead, turning yellow as they faded. A gash ran across her lower lip, tied shut with black-thread stitches.

'Sebastian's coming right back. I sent him to the

cafeteria for coffee. He was making me nervous with all his doting.'

Nell closed her eyes in a long blink. It would have been so easy to slip back into blackness and emerge again when everything made sense.

'Are you okay?' she asked, sticking to a whisper.

Lindsay laughed. It was a loud, ugly snorting sound as her eyes filled up with tears. 'Yes. Yes, I'm okay.' Her blue eyes looked so big and worried, and Nell couldn't stand seeing her this way. Lindsay never betrayed her calm unless she was angry. Nell had only seen this look in her sister's eyes once before, when giving birth to Reina had almost killed her.

'Oleg?' Nell asked.

'That piece of shit is still alive, too,' Lindsay said. 'I told the police where to find him, and you were right. The police were able to recover the video on his phone.'

'Good.' The word came out strained and breathless. Nell closed her eyes. 'That'll protect you from prosecution.'

'I need you to turn off crime writer mode right now,' Lindsay said. She gathered Nell's hand in both of hers. 'I've just spent three days sitting in this chair without anything resembling a shower, listening to your boyfriend read you shitty poetry because I didn't know when you were going to wake up. So you need to stop trying to solve your next crime and focus on getting better, because I need my sister.'

Nell stared up at her. Lindsay. She looked so tired. Her skin was pale, marbled by blue and purple veins. Her eyes were sunken, almost bruised.

'Are you really okay?' Nell said.

'I'm still dealing with that situation we previously discussed, if that's what you mean.' Lindsay's way of saying that she was still pregnant without having to spit out the actual word.

Nell was surprised to realise she was relieved, even though it meant her sister was still tethered to Matthew Cranlin. All of that seemed a lifetime away. They could sort it out later. Later, there would be fighting, arguing, crying – the way there always was when Matthew's name came up. But for now it didn't matter.

'Promise you won't leave my sight,' Nell said, and grabbed her wrist.

Lindsay put her hand on top of Nell's and laughed. Even her laugh sounded tired. 'Sister, a crucifix and a gallon of holy water couldn't purge me from this room.'

'Nell!' Sebastian's cry was hushed by the instinctive lull hospitals encouraged. He set two cups of coffee on a metal tray and ran to her.

'Hey,' she said, a moment before he took her face in his hands and kissed her. She felt his stubble against her lips, tasted the coffee on his breath.

He drew back to look at her. 'What do you remember?' he asked.

'Everything,' Nell said. 'That's my job, remember.' Already she was wondering about Oleg's trial, and how the press would cover this. The police would immediately know from the video that she was Penelope Wendall. They would come to question her about that night with Oleg in the woods, and all of the things he'd done leading up to it. It would be impossible to hide all of this from Sebastian; she had to tell him the truth, or he'd hear it from the police.

Sebastian was tracing her jaw with his thumb. He leaned down to kiss her nose, her forehead, before he took the empty chair beside Lindsay. Lindsay backed up just enough to let them have their moment, but she didn't leave the room.

'God, Nell.' He squeezed her hand.

'You must be so sick of always worrying about me,' Nell said, smiling tiredly.

'No,' he said. 'I want you to get better, and then we can spend the rest of our lives worrying about each other.'

Nell smiled, despite everything. Soon, he might not feel the same way. Once she was able to keep herself awake, she would tell him about Reina. She would tell him all of it, because she owed him that much, even if it cost her everything.

'Someone should get the doctor,' Sebastian said.

'Yes,' Lindsay pointedly replied. 'Someone should.'

Sebastian squeezed Nell's hand before he stood, and he kissed her again.

Once he'd left the room, Lindsay groaned. 'He's been insufferable,' she said. 'Like a slow song at the end of the dance and it just won't end. It goes on and on and you get more depressed the longer you have to listen to it.'

'You're jealous,' Nell said. 'He loves me more than you do.'

'I don't love you at all, you little rat,' Lindsay said. And then she doubled forward and laid her head beside Nell's on the pillow.

Nell inched closer. Three days unconscious and she had gotten the easier bargain. She hadn't dreamed, hadn't thought, hadn't felt anything. All the while Lindsay had kept vigil, doing the lion's share to protect them. It had been her role for Nell's entire life, and Lindsay had never resented her for it once. Not a single time.

❋

# THEN

Nell didn't pack more than she could fit into one duffel bag. Neither did Lindsay. They'd both spent a lifetime in Missouri. They'd both lived for a time in sprawling estates, with manicured hedges and swimming pools and housekeepers. But they had learned to never be sentimental about four walls and the people who lived inside of them, and now it was time to leave the past behind.

They listened to the radio for the first two hours, belting out the lyrics to Jay-Z and Shakira, pointing to each other and laughing when they sang out of key.

It was only after they'd crossed state lines into Illinois that Lindsay reached over and lowered the volume. She was quiet for a few seconds, and then she spoke with palpable difficulty. 'Whether you want to call yourself Penelope or Nell, you're still my sister, and I'm always going to be on your side,' she said. 'I need you to know that.'

'I know,' Nell said, and her stomach began to tie itself in knots.

'Then you know it's time,' Lindsay said. 'It's just you and me here. Nobody else. I need you to tell me what happened the day Reina disappeared.'

# 41
# NOW

One week after her ordeal, Nell was staring at her iPad as Sebastian wheeled her out of the hospital. Bas and Lindsay had tried to keep her from the news, but it had been futile. She was glued to every online article about Oleg, and was eager to visit Easter to get her take. After everything, Oleg had been the masterful liar of all the siblings.

'I really wish you'd put that thing away,' Bas said. He pushed her through the open glass doors, out into the winter air. It was cold, but the sun was bright and ice was melting on the concrete.

Nell tucked the iPad into her purse. A hospital orderly came to collect the wheelchair, and Nell stood. She'd almost expected to see paparazzi waiting for her in the parking lot, shouting, 'Penelope! Where have you been hiding all of this time, Penelope?'

But of course there weren't any. Oleg's case was months away from trial. It would soon come around through, and then she and Lindsay would be summoned to testify against him. The recording would be played for the jury, and everyone would know that Nell Way was the alias of Penelope Wendall, the Missouri teen acquitted of her daughter's murder.

The media would flood back into her life then, and there would be no stopping it. When they were alone in her hospital room, she and Lindsay whispered about it. Lindsay had nothing to lose, but for Nell the costs were high, and she had to accept that she could potentially lose a lot.

Nell had made an outline in her head, treating her own life like one of her books.

First, she would get back to her apartment. Surviving the hospital stay was step one.

Then, she would tell Sebastian the truth. All of it, including the things the jurors and the media never knew about her.

Then, she would call her agent to give him the heads-up that the media was about to descend. There would be outcry, calls for a boycott of her publisher. Jasper would eat it up. He'd find some way to turn it into a marketing ploy.

Then, she would deal with whatever came next. With Sebastian, or without him.

The car ride was quiet, and when they turned onto their block, Bas spoke for the first time since they'd left the hospital. 'Look at that, there's a space right in front.' He manoeuvred into a flawless parallel park and switched off the engine. 'You won't have to walk very far, and then you can get some rest.'

He reached for the door handle, and Nell leaned

over and gently grabbed his wrist. 'Wait,' she said. 'There's something I want to talk to you about.'

'Now?' He blinked. 'Can it wait five minutes?'

She shook her head slowly. 'I should tell you before we go inside.'

✳

# THEN

Nell didn't know, when she descended the staircase and entered the Eddletons' kitchen, that this would be the last day she spent with her daughter. If someone had told her that at the time, she might have muttered something like 'good'.

Reina was lying on the kitchen floor, arms and legs spread out so that she looked like a bony little star. Her bowl of applesauce and pear slices was untouched. The meal looked magazine pretty, with an artful sprinkling of cinnamon in the shape of a cursive letter R. Mrs Eddleton loved to do things like that.

Mrs Eddleton was sitting at the kitchen table, staring at her laptop and wearing her reading glasses. Nell never knew if she was ignoring Reina's tantrums or if she truly didn't see them, blinded as she was with love for her grandchild.

'Ready?' Ethan asked Nell, stopping only briefly

to kiss her cheek. It was something he only did when he wanted something from her.

'Ready for what?' Nell asked.

Ethan stepped over Reina's sprawled body and dumped the last dregs of his coffee into the sink. 'You're taking me to class. I told you last night, remember?'

Nell had only a vague recollection of Ethan knocking on her door while she was half asleep. He had just come in from some campus party and had no concept of the ungodly hour. He'd said something about loaning his car to a friend, to whom he owed a favour. Nell hadn't cared about the details. College. Friends. The world outside of motherhood – all of these things were alien to her.

'We have to leave now then,' Nell said, exasperated. 'I have to get groceries for your mother's church thing.'

'Don't forget the cake mix,' Mrs Eddleton said, typing furiously.

Years later, Nell would look back at this morning and wonder what might have happened if she'd done what she wanted, which was tell Ethan to fuck off and find his own ride to class, or to simply leave everyone – Ethan, Reina, the Eddleton house and everything in it – and speed off towards the horizon and never come back. The prospect of those what ifs would appear before her mind's eye like a banquet of shimmering gems.

'Thanks,' Ethan said. 'Meet you in the car.'

Reina screamed as Nell buttoned her into her coat. She screamed until she threw up the watery remnants of her breakfast in the car, and Nell had to turn around at the end of the driveway so she could go back into the house and change Reina's coat.

Nell sped down the suburban back roads. Not even eight o'clock and already her head was pounding.

Ethan was in the passenger seat, staring at the open textbook in his lap. He always studied in the minutes right before an exam, rather than in the days leading up to it.

'Reina,' he said. 'Cut it out.'

Miraculously, the screaming stopped.

Nell glanced in the rear-view mirror and saw Reina sitting in her car seat with her lips pressed together, her cheeks puffed out as if she was holding in a scream.

Ethan cut a smug look at Nell. 'Maybe if you tried, she would listen to you.'

Reina wasn't listening to Ethan because she respected his authority. This was just another of her many games. But Nell didn't bother trying to explain; it always ended in a fight.

They turned onto Gold Meadow Lane. It was a long strip of land that had belonged to family farms for generations, but now was being converted into condos. It was a straight drive to the university, but Nell came this way even when it added time to her errands if Reina wasn't in the car. She liked the way the grass seemed to stretch on forever, and she would pretend that she could build a house right in the middle of it. All that nothingness would be like a moat, protecting her from the life she'd somehow fallen into.

Now, though, the grass was torn up in several places, replaced by cement mixers and mounds of dirt. A sign by the road showed a painting of little grey condos above big red letters: COMING SOON.

Nell smelled it even before Ethan raised his head up and said, 'What is that?'

Nell closed her eyes in a long blink. Urine. Reina had wet herself. This had been the cost of her silence, and one of the many reasons Nell had long stopped asking her daughter to be quiet, or be still, or to behave.

Ethan looked in the rear-view mirror and Nell followed his gaze. Ethan's backpack was in the back seat, unzipped. Reina had taken a stack of papers from it and was now holding them pinned between her thighs.

Urine dripped down her legs and onto the upholstery. The pages were soaked.

Ethan gasped. It was a sound Nell had never heard him make, and in that moment she felt an odd spark of hope. He saw it, too. Reina had finally graduated to destroying something that mattered to him.

Nell flicked the turn signal and pulled over. Ethan was already jumping out of the car before she'd come to a complete stop. He threw open the door to the back seat and grabbed the stack of papers, holding them pinched between his thumb and index finger.

'Goddamn it, Penny! This was my term paper! It's the last day of the semester. If this isn't on Professor Gillan's desk *today*, I lose fifty per cent of my grade.'

Semesters. Professors. Grades. All things that used to matter to Nell but were now just pieces of a long-lost world.

She undid her seatbelt and rummaged through the trunk. 'Okay, calm down. I have some wet wipes.'

'Wet wipes,' he said, throwing the papers back into the car. 'Wet wipes aren't going to do anything, Penny!'

'Why are you screaming at me?' Nell tugged several wipes from the canister and got on her knees to scrub the upholstery at Reina's feet. 'I'm not the one who left his backpack unzipped. You know she likes to destroy things.'

Reina watched all of this with a blank expression. When Nell undid the seatbelt Reina went limp, but she didn't struggle when Nell tugged her out of the car seat and set her down on the grass.

The car seat was going to need to be dry-cleaned, but the floor hadn't taken much damage. That's what Nell was thinking when Ethan hoisted Reina up by her underarms and shook her.

'Why did you do that?' he burst out.

Reina hung suspended in his grasp. Her coat bunched up by her face, making her look like a suede turtle in pink fur lapels. Her mouth twisted into a smile, but even on her soft and pretty face, it looked wicked.

Ethan shook her. He shoved her hard against the door, and the entire car rocked.

Nell dropped the wipes and ran to him. 'Hey.' Her voice sounded strangely calm. She touched his shoulder. 'Hey, it's all right. We'll go back to the house and you can print it out again. So you'll be a little late. No big deal.'

Ethan's fingertips bore into Reina's coat. Her smirk was gone, and now the two of them were staring each other down.

For the first time, Nell was witnessing an act of defiance from Reina that was not aimed at her. Nell may as well have been invisible, standing there beside them.

Ethan was breathing hard, little clouds bursting from his nostrils. His eyes were dark with rage, and Nell realised that for the past four years, Ethan hadn't been blind to everything that was wrong with their daughter. He'd heard the screaming. He'd seen the destruction. He knew the things Nell told him were true. But he'd wanted to believe that they weren't. He wanted to believe that if he was patient, if he loved her enough, Reina would be the child he wanted.

Reina let out a whimper and started to squirm.

'Ethan.' Nell's voice was gentle. 'You're hurting her.'

He shook his head. 'I can't do it.' Spittle flew from his mouth when he spoke. 'I just can't.'

He threw Reina into Nell's arms. Nell felt the dampness of the urine on her hip when Reina latched on to her. For once, her daughter coiled her little body around her waist. Later, Nell would wonder if this had been a sign that Reina did love her, that she understood her mother's job was to protect her. And she would wonder if this, too, had been one of Reina's games.

Ethan climbed into the driver's side and turned the key in the ignition.

Nell pried Reina's hands from her shirt and set her down on the ground. There was a light dusting of snow, and maybe it would clean some of the urine from Reina's jeans.

'Ethan, stop.' Nell climbed into the passenger seat, leaving the door open behind her.

'I can't look at her,' he said. 'I can't look at her. I'll kill her if I do.'

Nell put her hand over his wrist. He was shaking. 'I know what you're feeling, Ethan, but it'll pass.'

He turned his head sharply in her direction. 'Does it, though? Does it ever stop?'

Nell didn't answer. She couldn't bring herself to lie to him.

When he leaned back in his seat, Nell worried that he would get out of the car and come for Reina again. She worried that he would grab her, or that he meant it when he said he would kill her.

Instead, he slammed his foot on the gas.

Nell nearly toppled backwards through the open door, but he grabbed her by the wrist and saved her from falling.

'Ethan!' She knew that she should have wrested out of his grip. She should have jumped out of the car and risked breaking both of her legs or even her neck, because Reina was still out there. She was still sitting in the snow and her own mess.

Nell wasn't sure what kept her from trying to reach her daughter. She wasn't sure what made her grab the handle of the car door and pull it shut, choosing to save herself instead.

## 42
## NOW

Hail bounced off the roof of Sebastian's car. Up ahead at the end of the block, a traffic light turned green and someone honked their horn. A group of teenagers in their parochial school uniforms passed by in a cloud of riotous laughter.

This was the first time Nell had told anyone other than Lindsay what happened that day.

Sebastian listened without a single interruption, and now he stared at Nell and the silence grew thick and uncomfortable.

He could have told her to get out. He could have sped away and left her there and sent his sister to collect his things so he wouldn't have to ever see Nell again. But when he finally spoke, he said, 'Did you go back?'

Nell nodded. 'Of course I did.' Her voice was hushed, like she was trying not to cry, although no tears came. 'Ethan sped the whole way to the university. He ran every red light and I don't know how we didn't get pulled over. And then, once we pulled up in front of the building, he started shaking his head. I think he was having a panic attack, but I'd never seen him like that. He had always clamped down his emotions so much that you'd wonder if he had any. He was saying, "What did I do? What did I do?"'

Nell could still see it clearly, as though it had only happened yesterday rather than ten years ago. In her mind, Ethan was still twenty-one years old. And when she thought of him, she still felt like that frightened teenage girl who got pulled along in everyone's current and could never find the footing to claw herself out.

'He begged me to go back for her, and I said that I would. I told him to go to class and I said that nobody had to know this ever happened. I would clean her up – I always kept spare clothes in the diaper bag – and I'd go to the store and everything would be fine. I told him I wasn't angry, that I understood. And I really, really did.

'But when I drove back to that road, she was gone. I remembered exactly where we'd left her because there was a big sign advertising new condos. I was sure I had the right place. There was nowhere for her to have gone. The nearest gas station was at least a mile away, and the construction site was abandoned for the winter. And it was daytime; there wouldn't be any coyotes or wolves.'

Nell could see this, too. Her beautiful field of grass that she had so admired. It was a crisp, smooth ribbon of eternity that made the entire world seem clean and empty. And somehow her daughter had been swallowed up by all of that nothingness.

'I thought someone must have found her. It was a small, safe little town where nothing bad ever happened. I thought that if I went to the grocery store like I'd planned, and I told someone that I lost her, eventually someone would come up and tell me that she'd been returned to the police and that she was *safe*.' Nell said that last word – safe – with venom, as though it had betrayed her.

'But no one found her. Her picture was all over the news. It was on every telephone pole. Every news website. It was in every state – it even went international. And still I thought, *someone will find her*. Someone will bring her home. How could it be possible that she just disappeared?'

Nell thought about Reina every day. The words she said to Sebastian now were not new to her. But suddenly she sobbed. The teenage Penelope and the adult Nell intersected. The hope of a young girl and the unflinching understanding of a woman. Nell knew all of the things that could happen to a child left alone in the world. She knew that there were things that could rival even Reina's ugliest tantrum. And she knew enough to understand that she would never know what her daughter had seen.

'But this case went to trial,' Bas said.

Nell nodded. She popped open the dashboard and found a napkin and blew her nose. 'Everyone

393

thought I killed her, and I figured it was the same difference. I could have stayed with her. I could have pulled the keys out of the ignition. But I didn't try.'

'Why didn't you say what really happened and Ethan's role in it?' Bas asked.

'If I'd taken the stand, my attorney promised me that I'd lose,' Nell said. 'The prosecution was just dying to get their hands on me. But if I didn't testify, they couldn't.'

'But after the trial,' Bas said, gently. 'Or now. When the press comes for you again with this upcoming trial, you could tell them the truth.'

She looked at him. 'No one would believe me. No one ever believed me about Reina,' she said. 'And it would only destroy Ethan's life. My trial is over; I can't be charged with the same crime twice. But if anyone knew he was with me that day, he would be arrested for child endangerment and I don't know what would happen to him. I don't want that.'

'So you took the fall, and he just let you.' Even though the engine had been off for a while now, Sebastian gripped the steering wheel. He stared through the windshield at the pellets of hail bouncing off the hood. He woke up in bed each morning beside Nell Way, but he had never met Penelope Wendall, the exhausted teenage mother whose C-section scar ran breastbone to pelvis too. It would take him time to reconcile the two people, until their overlapping images formed one shape.

For the first time all morning, there was a hint of anger in Sebastian's voice. 'You were public enemy number one, and he gets to just live a peaceful life.'

'No he doesn't,' Nell said, with certainty. 'There will never be peace for either of us. No matter how many years pass, we're both going to turn up the volume on the news whenever we hear that human remains have been found. He's always going to blame himself, the same way that I blame myself. We're both always going to wonder.'

She didn't know what Ethan had done in the near-decade since she'd seen him last. She didn't know if he'd met someone new, or if he'd had more children, or if he was afraid to. But she did know that he would always be more broken than he appeared on the outside. Just like her.

'Why didn't you tell me all of this a long time ago?' Sebastian asked.

'For the same reason I didn't jump out of the car that day, I guess. I was trying to save myself.'

Sebastian was still looking straight ahead when he reached over and put a hand on Nell's knee. 'We can talk about this a little later,' he said. 'It's getting cold in here. Let's go home.'

# 43
# NEXT

By August, Oleg's trial had concluded. Nell last saw him at his sentencing, when she sat beside Lindsay and heard the judge sentence him to fifteen years in prison for their attempted murder. She watched him shuffle between the pews with his hands cuffed in front of him. His white-blond hair was slick and shining beneath the courtroom's neon lights.

The trial date for Autumn's murder had yet to be determined.

Since then, an appeal had been filed by Oleg's state-appointed attorney, who was attempting to have him extradited back to Russia. If that happened, he'd be a free man so long as he never set foot in the United States.

For now, though, he was being held at Royal King's State Penitentiary in the men's housing unit.

Easter, cleared of all her charges, had been released and was being kept somewhere in isolation. All Nell's calls to the Hamblins' phone had gone unanswered. Nell's agent was insistent that she keep trying, and she would. But Nell knew of another way to get the information she'd need to finish the story.

It was a hot day, and the AC was blasting in Nell's new Subaru Impreza. She'd bought this car much to Lindsay's exasperation. If Lindsay had her way, Nell would be speeding up the interstate in a red BMW, letting the entire world know she was a woman of means. And this was true. After the trial brought her identity to light, Nell had gone into recluse mode. She still barely left the apartment, and had just returned from a two-month hiatus to the Bahamas with Bas, where they'd both enjoyed a break from the press. But Jasper had worked his magic while she was away, and the Hamblin manuscript was already sold before it was finished.

Lindsay was reclined in the front passenger seat, her bare feet up on the dash, pink manicured toes wriggling in the heat of the sun through the glass.

When Nell pulled into the driveway of Royal King's State Penitentiary, Lindsay looked over her shoulder. The baby had been quiet for the entire trip, but he was wide awake. His starry blue eyes stared up at the building that emerged before them like a gothic castle.

'Welcome to our family tradition, kiddo,' Lindsay said.

The baby laughed, bubbles of spit forming in the creases of his mouth. He was the happiest, goofiest baby Nell had ever seen. She often found herself scrutinising the way he looked out at the world. She waited for that cold, menacing glare to darken his face, but it never did. After he was born, a week had passed before Nell worked up the courage to hold him, and only at Lindsay's insistence. She'd been so terrified that the moment she touched her nephew he would turn into something irreparably broken too. But instead, he had been warm and fat and squirmy in her arms. He'd smelled like a clean diaper, and powder and warmth.

But even so, Nell worried for him. That worry eased a little each day, but she didn't know if it would ever truly leave her.

Nell parked the car, and Lindsay hopped out first. She opened the back passenger door and reached for her son, wiggling her fingers greedily because she couldn't wait to gather him up.

He'd been born with Robert's trademark auburn hair and long lashes, and a paternity test confirmed that this child was the product of one of the nights he and Lindsay had shared last summer after their divorce. Things were rekindling, but slowly. He was talking about moving back into the house, and Lindsay, who feared commitment almost as much as her sister, was considering it.

'I can't believe you wanted to bring him here,' Nell said wryly.

'Best to teach him what he's in for while he's still young enough to love me,' Lindsay said, hoisting him against her chest. 'Besides, the look on Bonnie's face will be priceless.'

In the visitation queue, Lindsay and Nell parted ways. They were here for different inmates.

Nell sat at the visitor's window with her hand on the phone, waiting. A minute later, Oleg was escorted to the chair on the opposite side of the glass. He picked up the phone at the same moment as Nell, and he regarded her with a flat, defeated stare.

'Hi,' Nell said. 'You approved my request to see you, but I wasn't sure you'd come.'

'Here I am,' he said. 'What do you want?'

Nell reached into the purse that was resting by her feet. She extracted her yellow notepad and set it in her lap. 'A year ago, you contacted me about a book. I'm here to write the final chapter.'

# ACKNOWLEDGEMENTS

Infinite thanks to the amazing team that helped bring this story to life: my agents extraordinaire, Barbara Poelle and Heather Baror-Shapiro, my wonderful, wonderful editor Miranda Jewess and the entire team at Viper and Profile Books.

## ABOUT THE AUTHOR

Ren Richards grew up in New Haven, Connecticut, and has an English degree from Albertus Magnus College. She is a *New York Times* and *USA Today* bestselling author, who has written more than a dozen YA and middle-grade books as Lauren DeStefano. Best known for her dystopian Chemical Garden series, she always dreamed of breaking into the adult suspense category.